Manchester-based writer Carrie Williams travels widely as a reviewer of hotels, restaurants and bars. She began writing for *Black Lace's Wicked Words* short story collections before progressing to novels.

She is the author of *Chilli Heat*, *The Apprentice* and *The Blue Guide*.

Also by Carrie Williams

Chilli Heat
The Apprentice
The Blue Guide

The
Apprentice

CARRIE WILLIAMS

BLACK
LACE

1 3 5 7 9 10 8 6 4 2

First published in 2009 by Black Lace, an imprint of Virgin Books

This edition published in 2013 by Black Lace, an imprint of Ebury Publishing
A Random House Group Company

Copyright © Carrie Williams, 2009

Carrie Williams has asserted her right to be identified as the author of this
Work in accordance with the Copyright, Designs and Patents Act 1988

The Random House Group Limited Reg. No. 954009

Addresses for companies within the Random House Group can be found at:
www.randomhouse.co.uk

A CIP catalogue record for this book is
available from the British Library

The Random House Group Limited supports the Forest Stewardship
Council® (FSC®), the leading international forest-certification organisation.
Our books carrying the FSC label are printed on FSC®-certified paper. FSC is
the only forest-certification scheme supported by the leading environmental
organisations, including Greenpeace. Our paper procurement policy
can be found at: www.randomhouse.co.uk/environment

MIX
Paper from
responsible sources
FSC® C016897

Printed and bound in Great Britain by Clays Ltd, St Ives PLC

ISBN 9780352347640

To buy books by your favourite authors and register for offers visit:
www.randomhouse.co.uk
www.blacklace.co.uk

To Nuala: love, thanks, admiration

Prologue

Sitting in one corner of the room, she reminds me of a spider waiting to catch a fly – watchful, unmoving, almost supernaturally contained. Even in anticipation, I think, she's cool and controlled. I stand naked, proud, before both of them, enjoying the thrill of two sets of eyes on me. Far from embarrassed, as I felt the first time, I am filled with a sense of my own power. In the lamplight my flesh glows like pale amber, and my breasts are as pert as young buds. I place my hands on them, let my fingertips flit around my nipples.

I hold his stare, which seems to interrogate me. Is he wondering who I am? Does he care? Is that what this is about, or is it the opposite: is it our very anonymity that's the point here? Or is it that he's asking me what to do, how to proceed, and, if so, does he not realise that it's not up to me?

I wait, as I waited before, as she has taught me to wait. It's she who's calling the shots here, and what I want is wholly irrelevant. But I do want this man, this . . . *boy*. For surely that's what he is? His smooth tanned skin, his large bright eyes, unsullied by too much life – he's eighteen, nineteen tops. I've never had a younger man, and the appeal is strong, both physical and mental. That he has some experience is obvious. He's too gorgeous, surely, to be a virgin. But there's an undeniable innocence to him – something to do with the cleanness of him, of his skin, and with the trust in his eyes. Like me, he's agreed to submit himself to her whims, or else why would he be here? Trickery, I'm sure of it, is not part of her armoury; I believe her to be upfront. I wonder what's in it for him, but I wonder only briefly.

'Take him,' she says, interrupting my line of thought. It's almost a bark, the decades of unfiltered French cigarettes having taken their toll.

It's the signal I've been waiting for. Stepping forwards, I adopt an imperious air – I am older than him, after all, if only by three, four years or so – and, placing my hand on his bare, hairless chest, push him gently back. He yields, allowing himself to tumble back onto the bed, looking up at me in mock-surprise, irony flitting around his eyes and mouth. *Come on then*, he seems to be saying, voicelessly.

She's dressed the bed for the occasion, this time in lustrous dark-chocolate satin sheets, like you see in boutique hotels in magazines. I climb onto it and kneel over him, taking his prick in my fist. But I know that she doesn't want to make it that easy for us. I look over at her, awaiting fresh instruction.

She's smoking again, face impassive. I wonder, again, that she doesn't want to join in, and then the thought occurs to me, for the first time, that perhaps she does, deep down. She's just paralysed by fear, hidden beneath a veneer of what could be mistaken for indifference. But why would an indifferent woman go to all this trouble? She must be getting something out of these things, however little it seems that way.

'Mount him,' she says simply, and I feel my pussy melt. I bring it towards his eager prick, let it graze at me for a moment, just to remind him of who's boss. Of course, I'm *not* boss, but in terms of the two of us on the bed I have more say than he does. Then I slot myself down over him, delighted to find that I fit him like a silken glove. He moans and, as I move around on top of him – from side to side, and round and round – I reach round behind my arse and take a good firm fistful of his downy balls.

For a while I drink in his face as I fuck him, gaze at those big wide eyes, bigger and wider now that he's inside me, at that smooth jawline, at that floppy chestnut fringe falling back from his face. Then I turn my head and look over at her, to see what she's doing as we fuck. And, as our eyes meet across the bedroom, I see not impassiveness but some kind of spark, a smouldering fire. This is getting to her. I feel jubilation inside. We are turning her on.

'Come now,' she says, and I nod, bringing two fingers to my clitoris. I press it for a moment, feeling its throb. Then I start massaging it from side to side. I'm gazing down as I do so, at my own hand. I can't bring myself to look at her when I'm doing this, when I'm about to lose it.

I don't look at him now, although I know that by this point his eyes are closed, falling back in his head in some kind of swoon. But his hands are firm on my hips, pulling me tighter in to him, and I sense from the rhythm that has established itself between us that he won't be long in coming either.

I arch up as my climax takes hold, throw my head back as I feel my face contort with something like pain.

'Oh God,' I hear myself moan, but the voice sounds like it comes from far away, almost from another realm. It's at that moment that the boy jerks his hips up, convulsive, puppet-like, and starts coming too, hands still fast on my hips. I fall forwards over him, hair trailing down over his face. I'm panting, feeling ravaged by my orgasm, yet I want him again, want the feeling back almost as soon as it's died away.

I look wildly over towards the corner where she sits. She's standing up.

'That's all. You may dress,' she says.

My lips form the word 'No', but her hand is reaching for the doorknob and I know that there's no use. That it's finished for her, and therefore for us. Like before, she's in a hurry to be somewhere else. Will she masturbate now, in her room?

'Come on, girl,' she says, a bit impatiently, and I grab my clothes from the floor and, still naked, hurry after her. As I pass her in the doorway, she turns back to the bed.

'Thank you,' she says to the boy, with a slight incline of her head. Her voice is somewhat cold.

He smiles over at her, nods, but says nothing.

She closes the door and we part ways at the staircase: she's en route to her study, me to the shower. As I'm making my way up, she reminds me that we are to meet at four, that she has some correspondence to dictate. I tell her I haven't forgotten, that I'll be there.

1

The Interview

My name is Genevieve Carter, and I have a confession to make. While my elder sister Vronnie, on whose very chic Heal's sofa I have been crashing for the last three months, thinks I've been pounding the pavements of London looking for a job in media, I've been sitting in cafés, making a latte last through entire afternoons, dreaming and staring out of the window. Or rather, I've been trying to write a novel – I've always wanted to be a writer. But so far it's been like banging my head against a brick wall – it just won't come. My notebook is full of false starts and phrases that go nowhere, doodles and lewd little sketches and ink blobs from my leaky Biro. My mind tends to wander somewhat.

Vron would be livid, if she knew. (*Big* understatement.) I've already outstayed my welcome. The fact that she's a fashion stylist on one of the big women's glossies at the tender age of twenty-five shows what a tough cookie she is. She decided what she wanted to be and went for it. I wish I was like her: decisive, go-getting, hard-nosed even. She climbed on other people's shoulders, lost friends, never looked back. Whereas since leaving uni and splitting up with Nate, my sixth-form sweetheart, I've felt lost, directionless. Sometimes I wonder if this thing about becoming a writer is as much about finding a place for myself, a role in life, as about writing itself.

Only this afternoon, I'm surprised to say, is a bit different. For once, I'm not mooning about in cafés – I'm actually doing what I told Vron I'd be doing, and going for a job interview. Leafing through the *Guardian* jobs page two, maybe three, weeks ago, I spotted an ad for an 'assistant/home help' for a novelist in West London, and I'm happy to find myself on my way to his/her house for an interview. Chances are slim that I will actually get the job, of course, but if I did then maybe being in such a creative atmosphere might unblock me. The pay's not bad either.

I look down at the piece of paper I clutch in my perspiring fist – a handwritten letter on fine paper, curt, to the point, stating the day and hour at which I am required to present myself. I reread the address – 167 St Petersburgh Place, W2 – then I look up around me, for the nearest street sign. Yes, I'm on Moscow Road. I need to hang a left further up, then I'll be there.

I study again the scrawled initials at the bottom of the letter. A.F., it could be, or A.T. Strange that the person hasn't written out their full name, that they don't wish to disclose their identity. I don't even know if it's a man or a woman. I wonder if it could be even be Sir Andrew Fogerty, but then I remember that the job ad stated 'novelist' and he's mainly a biographer.

As I round the corner into St Petersburgh Place, nerves hit me, and I have to do some deep breathing in an attempt to calm myself down. I walk slowly, and then, when I've located the right house on the left-hand side of the street, I realise I'm at least ten minutes early and I carry on up the road, wondering some more about the mysterious A.F./A.T.

I recognise her as soon as she opens the front door with its peeling, faded green paint; she's aged considerably since the last photos I saw of her. After all, it's been twenty-odd years since her last book that made any real impact – not too long after I was born, in fact. I've read them all, of course, and I disagree with the critics about her more recent output being sub-standard, lacking in the earlier inspiration. But up-to-date publicity photos have been scant, and she's hardly a household face.

'Come in,' she says simply, and I know from the look of gratification on her face that she knows that I know who she is.

'Thank you, Ms Tournier.' There's an undertone of ingratiation in my voice. I suppose that's natural in any interviewee, and unavoidable in one who's just come face to face with her literary heroine and the prospect of working with her, but I hate it.

She ignores the hand I hold out, is already turning away and walking back down the dark, narrow hallway. I watch as her trademark raven bob swings to and fro about her long, elegant nape. She still has a certain French chic, despite the decades she's lived in London, but I imagine she must dye her hair by now.

She leads me to the kitchen, where a long oak table is loaded with unread newspapers, unopened mail, paperback books and teetering stacks of paper. She gestures to the only chair free of such debris.

'Do call me Anne,' she says, as she turns away to fill and switch on the kettle.

I want to tell her how lucky I feel to be here, having been such a fan of her work for so long, but I'm horribly tongue-tied, and also afraid that if I strike up conversation I'll blather on idiotically in order to fill the silence. There's a forbidding aspect to Anne Tournier, which is not surprising given the laconic voice of her fiction but which doesn't encourage one to make the first move.

She turns back to me, hands over a mug steaming with tea.

'I assumed you didn't want sugar,' she says, but as I nod she's no longer looking at me. She's eyeing something on the table in front of her, something that I soon recognise to be my CV. I wince. Like everyone, I talk myself up on paper. I'm not sure whether what's written down bears much relation to who I am.

'Soooo,' she says, fumbling in her cardie pocket for her cigarettes. 'Pendleton Girls, Durham . . . All very impressive. You have had a charmed life. Privileged, would you say?'

I shake my head vehemently. I know the connotations and associations those names carry, but I honestly don't feel that my course through life has been assisted by my attending these places. In fact, I sometimes wonder if it's been hindered. Otherwise, why would I feel so ill at ease in my skin, so directionless?

I know, too, that Anne Tournier is strongly left wing, and although I consider myself to be the same – in spite of, or perhaps because of, my background and education – the last thing I want is to become embroiled in a political debate with someone known for her intellectual rigour.

'And . . . let's see . . . ' Her eyes are flitting across the page; already, it seems, she's lost interest in my life story. 'Ah yes,' she says, tapping the paper with one manicured finger. 'You're the one who wants to be a writer?' She looks up at me, blowing out a ring of smoke. 'Or one of them,' she says. 'Been published yet?'

I shake my head, feeling hopeless. Everything she's asking me makes me feel small and stupid.

'Why not?'

'I . . . I guess I never really finish anything.'

She flicks her cigarette ash into a nearby saucer. 'Maybe,' she says throatily, 'maybe you should forget about writing, at least for the time being. You're –' She glances down at the CV. 'You're only twenty-three. You should be living, not writing. And what can you write about anyway, until you've lived a little?'

I shrug, feeling even more stupid. She's right. What do I have to say to the world, after my private education, my limited love life? There was uni, of course, but what did I do there that everyone else didn't do: drink, read books, sit around talking crap about things I had little knowledge of?

'But Françoise Sagan . . .' I begin, desperate to show that I have some shred of intelligence.

Anne waves her hand dismissively. 'A fluke,' she says. 'A one-hit wonder. Never did anything again that even remotely lived up to *Bonjour Tristesse*.'

She's right, of course. Again, she's right. I look at her, and the intelligence in her keen eyes blazes out like fire.

She looks back down, and for a moment she is silent, as if she really can't find anything else to ask me about. It's true, I think humbly: my life is really not worth talking about. But do I need to be fascinating in order to do the job she advertised?

'Funny,' she says at last, ruminatively, rubbing her elfin chin with her fingers. 'CVs are basically all the same. Boring as hell. What's interesting about a person never comes out in a CV.'

'What do you mean?'

'Well –' She jabs at the printed sheet with one finger. 'I suppose what I'm saying is that this gives me no feel for who Genevieve Carter really is. I know that you like reading, writing. I know what you studied, etcetera etcetera. But I have no idea who you really *are*.'

She glances up, and there's an added fire in that shimmering, watchful intelligence. 'For instance,' she says, 'it tells me nothing about your experiences as a *woman*.'

'As a woman?'

'Your sexual experiences, for instance,' she breathes. 'What makes you tick, what turns you on.'

I must be blushing, for she lets out a little laugh. 'You're not a prude, are you? Oh *Dieu*, the English can be so uptight. It still amazes me, after all this time.'

I recover myself, hating to live up to a national stereotype. 'What . . . What do you want to know?' I say. It's an odd line of questioning for her to adopt, but then this is no ordinary interview. Why, for instance, doesn't she conduct it in her study? Why are we here in her cramped, paper-strewn kitchen, where there are not even enough free chairs to accommodate the both of us?

She gives a little shake of her head, setting her bob in motion. 'Oh, I don't want to know what positions you like, all that sort of stuff,' she says. 'But . . . well, I'm a novelist, so I'm incurably nosy, I'm afraid. Do you think you could put up with me? With my asking you personal questions, from time to time? Sometimes I don't even realise I'm doing it, it's so ingrained.'

'It depends on the sort of questions.'

'Well, of course you can tell a lot about a person by knowing about their previous lovers. It's one of the first things

I always ask mine, in fact. Who they've been with before me, what they were like in bed. Enormously instructive, as well as just plain fascinating.'

I feel one eyebrow arch. 'Well,' I say, 'there's really not that much to say about my relationships. I've only had one lover.'

'One?' She holds up an index finger, eyes round and incredulous. '*One* lover? And you are –' She glances at my CV once more. 'You are twenty-three? What have you been *doing* with your life?'

I shrug. 'I've been with the same guy since I was eighteen,' I say. 'We were in sixth form together. And I stayed with him right through uni, so . . .'

I pause. It feels like I am trying to justify my behaviour, when others might see it as laudable that I haven't slept around. Anne is making me feel, by the look on her face, as if that's really rather pitiful.

'He must have been a bloody good lover,' she says, lighting another cigarette, eyes small and shrewd, half-closed against the smoke.

I shrug again. 'I have nothing to compare it with.'

'And that is precisely my point,' says Anne, highly animated now, wagging her finger at me over and over. 'You can't know what you were missing. Weren't you ever . . . *tempted*?'

'Tempted?'

'To stray. To find out what lay beyond this . . . this . . .'

'Nate, his name was.'

'This Nate.'

I try to think back. 'No, I don't think I was. I was in love. It didn't occur to me to even look at other men.'

She chuckles, but there's also what looks like a sneer on her face. 'How very touching,' she says. 'But now?'

'Now what?'

'Do you regret that you wasted some of the best years of your life on one person, when it turned out not to be for ever? You'll never have the energy you had then, believe me.'

I take a sip of my tea, though it's lukewarm by now. 'There's no point in regret,' I say.

'That's a good policy,' she says. 'A good theory. One that's not too easy to put into practice, but . . . I digress. I suppose my point is that maybe, just maybe, you'd have something to write about if you hadn't spent – what? – five years with the same guy.'

'Maybe.'

'Anyway, as you say, the important thing,' she says, grinding her cigarette butt into the saucer, 'is not looking back. Which brings me to the main question I ask of all my interviewees.' She pauses, for dramatic effect it seems to me.

'Fire away.'

'How do you see your future?'

'I . . . I don't think too much about it. I just . . . I just want to write.'

'And what about men?'

'What about men?'

'Are you looking for someone to fill the gap, the hole left by this . . . this . . .'

'Nate.'

'Nate.'

I don't want to tell her that yes, that's what I feel I'm lacking: another Nate, someone to snuggle up to under the duvet, someone to walk through the autumn leaves with, someone whose hand I can hold in the cinema. She'll laugh at me, I know she will, or wither me with those calculating ice-blue eyes.

'I'm too young,' I say, 'to settle down. I need to discover myself before I even think about getting serious with another bloke, find out who I really am.'

She's staring at me, and her gaze seems approving now. 'You owe it to yourself,' she says. 'It's essential, it really is. A sentimental education, as we French call it, rather euphemistically. Now –' She looks back down at my CV. 'Could you start immediately?' she asks. 'I see you're not working at the moment.'

I nod, suddenly excited. Perhaps this has gone better than I thought. Suddenly it's imperative that I don't let this chance get away from me. I lean forwards over the table, wave one hand at my CV.

'I'm not working, and I'm keen to learn, and I'll do any courses I need to do to bring myself up to speed, at my own expense, of course.' I pause for breath. 'And I know you mentioned an hourly rate in your ad, but I'd be prepared to work for less if it means being able to work with one of my favourite writers.'

I'm sucking up, but I'm desperate. Anne's eyebrows are raised.

'Indeed?' she says, and again there's something calculating to her smile, and something appraising.

'I'm not just saying that,' I tell her. 'I really am a huge fan of yours. Ever since –'

'Well, then, I'm very flattered, and very happy that you chanced upon my ad. It seems that fate has conspired to bring us together.'

I grin. 'Does that mean I've got the job?'

She nods. 'You can start tomorrow if that suits you,' she

says. 'And did I mention that I'm offering lodging as part of the deal? I have an attic room at the top of –'

'I'll take it,' I say, and I feel giddy at the thought that life, my real life, is starting at last.

2

First Day

Vron is all too delighted to drop me off in Bayswater in her little black Porsche, on her way to Vogue House. She can barely conceal her pleasure at getting shot of me. I don't mind: it's all I can do not to skip up the path towards Anne's front door. But I force myself to take my time, to savour the moment, glancing up at the window of the attic room that I haven't even seen yet and that is to be my new home.

Five minutes later I'm standing on the threshold to that room, as Anne gestures around it with broad sweeps of one arm.

'I've never had much use for it,' she says, 'so I'm all too happy to have someone up here. It's warm and cosy, and there are extra blankets in the armoire. If you don't like the walls, you can always paint them.'

But I'm not even looking at the walls – I'm rushing for the front window, having suddenly realised that I can see a patch of Hyde Park and some of its treetops from it.

'It's perfect,' I say, and I have to hold back from embracing her. The instinct is there, but Anne, for all her talk of lovers and of uptight Brits, seems to be such a cold fish, physically, that I'm not sure she won't just stand there as stiff as a board, not returning my embrace and making me feel a fool. I wonder what she's like in the bedroom, whether the sex she has isn't all in the head.

'Then I'll leave you to it,' she says. 'Help yourself to lunch. Hettie always makes sure that the fridge is full of good things.'

'Hettie?'

'My housekeeper. She's around every day, does the shopping on the way, takes care of the Hoovering and the laundry, prepares lunch and an evening meal that I can reheat. She's a godsend.'

'And me?'

'Oh, there's nothing really to do today. You might as well just spend some time settling in, getting to know the area, perhaps? I need to work on a synopsis for the new novel.'

My ears prick up: I'd love to hear more about that. But I assume that I'll find out about it soon enough, in my guise as assistant.

'Are you sure?'

She nods. 'Don't worry,' she says. 'You won't be bored here. I have plenty to keep you occupied.' And with that she is gone, and I'm left alone in my new room, on the threshold of my new life.

I unpack, but it doesn't take long and, at a loose end, I go for a walk in Hyde Park, buying a sandwich and a bottle of water en route. As I sit munching under the trees, I can't believe my good luck at having found this job. Anne, though a strange mixture of aloof and overly personal, seems to be a lenient, undemanding employer: the 'home-help' aspect of things, mentioned in the ad, is clearly not going to amount to much, given the presence of Hettie, and it will be interesting helping out administratively during the conception of a new novel. Who knows, perhaps I will even have some input, in a small way? That would be amazing. I can already see my name on Anne's acknowledgements page. And the relief at being out from under Vronnie's feet and away from the sharp end of her tongue is immense.

As I open my bedroom door, I see a note on the floor that must have been pushed underneath it. I unfold it and read that Anne has a dinner guest tonight and would be delighted if I would join them for a meal and a celebratory glass of champagne to mark my first day. I grin. How could I refuse?

I kick off my shoes and lie down on the bed, wondering who might be coming to dinner. Anne, though no longer at the literary vanguard, has some famous friends – I know that from the books pages. I feel quite starry-eyed at the thought of them trooping through this house, at the thought of the parties that I might attend. I feel on the brink of something wonderful, as if life is a luscious basket of fruit that someone is tending towards me. I only have to reach out my hand and something delicious is there for the taking.

I must have dozed off, for when I wake the sky has darkened outside. Checking my watch, I see that it's almost seven – the appointed time for dinner, according to Anne's note. I jump up, rifle through my wardrobe. I want to look good but not overdressed: after all, this is just a simple weekday supper in a bohemian household. I fall back on an old favourite: a simple black shift dress that emphasises my curves. With a silver bangle or two and some teardrop earrings, it looks chic but not show-offy.

I'm nervous as I walk downstairs in my kitten heels: not only at the prospect of the mystery dinner guest, but because it's just struck me that I barely even know Anne – my interview was brief, and since then I've only seen her when she showed me to my room. All my anxieties about my boring, uneventful life come flooding back and I imagine myself sitting silently at the table, unable to think of a thing to say in such illustrious, intellectual company. Part of me wants to make an excuse and run upstairs and hide under the duvet.

As I approach the kitchen, I hear voices, one female, one male. For a moment I stay back, deferring the moment. Then I take a deep breath, push open the door and walk in.

I'm relieved not to recognise him, although he's so distinguished I think that I probably ought to. As he sees me, he turns, glass in his hand, and smiles.

'So this must be your lovely new assistant,' he says, voice deep, imposing. 'Genevieve, is it not? Delighted to meet you.'

He holds out a hand, shakes my hand firmly, authoritatively, and I note a roguish twinkle to his eyes as they sweep over my face, take in my low neckline. He must be in his late fifties, perhaps even his early sixties, but he is close-shaven and looks fit and spritely in his charcoal-grey suit, which reeks of Savile Row. His silvery hair has an expensive cut to it, and he's clearly someone who has taken care of himself, refusing to yield to the ravages of time.

'Genevieve, meet Jim Carnaby,' says Anne, stepping up behind him, and I smile and say, 'Lovely to meet you too.' I've heard of a James Carnaby, an art historian, and I guess that this must be he.

He sits down at the kitchen table, which I notice has been cleared – presumably by Hettie. I wonder again what exactly my duties will consist of, given that Hettie seems to take care of all the domestic tasks. A candle burns brightly in the centre, and – as Anne promised – a bottle of champagne keeps chill in an ice bucket beside it. Seeing me look at it, James Carnaby reaches over and pops the cork.

'To new adventures,' he says, filling the glasses that Anne has brought over. 'To fresh blood.'

'To fresh blood,' Anne and I repeat, although it strikes me as somewhat of a strange toast – like some strange rite involving menstruation and the phases of the moon. As we drink, Anne sets three bowls of soup on our place mats.

'Tomato and fresh basil,' she says. 'And no, of course I can't take credit for it. It's all Hettie's doing, as is the rest of the meal. Although I did plant the basil, way back.'

James smiles indulgently as he tastes it. 'There are talents more worthy of praise than those of the kitchen,' he says, and the pair exchange an affectionate smile. I wonder if they might be lovers, or might have been lovers in the past. Anne may seem icy, but her novels tell of a vast sexual experience. There's an erotic thread to all of them that rings true, that must be drawn from real life.

'And what about Genevieve?' he says, turning to me. 'What are your talents, my dear?'

I shrug, embarrassed. As Anne knows, I don't really have any and, whereas, if James and I were alone, I would be tempted to invent something to impress him or even just to have something to talk about, in her presence I feel stifled, circumscribed by the banal truth.

But Anne comes to my rescue. 'Genevieve is hoping to be a writer,' she says.

'Aaaah,' says James, taking another spoonful.

'A cliché, I know,' I say apologetically.

He reaches over the table – he's seated opposite me – and pats my hand. 'Sadly true,' he says. 'But if you have real talent, and something to say, then you mustn't be put off. Now, what do you write about, young lady?'

I look down at my hand. He hasn't removed his. He pushes his empty bowl away with his free hand. I glance up at Anne to see if she's noticed what's happening, but she's turned away to remove some warm plates from the oven, then ladle on to them what looks to be some kind of rich beef stew. When she returns to the table with two of the plates, she can't fail to see it, but she doesn't react at all.

The arrival of the main course seems to let me off the hook as far as James's last question is concerned and, when Anne sits down with the third plate, we all tuck in. James, whose hand has let go of mine so that he can eat, serves the last of the champagne, and when that's finished he pours us all generous glasses of red wine from an expensive-looking bottle. Unused to drinking much, I'm already feeling more than a little tipsy.

For a few minutes – perhaps Anne and James sense my discomfort and also my imminent drunkenness and decide to give me some space – I enjoy a reprieve while Anne questions James about a forthcoming tour of universities to promote his new book, which is called, I learn, *Roués in Nineteenth-century French Art*. I smirk when I hear that. Is James, despite his age, just another of the womanisers of whom he writes? Not that there's anything wrong with that – part of me admires someone who has looked after himself so well, who has retained his appetites rather than retreating into a world of pipes and slippers. But it's just funny to hear that he's devoted a whole book to the study of rakes in a given place and time, and given it an artistic spin.

'I'd be interested in reading that,' I say, before I can think better, and James smiles at me across the table.

'Oh good,' he breathes. 'At least someone is. I'll drop you in a copy sometime.'

As he speaks his hand comes down on mine again, and I feel the slightly leathery flesh of his palm on the back of my hand. It's not an unpleasant sensation, but I shoot another glance at Anne, who can't possibly have missed it this time. To my surprise she's smiling, albeit a rather faraway, distant smile, and her eyes are assenting. To reinforce her expression, she nods at me. She seems to be giving me permission to submit to James's advances.

I feel a sudden flood of panic in my veins. Do I want him? I've never even contemplated sleeping with an older man, with a man this old, but then the opportunity has never presented itself. I've certainly never looked at a much older man in the street and wanted him. But not all older men are like James Carnaby. There's a definite lure. Or is it just the wine, or the thrill of being shown attention by a well-known writer? Am I mistaking gratitude for lust?

We have a little cheese in place of dessert and then James takes my hand and leads me through into the front living room, where a candle burns in a scarlet glass on the dark-wood coffee table. As he guides me to the low-slung sofa, I catch a glimpse of myself in the mirror over the hearth: my cheeks are glowing. I'm full of red wine and red meat, but my own blood is pumping forcefully through my veins in anticipation of what is to come. There's no denying that I'm sexually aroused beyond my wildest imaginings.

Anne appears as we sit back on the sofa and settles into an armchair opposite us. She's holding a half-full glass of wine and smiling indulgently, as if we are two slightly naughty but beloved children whose whims amuse her. James has one arm draped around my shoulders, and his wrist and hand hang down towards my cleavage. I stiffen as I feel him lower it further, play with the low neckline of my dress and then creep inside. Slipping into my lacy black bra, his fingers close around one of my nipples, brush the tip of it. I let out a sigh that comes out more like a moan. Opening my eyes, I look over at Anne, a little shamefaced, but her gaze is now directed at my breasts and at what James is doing to them. Her lips are parted slightly. She takes a sip of wine, and I see her muscles open and close beneath the slightly loose skin of her throat. Her expression itself is blank.

I lean woozily back against James's chest, bring my hand to my crotch. Again, it's something I can't help but do. I've never felt so out of control of my own actions and reactions in my life and, in some deep, dark part of myself that I hardly recognise, I'm loving it. I can't even blame the alcohol: I've drunk more, much more, than this in the past, and I'm still reasonably compos mentis. But it's as if I've been picked up by some kind of tide, and it's carrying me along and there's nothing I can do but submit.

James pulls me up onto his lap, and I can feel the hard knot of his cock in his trousers nudging me between my arse cheeks. I'm very wet now, and desperate to fuck him. The thought brings me up short, and suddenly everything seems very surreal. The whole situation is mad, beyond mad. But there's no stopping me now. I don't want this to end until I've had James inside me. Only, perhaps we ought to go somewhere more private?

James obviously doesn't agree, for he pulls up the skirt of my dress until my thighs are uncovered. In response, unable to help myself, I part my legs. I daren't look at Anne now – I feel humiliated by the rampancy of my desire, by the fact of how far I have shown myself willing to go in front of her very eyes.

James reaches down between my legs. For a moment his fingers pluck at the wet gusset of my knickers; no doubt he can feel the hard little bud of my clit trying to poke through the flimsy fabric, desperate to be touched. Then he pulls the gusset aside, revealing my wet lips, my open pussy. Anne, opposite, must have a full-on view as he massages my clit. But I still can't look at her. My head is thrown back against James's shoulder as I gyrate my hips, pushing myself harder onto his fingers, until at last he slips three, four inside me. With his thumb still jiggling my clit from side to side, I come so hard I see stars.

For a while all is silent. I lie back against him, eyes closed, panting, legs still splayed while my contractions die away. James is clutching me to him, one hand closed around a breast, his mouth nuzzling my nape, taking playful little pecks at me. His cock is still hard against my arse, beating a kind of pulse, and I know that I don't want this to be over.

A hand comes down on my bare thigh. I look up, and it's Anne, still smiling faintly, enigmatically.

Oh no, I think, and I wonder how to tell her I am definitely not up for a threesome with the two of them, that I might fancy James but I don't fancy her.

She seems to read my mind, for she shakes her head. 'But you will be more comfortable upstairs,' she says. She takes my hand and helps me up from the sofa; the bottom of my dress falls back down over my legs. Leaving my shoes where I kicked them off, I allow myself to be led upstairs. Her hand is firm around mine. She doesn't speak, and neither do I.

At the top of the first flight of stairs, she opens a door and gestures me into what I take, from the lack of personal items there, to be a guest room. The curtains are drawn, and incense already burns in a little holder on the mantelpiece – it's clear she's prepared the space in advance, that she's paid careful attention to setting the scene. She seems to have been pretty certain I'd submit to James's advances.

'Make yourself comfortable,' she says at last, breaking the silence, and she gestures towards the bed. On it I see a crimson silk robe that matches the colour of the bedlinen. I look at her anxiously, feeling absurdly shy at slithering out of my dress given what she's just seen. Somehow things are different now that James is not here.

As if sensing my mood shift, my hesitation, Anne fades back and out of the room. 'Relax,' I hear her breathe as she leaves me to my own devices. 'James has a reputation for knowing how to please a woman. You're in safe hands.'

As she closes the door behind her, I sit down on the end of the bed and finger the robe. It's of exquisite quality, and I imagine Anne shopping somewhere in Knightsbridge – Harrods perhaps – picking it out from the rails. It looks unworn, and I wonder if she chose it especially with me in mind.

Hearing a noise on the stairs, I strip off quickly, then fold my clothes and place them in a neat pile on the easy chair in the corner. I slip into the robe. It feels delicious against my bare skin. I sit back on the bed and let myself recline until my head's on the soft pillow and I'm stretched out, feet towards the door.

James appears, a tall lean figure in the doorway. Silhouetted by the brighter light of the hallway, he's nothing more than an outline, mysterious, even more alluring. I'm glad to have him alone. I smile shyly at him, wondering what on earth I'm doing here, what I'm supposed to do. For a moment Nate flashes up in my mind's eye. I wasn't lying to Anne when I said that I loved him, and in many ways I'll never stop loving him. But I do wonder now if it was good for me, meeting him so young, being exclusive with him for so long, denying myself.

James sits on the end of the bed, puts one hand on and then around my ankle. Even that, such a small act, elicits a purr of pleasure from me. He's not even undressed yet, and already I'm leaking onto the robe beneath me, I'm so bloody turned on. And turned on by a fifty- or sixty-something! What would Nate think if he could see me now? What would I have thought myself, if someone had told me this was going to happen?

And yet here I am, giving myself fully, willing to go wherever James wants to take me. He, however, seems to be stalling for time, running his hands up and down my shins, massaging the backs of my calves with strong, confident fingers. It's good, of course, but I want so much more than this and I don't know if I can hold out. I spread my legs, pull the robe up. I want him to know how much I want him.

There's a light rap on the door, but, by the time James calls, 'Come in,' without betraying any surprise, Anne is already halfway into the room. She makes her way over to a wicker chair in front of the window and sits down without a word.

I stare at her, but my natural impulse to close my legs is stymied by James's hands on my knees, bracing them apart. Part of me wants to sit up and tell Anne to bugger off, to just leave us to it. But this is her house, her bed, her friend. I'm fairly sure that, if I objected, she'd call a halt to it all, and I couldn't bear that, not now that I'm so close to having James inside me. James, for his part, is looking over his shoulder at Anne, apparently still awaiting instructions. Returning his gaze, the latter nods.

James advances up the bed, takes hold of my pliant thighs and begins jabbing at my pussy lips with his tongue, lapping at my juices, then flicking at my clit, over and over. I raise my hips to meet his mouth, to welcome it, and he slips his hands under my buttocks to support me, his grip firm on each. Feeling my gown fall away from my chest, I take one of my breasts in each hand, squeeze the hard little nuts of my nipples. I've never felt so horny in my life.

It's not as if I've forgotten, as I lie alternately whimpering and swearing, that Anne is there – that would be impossible. But somehow it doesn't seem to matter. What James is doing to me is all that counts, has unshackled me from all other care or concern. I didn't know it was possible to feel this turned on, and I'm not letting him stop.

Beneath his expert tongue I judder to three, four climaxes, my fingertips sunk into his shoulders through his crisp, elegant shirt. My knuckles bear the imprints of my teeth, and tears are pouring down my cheeks. I feel as if I'm being ravaged by some incredible force of nature. And all this with his tongue alone! What's going to happen when he's inside me?

I'm not, it seems, to find out. Anne appears beside us, as if from out of a dream, and touches James lightly on the shoulder.

'Your taxi will be here soon,' she says in a low voice, as if talking to a sleepwalker or someone who's been hypnotised.

James sits up without a word, but he doesn't appear to feel angry or cheated at all, as I do. Anne's hand has remained on his shoulder, while he rests one of his on her forearm. For a moment, in the low light, they just look at one another – kindly, it seems to me.

Lying there, post-orgasmic on my flooded robe, my sex still on display, I feel ridiculous, and suddenly frozen out, unsure of my role. I was James's lover, but only for the time that Anne, it seems, allowed me to be so. Now she has decreed that it's over, and there's nothing I can do about it. I can't tell her how much I want – *need* – to see James naked, this man who has made me come so exquisitely. Can't tell her how curious I am to see the body of this man who has been able to make me feel this way, to know what it is to have his dick inside me. I wouldn't know the words to use.

Turning back to me, James looks at me tenderly, brushes my hair back from where it is sticking to my sweaty brow and kisses me on the mouth. There's a hint of a tongue – just a hint, but enough to make me hope that this is not over. Then he stands and follows Anne out of the room and onto the landing.

I lie on the bed and listen to their footsteps as they head downstairs. For a while there is the low murmur of their voices in the hallway, but, as I try to catch a word here and there, I start to feel woozier and woozier. With my fingers I play at my pussy lips, and before long I have my knees up again and am biting on the back of one hand as I come to the tune of my own fingers, still thinking of James's tongue on me, of his cock.

When I wake up it's the middle of the night and I have a raging thirst. The door is closed and a sheet has been pulled up over me, but my hand is still between my legs. A glass of water has appeared on the night table beside me, too. I drink it avidly, telling myself I'll go back to my own room. But before I can act I've lain back on the bed and am sinking into sleep again.

3

The Morning After

I sleep late the next morning, and jump out of bed in a panic, worried that Anne might be mad at me. Here I am, on only my second day here, and she might be pacing in the study or in the kitchen downstairs, full of ideas or letters that need dictating or any of the other stuff for which she's hired me.

I shower and brush my teeth hurriedly, slip on a clean shirt and jeans, and head downstairs. My hair is pulled back from my face, which is free of make-up. But despite this, and despite the scrubbing I gave myself under the water jets, I feel dirty. I dread, as I descend to the kitchen, seeing Anne again after the events of last night, after her witnessing my abandon.

She's not there, and her keys are gone from the little enamel dish on the bookcase by the front door, where I noticed she keeps them. From which I deduce that she's gone out. I feel a definite relief, although I know that I'm only putting off the inevitable and that in many ways it would be better to get it all out of the way now rather than let it ruin my day, this lurking niggle, like faint nausea, in the pit of my belly. It stops me, this feeling, from finishing the toast I make myself in the kitchen, although I manage to stomach a cup of tea, which clears my head a little.

Then, at a loss in the absence of Anne and any tasks – I look around for a note but she hasn't left one, and from the sitting room I can hear the sound of the Hoover, meaning that Hettie is in the midst of cleaning up – I decide to go out for a run in the park to get some oxygen pumping through my veins and make me feel clean again.

Changed into tracksuit bottoms and a vest top, a bottle of water in one hand and my iPod on my hip and in my ears, I leave the house and turn right for the park. It's a bright late-morning, perhaps a little too warm for running, but I set out at a slow pace and resolve to carry on for a good twenty minutes, to think of nothing but my body, the stretching and relaxing of my muscles, the filling and emptying of my lungs. I want to get into the zone, and so banish thoughts of Anne, and of James Carnaby.

I enter Kensington Gardens via the Orme Square Gate and head east, running parallel to the Bayswater Road, past the children shrieking with delight in the Diana Memorial Playground, hanging from the rigging of the mock pirate ship that I can glimpse through the trees. Down by the fountains near Lancaster Gate, I halt for a swig of water and to tie an errant shoelace, and then I turn in along the Long Water and run past the Peter Pan statue, before looping back west and circling the Round Pond to bring me back to where I started. I'm not a natural runner, and keeping my breathing measured and regular is such an effort that I really don't have the mental space to let Anne and James in. When they threaten to do so, I accelerate, push my body a little harder, banish them from the edges of my consciousness, even though I know they're squirming away inside my head in spite of me.

At last, feeling cleaned out by the blast of oxygen, I walk out of the park and down Queensway, past the ice rink and the roller-blading concessions, and along past Whiteley's domed shopping centre. I turn left onto Westbourne Grove and head for the Lebanese juice bar, where I order a mixture of freshly squeezed orange, mango and papaya to rehydrate myself. Sipping it slowly through a straw, I gaze out of the window, watching the world go by. When memories of the events of last night start creeping in, I grab one of the newspapers from the counter and try to concentrate on that.

It's when I look up, ten minutes later, that I see Anne walk past, almost as if my thoughts have summoned her up. As I watch her progress across the shopfront, I think how ordinary she looks. She has that edge of chic, of course, that Frenchness to her. But lots of people in London are chic. And lots of people are foreign. She doesn't stand out in any way. And she certainly doesn't look like someone who sat and watched two people having sex last night, or almost having sex. I think again of her eyes on my breasts, of the contracting of her throat, and my own throat goes dry. *What have I done?* I groan under my breath. *What the fuck was I thinking? How can I ever go back there?*

I order some baklava from the alluring display cabinet of Middle Eastern *mezze* and sweets but, as with the toast earlier this morning, I only toy with it, the butterflies in my belly winning out over my hunger. I have to face Anne, I tell myself at last. Even if it's to go back and be sacked. I am supposed to be on duty, and here I am playing hookie already, even if I did check to see if she'd left me any instructions. I should at least have left her a note to tell her where I was going.

No, there's no avoiding going back and seeing her; I feel like running away, but all my possessions are there, in the attic room. Short of following her and waiting until she goes out, then rushing upstairs to fetch my stuff and doing a runner before she gets back, a confrontation of some kind is inevitable. Tossing a handful of coins onto the table to cover my bill and a tip, I stand up and walk out.

My heart is thumping painfully as I unlock the door to the sound of Radio 4 from the kitchen, suggesting that Anne is indeed home – Hettie, from the sound of it, is hoovering upstairs. My instinct is still to run upstairs, grab my possessions and just leave, but there's another voice inside me, reminding me of how much I might have to gain from this job, this association with a literary figure. We had all had too much to drink, I reason with myself, and got carried away. After a day or two it will all be forgotten. I enter the kitchen.

Anne is at the sink, but as she hears me enter and let out a little cough, she turns around and meets my gaze frankly, with no trace of embarrassment. My own cheeks, I can feel it, burn. My legs feel wobbly, my mouth painfully parched, like sheets of paper sticking together.

Anne doesn't say anything, which doesn't help, but instead carries on just looking at me, a little questioning, as if intent on waiting for me to speak first.

'I . . . I'm sorry,' I manage at last.

'Sorry for what?'

Anne is a no-bullshit kind of woman, I say to myself. She won't ease life for other people, defer to the social niceties to help them out. She's straightforward to the point of brutality. Part of me admires her for that at the same time as hating her. How dare she be so cool and unmoved when she can see how hard this is for me?

'For . . . er . . . I looked for a note, but . . .'

'But what?' There's an impatience to her tone. She thinks I'm an idiot.

'I just – I went for a run. There didn't seem to be . . . You didn't tell me what I needed to do.'

'Needed to do?' For a moment she looks confused, then she smiles – a hard, pinched, even pitying smile. 'Oh, I *see*. Work, you mean.' She looks around her. 'It's fine to go for a run. There's not actually much to do right now, in any case.'

Her eyes alight on the mountains of books and papers on the dresser, apparently shifted there from the kitchen table before we had dinner with James last night. 'I suppose . . .' she says a little absently. 'I suppose I wouldn't mind if you sorted all this mess out.'

'What shall I do with it all?' I say, trying to hide my disappointment at this onerous task.

She eyes the piles, shrugs. 'Oh, I don't know,' she says airily, waving one hand as if swatting away a fly. I can tell she doesn't really care about the mess, that it's accumulated for months and months and that she's just trying to find me something to do, something to justify my being here, the hourly rate that she's paying me.

'Fine,' I say, to put her out of her misery. 'How about if I shelve the books, and organise the paperwork into piles? Then you can see if stuff needs acting on, and let me know if I can deal with any of that. The rest I can file.'

'Sounds wonderful,' she says, but already she's turning

away, preoccupied by some thought that's crossed her mind as I spoke. I watch her a little enviously. To be filled with creative impulses and ideas and to have the talent to follow through with them – what a joy that must be. I think again of my false starts in cafés, of my struggles to find a subject worth writing about. Anne must be right – I just haven't lived enough to have anything worth saying. Which is all the more reason to treasure this job and my good luck in finding it, and not to blow it because of my quibbles about last night. Alcohol does funny things to people. I only hope the other two drank enough wine to have only hazy recollections of what happened. Like a dream, it will hopefully fade away over time, until nothing remains but the faintest and most blurred of images.

Anne has left the kitchen, no doubt keen to get to her study. I stare down at the table, repress a sigh. I'd dreamed of being at the creative coalface, and tidying and filing is not exactly going to set me alight. Still, there's always time to be more involved with the creative side of things once Anne is further advanced in her novel. She mentioned that she's only now at the ideas stage, and presumably things will get more interesting and there'll be more scope for me as she progresses.

It doesn't take me long to work my way through Anne's mountains. Most of the paperwork can be instantly relegated to the bin – the circulars from local political parties, the out-of-date theatre mail-outs, Anne's reminders to herself for events now firmly in the past. The rest – unpaid bills, letters from readers forwarded from her publisher, literary periodicals still in their cellophane wrappers – I divide into piles, which I arrange across the table in order of urgency.

On top of each I put a note: 'Outstanding bills – URGENT', reads the first. Then I turn to the books.

Anne reviews English-language fiction for a handful of reviews in Paris and elsewhere in France, and much of the teetering pile is made up of unbound proof copies sent to her by publishers. Looking at the titles, I realise that some of them are now too old for her to even bother reviewing. Those I put into a separate stack by the wall, with a note to that effect. The rest I sort into date order and leave in the middle of the table. What appear to be non-review copies, things Anne has bought herself but not got around to reading, I carry into the living room to distribute among the bookshelves. There's a chance that she wants them in her study, but, if I have to ask her, then she might as well be doing this herself. I know already that part of my role is to take certain executive decisions. I remind myself that if she cared that much she wouldn't have left them pell-mell on the kitchen table anyway.

The fiction I slip onto the shelves wherever I find room – a brief look tells me that Anne is not the kind of person to organise her books alphabetically, or by subject matter, or whatever. I make a mental note of where I place each one in the event that she asks me for a certain title in the future, but I don't anticipate that she will. I'm happy just to have something to focus on to stop my thinking about last night. I'm feeling calmer and more phlegmatic about it all now that I've seen Anne again, and resolved to just get on with my job and write off our first evening as a freak incident.

Then I get to the bottom of the pile, and I'm brought up short by a book that I hadn't even noticed during my first sorting. It's a large and handsome hardback titled *Peek: Photographs from the Kinsey Institute*. The cover bears a sepia image of a woman, head thrown back, gown falling off her shoulders, bare breasts accentuated by what appears to be a wooden photo frame held up in front of them, outlining them. Glancing quickly at the door, I open the book and flip through it, feeling a bit like a naughty schoolgirl. I see a woman dressed as a dominatrix, wielding a whip over what appears to be a soft toy – a dog placed in a sit up and beg pose. I see a blur of naked legs viewed from above, in a multiple exposure. I see a group of nude men, posed around a column as if holding it up, akin to Greek statues. I go and shut the door to the hallway, come back and sit on the sofa, turn to the introduction.

The Kinsey Institute, I learn, is a research body – part of Indiana University – investigating 'human sexuality'. In the 1930s, its founder, Alfred C. Kinsey, started to gather photos and artworks to form a 'documentary collection' supplementing his team's 'observed data'. Dating from the 1870s on, the works came from all kind of sources – from artists themselves to law-enforcement authorities – hence their eclectic nature. The ultimate aim was a detailed classification scheme of sexual practices.

I flip through again: some items (the cream of a collection of almost 50,000) are subtle and evocative, others graphic to the point of brutality. This time I linger on items that leap out at me: some French erotic postcards from the late nineteenth century, a gorgeous male nude study from the 1950s, a photograph of some naturists in the snow, engaged – rather surreally – in archery. There is also an interesting-looking essay on sexual photography by an expert in the field, which I resolve to read when I have more time.

I look around at Anne's many bookshelves, seeking a spot where this one will fit. In the corner of the room, at the bottom of a sturdy bookcase, I notice a double-height shelf with a range of large-format art books. I steal over, cock my head to one side and let my eyes run over the titles: *Paul Gaugin: an Erotic Life*; *Gustav Klimt: Erotic Sketchbook*; *Ars Erotica: the Best Modern Erotic Art*; *Venus: Masterpieces of Erotic Photography*; *Private Collection: A History of Erotic Photography 1850–1940*. It seems my employer has a bit of a one-track mind when it comes to art.

I slip the Kinsey book on to the shelf and take out another one almost at random, then return to the sofa. I open the book, and my gaze falls on a picture of an older man, sitting in an armchair, facing the camera. The image is in black and white, as all the best nude photos seem to be, and his flesh glows like ivory. You can't see his sex itself, but his eyes are proud and provocative. He knows that he is still desirable. Inevitably, I have a clear and detailed flashback of last night, of James Carnaby's face between my legs, of his tongue on me, making me come over and over. My desire to see him naked was so strong it shocked me. I could never have imagine wanting that. Seeing this fifty-something man in the book makes me feel cheated all over again.

I rest the book on my knees, biting my lip and glancing towards the closed door again. One of my hands slips between my legs. I press it to my pussy, let out a moan of frustration. I wanted James so much, wanted him inside me. I can't believe that Anne allowed us to go so far and then whisked him away from me. That he submitted to her on that. Wasn't he gagging for me too? I don't even need to ask the question: I felt his cock throbbing for me like a little heart, even while we were still downstairs.

I keep moaning and rubbing at myself through my sweaty tracksuit bottoms even as I'm wondering at all this, a bitter taste in my mouth. What was in it for James? Sure, he got to go down on me, but didn't he leave as horny as fuck, as frustrated as me? He didn't look that way: he looked calm and composed.

I realise, as this occurs to me, that James must have known what was going to happen before we even began. That he knew that Anne wasn't going to let us go all the way. Again, what was in it for him?

My orgasm is already mounting as another thought, grimmer still, shoots into my consciousness – the realisation that I never actually heard him leave the house after the pair exited my room. I remember hearing voices in the hallway, but then I had to attend to myself, bring myself off again through sheer frustration at being cheated of James's cock. Then I zoned out, all floppy and sated. What if the stuff James and I did was just an appetiser – Anne's way of getting him all fired up to pleasure her? Could it be that watching her lovers at work with someone else intensified her desire for them? If so, then I have been used most shabbily.

The sound of the telephone interrupts me, and I'm grateful. I was on my way to a sad, cross, niggardly orgasm, a measly compensation for what should have been mine. Suddenly I don't want to think about James any more, of his complicity in Anne's warped little games. I don't want to come thinking of this man who could be old enough to be my grandfather.

I replace the book, walk over to the phone in the opposite corner of the room. I already know that Anne won't be answering it, that she eschews having a handset in her own room in order that she's not disturbed when the creative juices are flowing. And Hettie is out in the garden, pegging clothes on the line. There's an answering machine, of course, but I suddenly feel guilty again – I'm here to work, to assist Anne, not to sit around ogling pictures of naked men and bringing myself off.

'Hello, Genevieve speaking,' I say when I pick up, suddenly unsure whether it's a good idea to mention Anne's name when answering the phone, for reasons of privacy. Do novelists get stalked?

There's a pause on the other end, an intake of breath, and then my stomach flips as I hear a familiar voice.

'Genevieve,' says James quietly, and for a moment I imagine he's savouring the feel of my name in his mouth.

'Hi,' I reply, when it's clear he's not going to go on. My own voice comes out funny: squeaky and cracked at the same time. 'Er, Anne's upstairs. I don't know . . . I . . . is it all right to disturb her?'

'Oh no,' says James, and his voice comes down the line at me like molten honey. 'Oh no, you mustn't disturb Anne, not while she's working. I was just going to leave a message on the whatnot.'

'I'll take a message then,' I say meekly. 'I'll just fetch a –'

'No, no,' he says, quickly but still quietly. 'It wasn't anything important. In fact . . .' He pauses, as if he's not sure that what's coming is appropriate. 'In fact, I'm . . . I'm glad that you picked up.'

He pauses again, and I open my mouth to speak but nothing comes out. For a moment there's a silence so profound I can hear my own blood rushing in my ears.

Then James speaks again. 'I was wondering . . . You'll think me an old fool, but I was wondering if we could meet?'

I breathe in sharply. This was not what I was expecting, and the thought fills me with dread as well as desire. But James and I have unfinished business and I know that, if I don't accept his invitation, I'll be plagued by 'what-ifs' for the rest of my life.

'Sure. When . . . Where?'

'Are you free tonight?'

'I guess so. She hasn't . . .'

I falter, and he goes on in my place. 'She doesn't own you,' he says, 'just because you live in her house. Your time is your own, in the evenings.'

I nod, but I don't say anything.

'So let's say eight o'clock? We can have a bite, if you like. I haven't forgotten I promised you a copy of my book too.'

'OK, that would be nice.'

My voice must sound hesitant, unconvinced, for he adds, 'Don't worry. It will be discreet. I know you don't want to be seen around with such an old man. But I know the perfect place – are you familiar with the Prince Alfred on Formosa Street in Little Venice?'

'A pub?'

'Yes. It's easy enough to find with an *A–Z*, if you don't know the area. You'll see what I mean about discreet when you get there. Bye for now.'

He hangs up, and for a moment I just stand there, the handset still in my hot palm, sticky with perspiration. Then I start at a noise in the hallway and, after replacing the phone quickly, turn back in time to see Anne coming through the doorway, plucked eyebrows raised.

'Did I hear you on the phone?' she says.

'Er, yes,' I say, struggling not to stammer or let my voice get all squeaky again. 'It was just one of those annoying sales things, a recording. I hung up. Don't they charge you for listening, even though it's them who have called you?'

'Oh, those,' she says. 'Damned if I know anything about

all this modern technology.' But already she's breezing out of the living room and heading towards the kitchen, asking Hettie about lunch.

I grimace as I listen to her recede. Day two and already I'm keeping secrets from her. This job threatens to be a whole lot more complicated than I envisaged.

4

Return of the Sugar Daddy

I lie on my bed, trying to steady myself. Having grabbed something to eat, Anne headed back up to her study, without giving me any further tasks. Perhaps she didn't realise I'd finished sorting out the dresser, and I should have pointed out that I was at a loose end again. But dizziness overcame me, and I had to come up to my room and try to calm my racing mind.

For a few moments I feel truly lost, and I curse having seen the ad for this job. I toy with the idea of going downstairs again and dialling 1471 to get James's number, then calling him back and cancelling our date. The very word 'date', as I hear it in my mind, makes me shudder. A girl like me, fresh out of uni, going on a date with a possible sexagenarian? I see Vron's face in my mind's eye, incredulous at first, then mocking. 'What the *fuck* do you think you are playing at?' she'd bray. There'd be no point telling her that this is no ordinary sixty-something man, no point trying to convey to her the way it felt as if a lifetime's experience of pleasing women was condensed into what happened when he opened his mouth and applied his tongue to my clit.

But then I blank out Vron's face, blank out Nate's face – the latter confused and hurt as well as disbelieving. This has nothing to do with them. This is about me. And I feel that I am owed closure on this, after Anne intervened to put paid to our encounter. Even if nothing happens between James and me tonight, I will know, at least, the outcome to our little story. Know what there is between us, if anything, without Anne's interference.

And also, there is something in me that I'm not too sure I have really felt before, or registered as a part of my make-up, and that thing is plain curiosity. Curiosity about this older man and the feelings he brings forth in me. But also curiosity about him: what his body is like, how he uses it. It strikes me that I've always taken the safe option, the obvious route. Being with a much older man is something that has never occurred to me, betraying a failure of imagination on my part. But now that my interest is piqued I need to know what it is like.

Resolved not to miss out because of my nerves, telling myself I'll go to the pub early and have a stiff vodka or two before he arrives, to take the edge off it all, I feel stronger, and my morale returns – and with it my libido. Energy washes through my veins, renewing me, and I think again of some of the pictures in Anne's books, and particularly of the provocative look in the older guy's eyes. I love his fearlessness, his obvious pride in maintaining his body and not letting himself go or fade out of public view just because he's no longer young.

How blinkered I've been. The world must be full of attractive older men that I've been editing out, focused as I have been on 'suitable' men. When I was with Nate, I barely glanced at other men, let alone entertained fantasies about them. But I realise now that, even since we've split, I've only really looked at men who are like him. It's as if I've forced a type on myself, just because Nate was attractive to me. By doing so, I've been depriving myself of a world of much more interesting opportunities.

I close my eyes. There's no point in regrets, as I once said to Anne. And whatever comes of this whole crazy situation, of this weird job in this weird house with this weird woman, I have learnt something about myself already, something that has allowed me to advance as a person. Which can't be bad.

I doze for a while, letting my hand idly flit about my crotch. Lazily I tweak my tracksuit bottoms down. There's nothing underneath – to avoid VPL – and my fingers slip easily into the folds of my labia, into my wet hole. With my thumb I rub gently at my clit; then I increase, gradually, both the pressure and the speed. I daren't let myself dream about what might happen tonight with James, so instead I think of the man in the book, of his alabaster skin, of the barest hint of pubic hair between his crossed legs, of his frank, inviting gaze.

As I look at him, he rises from the chair, and I see his dick, as proud as his eyes, bobbing, questing. He walks towards me. I moan, jiggle my clit a little harder, a little faster. I spread my legs wide, push my fingers in further, wanting to make the feeling last, before I go crashing over the edge, riding on the wave of my orgasm. I try to keep quiet, but guttural little cries bubble up in my throat and escape from my mouth.

He's bending over me now, the man from the photo, and my fingers become his dick inside me, my thumb on my clit becomes his, and I throw my head back in ecstasy and enjoy the feeling of falling away as my climax takes hold.

I lie panting, my hand on my mons. As my breathing settles, I'm sure I hear a shuffling noise from the direction of the landing. I hold my breath, eyes fast on the door. Anne's there, I think, and for a moment I'm convinced she's going to come in. I sit up, slither down into my tracksuit bottoms where they have bunched up around my thighs. I look at the door handle, waiting for it to turn. There's no lock on my room, I realise – it didn't occur to me last night – but I don't think I would have had the presence of mind to use it anyway, when I got back up here.

Nothing happens. I swing my legs over the side of the bed, stand up and reach for a towel to take to the shower with me. It was only the cat, I say to myself as I shoot a quick glance back at the door. There really wasn't anybody there.

I intended to be at the Prince Alfred ahead of James, in time for a couple of stiff drinks, but it takes longer to walk to Little Venice from Bayswater than I anticipated. Or rather, with all the sexy new apartments and bars that have sprung up around the new Paddington Basin and alongside the canal, I find myself waylaid en route. It's a blissful summer evening – still warm, but with a freshening breeze – and for a while I sit on the bank and watch the comings and goings of the barges, tilting my face up towards the sun as it begins its slow descent.

While I'm sitting here, a couple passes by, arms hooked around each other, white teeth flashing as they exchange loving smiles. For a moment I feel a pang – this is what I had with Nathaniel, for a long time. I'd do anything to recapture that sense of security and protection, that feeling of being completely in tune with someone, if only for the space of an evening. But I can't hope that of my meeting with James. I can hope that the spark is still there between us – that there *was* a spark, and that it wasn't just the wine talking. But that easy, unforced companionship that I had with my first love and erstwhile soulmate seems to be beyond the scope of what exists between James and me, given our circumstances. It's not even really the age gap: it's how things started, in a conflagration. With Nate we flirted and wooed each other for months, gradually inching towards sex, as afraid of it as much as we wanted it. It was as if we were both aware of how precious the thing that we had was, and wary that giving ourselves to each other physically might wreck that. Might dispel the mystery that we held for each other.

With James, things began with fire, a sort of violence. There was no romantic preamble, no emotional foreplay. Suddenly I found myself on his knee with his hand between my legs and his cock pressing into my buttocks. Even if things carry on, there will never be that slow burn, that gradual ascent into intimacy and trust, that I had with Nate.

My eyes follow the couple along the bank of the canal. Blinking away tears, I get to my feet and cross the bridge that will take me to the pub. I look at my watch and, seeing that it is two minutes to eight, feel a surge of excitement tinged with terror at the thought that James is probably already waiting for me.

I walk in, and for a moment I'm confused – the pub seems minuscule. Then I do a double-take and realise my mistake: the place is actually divided into a number of small snugs around a central bar, the wooden partitions between them inset with waist-high hatchways so you can move between them.

I'm standing in one of them and I lean forwards over the bar, craning my neck to try to see into the other snugs and assess whether James is already here. Suddenly hands rest on my hips from behind and there's a whisper of breath on the exposed nape of my neck, where I've pulled my hair up into a chignon to match my austere but hopefully sexy outfit – a figure-hugging black pencil skirt and a crisp black shirt with wide lapels.

'Ingenious, *n'est-ce pas?*' comes the voice, and I turn around and smile, shyly, at James.

'Hi,' I say, struggling to catch my breath.

He gestures around us. 'Now you see why I chose this place. Doesn't it remind you of compartments in a train?'

'I guess it does, now you come to mention it. What . . . Why . . . ?'

'It was a Victorian thing, a way of separating the sexes as well as people from different classes. There used to be things called "snob screens" over the bar counter too, for added privacy from the bar staff. Now, of course, it makes a perfect spot, on a quiet weekday night, for a tryst.'

I feel my belly leap. Is this what this is: a tryst? Suddenly my life seems exciting, one worthy of a would-be writer. Yet much as I might have felt I wanted that, my legs have started shaking. I'm terrified of what might be about to happen. Am I going to have an affair with James Carnaby? And, if so, what does he see in me? What do I have to offer a man like him?

He turns side-on to the bar, still looking at me, and asks me what I want to drink. My first thought is a Staropramen and a vodka chaser, but I decide that that sounds a bit studenty, and certainly unfeminine, and ask for a large glass of white wine. Already I'm annoyed with myself at being concerned about making a good impression, at foregoing what I really want because I'm afraid of what James will think of me. Why can't I relax and be myself? Why do I always feel this need to match people's expectations?

James turns back to me, two drinks in his hand, one of them a tall glass of foaming amber beer. It looks delicious. I could kick myself.

'Are you OK?' he says, sensing that something is wrong, and for the first time since I've got here I meet his gaze. At once, feeling like I'm being sucked into a black hole, I forget all about the beer as I struggle to maintain my composure. James has gorgeous warm brown eyes that inspire confidence. He looks, as he stands there questioning me with them, as if he really cares. As if I am the only person in the world for him right now.

'I'm fine,' I manage at last.

'Shall we?' He gestures with his head to the right, and I follow him as he dips through one of the hatchways and then another to find us a deserted snug. Reaching the one at the end, he places our glasses on the table and then swings back to close the hatchway against the rest of the world.

I study him as he goes. He moves athletically as he bobs through the hatchways, with surprising litheness for a man his age. I guess he must go to the gym on a regular basis to remain so lean and limber. His hair, though well and truly grey, is expertly cropped and shaved at the neck, giving him a clean, youthful look. His clothes are casual but smart: well-fitted Paul Smith jeans and a pale linen jacket over a cream shirt. Brogues glimmer on his feet, polished and of impeccable quality. He's a man, it's clear, who has the good taste to spend his money wisely. A man who knows what suits him and how to show himself off to best advantage. For the first time, I find myself wondering about the women in his life.

I know next to nothing about him, I realise, despite his being a literary figure of some renown. He's written well-received tomes on various aspects of art history, including a very famous work on the nude in Western art, and has curated numerous exhibitions. But of his private life I know nothing. Is he perhaps a widower? And how come he's currently single, given his looks, fame and money? Or isn't he currently single at all?

My worries must be inscribed on my face, for James reaches over to give my hand a reassuring pat and, just as he did the first time at Anne's house, he lets it linger, his eyes probing mine.

'How has your day been?' he says, and I cast around for something sensible to reply. I can hardly tell him I spent much of it looking at nude photos and thinking about him, having a wank in my room as Anne – the more I think about it the more I'm convinced she *was* there – listened in.

'Busy?' he prompts me. 'Anne working you hard?'

I shrug. 'Not very. I tidied her piles of crap for her.'

'Oh good.' He laughs. 'That confounded kitchen. A nightmare. Anne's really not very good at the domestics, and even with Hettie around it's a losing battle. What else did you get up to?'

'I . . . I went for a run. She wasn't around and I didn't know what else to do. She – I'm not sure what she wants of me, to be honest.'

James takes a sup of his beer, and his eyes leave mine and wander over to the window. I follow his gaze. Through the etched glass a tree is fluttering and flapping in the rising breeze.

'Oh,' he says a little vacantly, as if his mind is suddenly elsewhere. 'I'm sure it will all become clear in time. I'm certain Anne has plans for you.'

I stare at him. Suddenly there's a sinister edge to everything: to his voice, to this meeting, to the telephone call. I remember how this confident, self-assured, worldly man was ready to defer to Anne's wishes at the height of our sexual excitement, and I wonder again what's in it all for him. Is this really a date or is James playing games with me?

'Like what?' I ask, surprised by the sudden harshness in my voice. 'What plans?'

He looks back at me, but his eyes seem unseeing. 'How should I know?' he says. 'But she wouldn't have placed the ad if she didn't need help, would she? I'm sure you'll get the hang of things soon enough.'

'Yeah,' I mutter, looking down at the table, tracing with my fingers the damp circle on the beer mat where my glass has stood.

Sensing that I am going away from him, that the good mood we started out with risks being lost, he leans into me, and I can feel his breath on my face, minty and fresh but tinged with the beer he's been sipping. It's all I can do not to swoon. My hand tightens on his as I feel his free hand beneath the table, alighting on my knee, pushing up my pencil skirt and then making its way up my inner thigh. I grab my glass and take a huge gulp of the honey-coloured Chardonnay, then another.

'Your legs have started to shake,' says James in a low voice.

Is it any bloody wonder? I want to shout, but instead I look panicked over towards the section of bar that fronts our snug. Luckily, we're in the very last one, and the few staff on duty on this quiet evening seem to have congregated at the other end, where the main doors from the street are. Nobody can see us, thank God.

He leans in further, nuzzles my throat, and I moan and start shuddering, my whole body convulsing. This is where it really gets me, and he's found it – my main erogenous zone, the place where madness begins. With one hand I steady myself against the wall, with the other I reach out wildly, flailing, almost sending my drink flying from the table as I seek something to grab, to anchor me to the Earth. My head is thrown back, and I'm at his mercy now, totally, still aware that we could be seen by a passing member of staff at any moment but unable to do anything to prevent that happening. Unable to countenance the act of calling this to a halt, of insisting we go somewhere more private.

Still steadied against the wall and the table, I bring one knee up against my chest, shucking my shoe off as I do so. I slip one bare foot between James's inner thighs and with my toes stroke the bulge of his cock and balls in his designer jeans. His breath sharpens on my neck, speeds up, becomes irregular. I let go of the table edge, bring my free hand down and unzip his fly deftly, then slip my hand into his trousers and down his pants. His dick, blood warm and hard, stiffens further as I take it in my sweaty palm. I yank at it.

'I want you,' I whisper urgently. 'I want you now.'

He lifts his head a little and shoots a glance over his shoulder.

'Don't worry about them,' I command him. 'There's no one there.'

I've let go of his cock, am struggling to bring my knickers down over my thighs, to reveal myself in all my sodden glory, ripe and ready for him. But he's distracted still, his mind suddenly elsewhere. I am the driving force now, despite it being he who initiated this.

I leave my knickers where they are, wrap one hand around the back of his neck and try to coax him towards me. I no longer care where we are, or what damage may be incurred by the furniture, the glassware.

Then suddenly I know why James's attitude has changed. All of sudden it's like a sixth sense has fired up in me, and I know, I just *know*, that Anne Tournier is on the other side of the wooden partition, listening in on us. I don't know how I know, exactly, but there is something in James's face, in the way he held his body as he turned to look around, the way his attention seems to be directed more towards the neighbouring snug than towards the bar, as one would have expected to it be, that gave the game away.

And with that comes the suspicion that this has all been a set-up – that James phoned with Anne's prior knowledge or probably even at her bidding, in the hope that I would answer and that he could set up this meeting. This was never a tryst, in the strictest sense of a secret date. But it does, I think, remembering something I learnt at uni, match more closely the idea conveyed by the original French word *triste*, meaning a waiting place in a hunt. For what is happening here if not that I am being preyed upon by Anne in some way that goes beyond my comprehension?

Of course these thoughts only really come to me in flash form or with hindsight, for I'm preoccupied both with the sudden certainty of Anne's presence behind the screen and the awareness of the ludicrousness of what I've been trying to do – which is to fuck James right here in this pub, sprawled against this rickety table sticky with beer. I've got carried away to the point of utter recklessness and disregard for the social proprieties, and now the reality is catching up and I feel foolish and exposed.

I whip my skirt down, my knickers still bunched around my lower thighs. 'She's here, isn't she?' I hiss, and James looks back towards the half-height door and nods.

As my gaze follows his, the door slowly opens. Although I'm expecting it, the sight of Anne's face sends a jolt through my body, like an electric shock.

'Wha–?' I begin. But, before I can go on, James, having quickly zipped himself up, is walking towards Anne, reaching out to hold the door open for her, his body language betraying no shock or even surprise.

Bent forwards from the waist, Anne slips through and then straightens up. Her eyes are fast on James's, and something passes between them, some information conveyed in a language I don't know, that is foreign to me. It's not amusement, or embarrassment on James's part. It's just a kind of knowledge, an understanding of some kind; something that speaks of years of a friendship with depths at which I can't even guess. These are looks resplendent with secrets.

As if remembering, in some kind of psychic synchronicity, that I am there, they both look towards me, where I stand by the table.

'Hello, Genevieve,' says Anne coolly, as if her intrusion on this scene is perfectly natural. No explanation is proffered for her sudden appearance. I'm so stunned by this that I'm unable to reply.

James takes up the baton. 'How about if we go back to my flat?' he says, and Anne nods.

'Lovely,' she says. 'I trust you still have some of that Hennessy, the Private Reserve?'

James smiles, holding open for us the door that leads directly out from our snug onto the street. 'I've been saving it just for you,' he says. 'It's worthy only of a very special lady.'

Anne laughs, a high, slightly forced or false laugh it seems to me. 'Superb,' she says, linking her arm through his. 'Genevieve, you absolutely must try some. It's indescribable, a mix of dried orange and roses, roasted almond and vanilla.' She looks me deep and hard in the eyes, as if she's trying to tell me something, but at the same time her gaze is curiously expressionless. My stomach lurches: for a moment it's as if I'm staring into the void.

'Vanilla,' she goes on, 'is an aphrodisiac, of course.'

I look back at her, still lost for words.

James, intentionally or not, comes to my rescue. 'It should be something special,' he says, 'at that bloody price.' Now it's his turn to look deep into my eyes. 'Seventy-five quid a bottle is what that little beauty costs. Your boss has expensive tastes.'

Anne laughs unconvincingly again; the sound resembles a bell, clear and over loud in the deserted street along which we walk.

'But I'm worth it, aren't I?' she says, rolling her eyes first at James, then at me.

Walking along, I'm glad that Little Venice is so quiet tonight. We must form quite a curious threesome: me, Anne and James. A timid young thing in her twenties, a jaded and world-weary French novelist in her fifties, and a distinguished-looking art historian possibly in his sixties. But of course the casual passer-by would take us for a girl – a student or young professional – out for an evening stroll with her mum and dad.

Yet a threesome, precisely, is what I imagine I am on my way to. James's phone call was pure ruse – a way to get me out of the house in order that Anne might follow me, finding her own kind of titillation in that. I can't imagine why else it should have come about this way. Anne's appearance – her *interruption* – was certainly no accident or coincidence; nor can James claim that she must have listened in to our telephone conversation, for nothing in him showed surprise at her arrival. No, the two of them cooked it up between them, perhaps for the sheer novelty value of it all. Anne must get bored at home all day.

I shrug, fatalistic now. Let her have her fun, I think, and as the thought passes through my mind I'm surprised: it's not as if I've had that much to drink. I could use that excuse yesterday, but not today. Or not yet: already I'm tasting in my mouth, in the back of my throat, the burn of the cognac I've been promised, and along with it the lure of sweet forgetfulness.

After ten minutes or so, James and Anne slow down and then halt before an imposing red-brick block of flats on a wide avenue. James rattles his pockets in search of his keys, and then opens the heavy front door and gestures us to go in before him. As I walk behind Anne, I look up into his face, and there must be a question in my expression, or at least doubt or hesitation, for he smiles reassuringly, and for a moment his hand comes down to rest on my shoulder, ever so lightly.

We take a shiny modern lift to the top floor, where James's flat turns out to be. It doesn't take long to make the ascent, but the atmosphere has grown perceptibly more tense since we left the street, or perhaps it's just the fact that we are suddenly packed together in a small space, our bodies almost touching, our breaths mingling, the tinge of sweat in the air, from one or from all three of us – who knows? I'm careful to avoid catching my own eye in the mirror at the back of the lift, knowing that if I do I might well bottle it. Or perhaps I just won't recognise myself, and that, surely, is the first step on the road to madness?

Part of me, of course, wants to bottle it. Part of me recognises how laughable this is to start with, and also the demeaning nature of it all – already it's clear that Anne is using me as some kind of puppet or toy. But bottling it, I remind myself, would bring my new world, my chance at a new life, crashing down around me, and I know I would regret that – at least if I did it prematurely, without giving it my best shot. I don't, after all, know what Anne and James have in mind, and I'll never know if I bolt at the first hurdle like a frightened horse.

We step out into a long corridor, at the end of which James opens another door that takes us into his apartment. Despite the traditional nature of the building, the space inside has been opened up and much ingenuity put into creating a modern layout. The main living space is open-plan, with a large seating area with several dark-leather sofas and armchairs arranged in a circle into which a large stainless-steel arc lamp dips its head like a metallic swan. The effect is 1970s Paris. There's no television, or none discernible. To the right of the room, on the side that must face the street, is a long stainless-steel island that forms a sort of breakfast bar cum kitchen work surface. Parallel to it along the wall are some units in pale Scandinavian wood, and an oven, hob and sink – all, again, in sparkling stainless steel. The kitchen is impeccable and looks hardly used. Nothing – not even a bottle of olive oil or washing-up liquid – has been left out to disrupt the minimalist effect.

James sees me looking around and taking all this in. 'Welcome to my little nest,' he says. 'It's nothing special, but it does for an old bachelor like me.'

'It's lovely,' I blurt, but already the word 'bachelor' is whirring around in my head, reawakening my unanswered questions of earlier. What exactly is James's role in all this, in this game of which Anne is so clearly the ringleader? What's in it for this worldly, successful man, who despite his age could most likely seduce any woman he desired?

He shrugs. 'It'll do,' he says faux modestly.

Anne, in the meantime, has ensconced herself on one

of the squishy leather armchairs. 'How about some of that cognac?' she calls across, her lips pinched in a meagre smile, as if she disapproves of our small talk. *Just get on with it*, her face seems to say, and the butterflies start up in my stomach again as the uncertainty of her motives and intentions fires up in me once more. I very gladly accept the glass of amber liquid that James proffers me.

'Chin-chin,' he says, having handed Anne her glass and then turned back to his drinks cabinet to get his own. He and I clink glasses; as we do so, he looks me hard in the eyes, as if trying to send me some sort of telepathic message. I smile nervously, and he smiles back. Then he gestures towards where Anne is sitting.

'Do sit down, Genevieve,' he says, and I turn around and plump myself down opposite Anne, without looking at her.

James fiddles with a swanky Bosch hi-fi system set on a low Oriental-looking table in a corner of the room. After a few seconds, something soothing comes on, something that has at least some measure of a calming effect on my jangling nerves.

'Ah,' says Anne, and I risk a glance over in her direction. She's leaning back against the chair, chin tilted up a little, eyes half-closed. I wonder what scenes are playing themselves out on the inside of her eyelids.

'Górecki,' she adds after a few moments. 'A perfect choice.' She takes a swig of her cognac.

Watching her, I do the same. Then I take another.

Seeing how fast I'm getting through it, James crosses the room with the bottle and refreshes my glass, giving me a more than generous measure. As he stands beside me, letting the fiery Hennessy flow from the bottle, he places one hand on my shoulder. This time it stays there. We look at each other and time seems to stand still. I have to have you, I think, and I wonder if he can read my thoughts in my eyes, hear them in some way or other.

He nods, and I understand that he has understood, that he knows I would do anything to have him, fully, and that includes sharing him with Anne. If the only way she will concede him to me is piecemeal, then so be it. I'm prepared for that sacrifice.

The alcohol is working its magic, making me brazen, for I feel a tingling sensation through my veins, through my whole body, and I hear myself say, 'Where's your bedroom then?'

James jerks his chin over towards a spiral staircase in the corner, half-obscured by a tall and leafy pot plant. I stand up, dizzy with the feeling that suddenly it is me who is leading events, who has taken up the reins. There's a power in it, but also a kind of panic. Panic at having to keep up the role now that I have assumed it.

I stride across the room towards the staircase, forcing purposiveness and resolve into my movements, despite the jelly-like feel of my legs. James is following me. I reach the staircase and start to climb, and about halfway up I turn my head and survey the scene below.

Anne is still sitting in the chair, sipping her cognac. She seems completely unmoved by the fact that we are leaving her, seems not to have even registered it, although I know that it can't have escaped her attention. Above all, she is showing no signs of intending to follow us. Maybe, I think, and dare to hope, this time she is satisfied by her comfy armchair and her expensive drink.

Reaching the top of the staircase, I find myself in front of a set of double doors that are already open on to a circular room, which I realise must be set in a little turret. The bed, circular too, must have been commissioned to fit the space. It's a stunning room with a domed ceiling and windows all around – a sort of eyrie from which one can survey both the street and the communal gardens behind. The sky has darkened considerably now, and the streetlights are flickering into life on one side of the turret. On the other, the trees waving their branches in the wind are mere shadowy presences.

I turn towards James, who has followed me up the stairs. As I do so, I lower myself to a seating position on the bed. Beneath my hands I can feel the finest linen. James certainly hasn't skimped when it comes to his living arrangements. I look around again and notice that there is nothing else in this room beyond the bed.

'Is this your room?' I ask.

He nods.

'Then where –?'

He interrupts me. 'There's a dressing room downstairs, beside the bathroom, with wardrobes and so on. It doubles as a guest room too.'

'Will Anne – ?' I begin, but again I am interrupted, this time by a gesture – that of James holding up one finger against his lips. Then, as if relenting, or perhaps reacting to the expression on my face, he glances back over his shoulder and speaks.

'You don't *have* to do this, you know,' he says, in a voice barely louder than a whisper.

'I do,' I say. 'I do know, but . . .'

I'm not sure how to go on. *But I don't want Anne to be involved*, is what I was most probably going to say, but I'm scared that, if I say it, this whole thing will be called off, abruptly and without any chance of reprieve. Anne, it seems to me, is my only conduit to James and, if I demand her exclusion, I'm scared there'll be no way back to him.

Already James has moved closer to me, is easing me gently down onto the bed with his hands. Large and firm on my shoulders, they bolster me. I'm convinced he means me no harm, emotionally. Similarly, the look in his eyes is a guarantee of his sincerity. He wants me, as I want him, no matter at whose instigation this situation has come about.

I lie back, unfurl myself against the bed, luxuriously. Throwing my head back into the pillows, eyes closed, I submit myself to the caress of James's mouth as he peppers the tender flesh of my neck and throat with his lips. Moving around, he nibbles at my ear lobes, roots around my shoulders. All the while his hands are busy with my shirt, unbuttoning, shifting it off me and out from under me, before turning their attention to my bra – reaching round and expertly unclasping it to let my breasts spring free.

Coming up onto his knees from where he has been bent over me, James strips off his jacket and shirt quickly, throws them to the floor. The way in which he does so – casually, flippantly, as if they were cheap rags and not the finest garments money can buy – turns me on. He undoes his jeans, but doesn't pull them down, rushing to grab his cock out of his boxers. He's in a hurry for me, as I am for him. I tear off my blouse and bra, then reach down, pull my skirt up and start struggling to push my knickers down, wanting him to enter me quickly, before Anne can intervene. He helps me, pulling them down from my lower thighs and off over my legs, throwing them aside as he did his own clothes. They land on top of his. Crowning, in all their polka-dotted glory, his sober coloured attire, they provide a stark illustration of how far apart we are, James and I. And yet we burn so hard for each other, across the decades that separate us.

I would love, I think as I reach for him, to know the story of James's life, his erotic biography. Maybe one day he will tell me. Perhaps one day, when all this is over, we will be friends.

These are the thoughts that tumble through my mind as I raise my knees and open myself to him, guiding his prick towards me with one hand. Already growing frenzied, I have the other hand on my sex, two fingers jiggling my clit. Although the last thing I want to do is attract Anne's attention, I can't stop the low moans that are escaping from my throat. I don't remember ever feeling this fired up with Nathaniel, though I'm sure it must have been like this in the early days. Or perhaps not – perhaps I need this feeling of transgression, afforded by James being so much older than me, being practically old enough to be my *grandfather*, to get really hot. Nate and I were soulmates, and perhaps for that very reason unable to achieve the true excitement that difference brings. I'm not sure now that he ever held any real mystery for me. I never missed that, having never known it. But suddenly mystery seems very desirable.

I pause before guiding James inside me and, opening my eyes, I find that he is looking into my face as if questioning me. He seems to be wondering what I am thinking, and I hope that I am mysterious to him. It strikes me that he might never have had a woman as young as me, or not since he was young himself. Perhaps this is all as new to him as it is to me. The sense of being on the threshold of a discovery is palpable.

Yet while all of this has been winding its way through my thoughts, I've become aware, just as I suddenly knew in the pub, that Anne has grown near. I haven't heard her catlike creep up the stairs, but then I have been moaning in spite of myself, and the rustle of the leaves against the windows has been echoed by that of the crisp linen sheets on the bed.

I turn my head away from James's gaze and look towards her in the doorway, but, to my astonishment, without any real disappointment. There's an inevitability to it all that precludes that.

Anne returns my stare dispassionately, almost as if her mind is elsewhere, as if she's here physically but not mentally. I wonder what thoughts are ticking through her mind, what images flutter there. For it's obvious that this is something complicated for Anne, something beyond mere lechery and voyeurism. This, after all, is the author of such multilayered and emotionally complex novels as *Night Moves* and *Inside the Doll's House*. Nothing is ever simple for the characters in Anne's fiction, especially when it comes to sex, and I can't imagine it can be for her.

James, meanwhile, hasn't questioned why I've stopped, why my attention has been diverted away from him, from which I deduce that this is no surprise for him either. How could it be otherwise, when Anne accompanied us home? This thing, whatever it is, is not a thing between James and me, but a thing between James and Anne, first and foremost. It is me who has been blind to that, thinking that I could have him to myself, if I hung on in there long enough. I thought that Anne was instrumental in all this, but she's more than that – she's integral. Without her there would be nothing.

James is still staring at my face, but I don't look back at him. I can't. I don't want him to see my humiliation at having let myself be carried away on this wave of desire and longing and falsity. But more than that, I'm riveted by Anne and the whole issue of what she's going to do next, now that she's entered the scene that she's set, like an author walking into one of her own books and subverting the plot. Is she finally going to let down her guard and join in? Am I going to see my literary heroine naked, and even get it on with her? I'm terrified and freaked out by the possibility.

Anne steps forwards, and for a moment it's almost as if she's in some kind of trance. But then she seems to come to life again, and it's at this point that I notice that she has something under one arm, some kind of leather valise, chestnut brown and glossy in the low light. Pulling it out, she steps towards the bed and lays it down next to us, without looking at us. For a minute or two she merely regards it, and it strikes me there's a certain wistfulness or even sadness in those ice-blue eyes. I probe them with my own, but like the sea they seem both limitless and opaque, resistant to my questioning. Anne has a past, I think, that I will never fathom. Ditto James. What has brought them both to this point will never be entirely clear to me.

James is still kneeling over me, his prick still enclosed in my fist. Although my mind has wandered from him, the tension of the moment has kept my grasp on him firm. I finally manage to look back into his face. He's observing Anne now and, though his body is rigid, his expression tells me that he, at least, knows what is about to happen, or at least its essential flavour. He's not in the dark like me. I look back at Anne.

With a surgeon's careful movements and precision, she unzips the case and folds back the lid. I gasp. Displayed inside is a panoply of the most exotic and refined sexual toys that I have ever seen. Not that I'm an expert in the field, an aficionado. To date my experience has been limited to a straightforward vibrator that Nate bought for me, to 'keep me company' when he was away. I used it, but not that often. He was keen for me to try it on him too, but we never got around to it. I guess we were both a little embarrassed. Funny how shy you can be with someone you think you know so well yet how uninhibited with total strangers.

Anne clears her throat, as if calling my attention back to the present. Inside her box of tricks, I see one object that looks like it must be used for spanking, and another that resembles a riding crop. There are also some black leather wrist cuffs, and a gold moulded mask, again in what looks like leather. But it's the exquisite polished-wood dildo that has most caught my eye. At its sculpted tip it resembles the bulb of a penis in slightly elongated form, then it thickens a little towards the centre, dips in like a corseted waist and finishes in a ripple of three bulges at the base. Its combination of ridges and ultra-smoothness have me longing to try it out.

From beside it, Anne takes out a small, square brown bottle of what I take to be lube. She removes the top, slowly, and the air fills with the scent of honey. I swallow drily, eager for things to get moving again, in whatever form she decrees.

She holds the bottle up and tilts it, and, as she watches the slow drip-drip of the mellifluous liquid, it's as if she's relishing making me wait, in having this power over me. Or am I just being paranoid?

James's eyes are following Anne's movements, a half-smile creasing the bottom half of his face, mischief firing up in his eyes.

'Looks like somebody's paid a visit to our secret place,' he mutters at last, and he sounds hoarse with desire. His words rent the air; it's as if a curtain has been torn, revealing a new world behind it.

Anne smiles too, in her restrained, almost secretive fashion. 'Calla Lily,' she replies, her voice as hushed as if she were in a church service. And indeed, there's a sort of reverence to the atmosphere now, an air of holy ritual. A transcendence of the ordinary.

'But no,' she continues, still smiling to herself, not looking at James. 'I didn't have a chance to go,' she said. 'Not this time. So I ordered online.'

The image conjured up is almost comical: one of Anne, this great if under-appreciated novelist, sitting up in her study, supposedly writing great works of literature but instead getting all warm and moist as she browses designer sex toys, clicks on a few of her favourites and then feeds in her credit card details. I think of her awaiting the postman with particular excitement, and of the frisson she must feel as she opens the door and takes from him a package that, this time at least, contains something a little naughtier than the usual stack of new novels to review.

The dripping stops, and time seems to stand still. I look up at James to find him gazing at Anne, a little like an obedient dog awaiting an order from its master. There's a kind of devotion in his eyes, and a submissiveness, that makes me wonder anew at where he's coming from in all this, what lies beneath it all. What is his erotic history, and is he even conscious of his motives and desires or does it all lie far beneath the surface, impervious to attempts at excavation?

Anne nods, but, as she does, her eyes turn from James to me, it's me that she's looking at as she greases the dildo, running her elegant fingers, finished in a chic French polish, slowly up and down it. It's too much, and I have to look away.

Then she holds a hand out to James and he takes the

implement silently. He turns to me, makes as if to bring it towards my pussy where I still lie beneath him, legs parted, nearly forgetting myself in all this drama and expectation.

'No!' says Anne imperiously, and we both look towards her. She's standing by the bed as before, looking down on us.

'Then . . . ?' prompts James.

'Turn her over,' she says curtly, and I shudder at the robotic aspect to her voice. Again, I think, it's as if she's in a trance, been taken over by another power. I think of watching the film *Invasion of the Body Snatchers* and how I got the creeps every time one of the characters realised a partner or a friend wasn't the same person as before.

But Anne hasn't been taken over by alien life forms. Anne is acting according to some all-consuming inner need, some kink in her that gets off on watching, on controlling proceedings without actually taking part. I'm the first to admit that, lacking in worldly wisdom as I am, I don't know whether this is a rare thing or not. I'm aware of the existence of dominatrices, dungeons and so on, and of the need in some people to control and in others to submit, but this is my first experience of someone who seems to get off on that kind of behaviour, and I am struggling to understand.

James is quick to obey her, sliding one arm under my lower back, wrapping it around me and then levering me over. My skirt flips back down as he rolls me, and he whips it up to expose my bare rump. I close my eyes, my throat dry with apprehension and desire, my heart pounding with sudden violence.

I start, as if electrocuted, when I first feel the caress of the oiled wood against my tail bone. Then I let out a rending, long-drawn-out moan as the implement is pulled down between my arse cheeks, tracing a vertical line over my sphincter and over my perineum to my pussy, where it stops to tease and tantalise.

'Aaarrrgh' is all I can manage, desperate now to be filled by this beautiful dildo. But James is hesitating. I look over my shoulder, ready to plead with him to go on, to beg and to abase myself if necessary. He's oblivious to me though: his eyes are locked with Anne's. Again I get the sense of some sort of coded message passing between them, or rather from Anne to him. James, I see, is unable to really act until Anne accords him her permission.

And at last, after what seems like interminable minutes, she nods brusquely again, and then the dildo seems to tremble at my hole before pushing slowly inside. I raise my rump higher as my muscles inside clench around the magnificent toy, welcoming it, ensuring that it can't be withdrawn – not now it's finally inside me.

It feels, as James starts to push it in and out, gently at first and then with increasing speed and force . . . it feels . . . Words, which I have always thought of as my strongpoint, start to fail me. The only thing I can think of as it works its magic against my inner walls is the word 'heaven'. This is what it must feel like to go there.

As James creates a rhythm, I try to fall in with it, pushing back on the dildo to meet it, creating a kind of rapturous unison. Although I can already feel it building up, I fight to delay my orgasm. I want it so bad, and I know that were I to lay a finger or two on my clit I'd explode, go off my head with joy. But I've waited for James to be inside me for so long, in one form or another, that I don't want to come and bring this to an end.

James's free hand is on one of my upturned buttocks, his fingers digging into my flesh, driving me bananas. His

thumb is creeping ever closer to my arsehole, encroaching
on the milky flesh between my cheeks, and I wonder if he'll
dare enter me with it – whether that is on Anne's agenda
or whether he'll be thwarted again, called away at the last
minute, like a dog that's gone after an illicit bone. I realise
that that's the second time I've thought of James as a dog
at Anne's beck and call, and for a moment I feel a curious
mixture of pity and disdain. Pity at the fact that he feels
compelled to obey her orders and disdain at his allowing
himself to be controlled like some kind of puppet – or puppy.

That, in turn, makes me wonder what he really thinks of
me. He's been nothing to date, if not kindly and respectful.
He even gave me the chance, this evening, to let myself off
the hook if I wasn't happy with the way things were going. A
chance I didn't take. I wonder if he feels pity for me too, or
disdain. Or whether he understands the reasons that keep me
here when I barely even intimate them myself.

His thumb pad is against my sphincter now, pressing,
pressing, and I'm growing delirious with need. I push back
against him, accepting, even inviting him in. I've never had
anal sex before, although Nate tried once. I just couldn't
relax. Now – perhaps aided by the cognac – I am more than
willing. My pussy and arse are tingling with want.

There's a rustle, and I turn my head. Anne is holding
something out towards us. By now the light in the room
has fallen substantially, and it takes me a moment or two to
realise that it's the paddle that I saw in her case. I tense; this is
territory, I think panic-stricken, that I have never considered
going into. This is something deeper and darker than I have
ever contemplated. It might seem like an innocent bit of fun.
What harm can come of a bit of spanking between friends?
But I've read accounts suggesting that it's an area in which

things can rapidly get out of hand. What, I say to myself, if I like it too much?

But I'm mistaken: Anne doesn't intend for me to be spanked, since it's to me that she hands the implement. My surprise and hesitation must be etched on my face, for she nods in encouragement. My hand is quivering as I take it, but I'm strangely reassured by the fluid beauty of the object. Like the dildo, it is made of sleek chocolate-coloured wood. It reminds me of a hairbrush, and I titter a little nervously at the lascivious images that spring into my mind: of private schoolgirls and reddened arse cheeks.

'What's the joke?' says Anne a little sternly, and I remember where I am and wonder what's expected of me. Anne continues to eye me disapprovingly, and I'm taken back ten years to boarding school and being called in to see the headmistress for misdemeanours I don't recall. Mrs Scholes was her name, although nobody knew of the existence of a husband. Some of the girls said he'd probably killed himself when he'd realised what a dragon he'd married.

'Turn him over,' Anne barks, and I realise that the roles have been reversed. James realises too, slipping the dildo out of me. I turn over. James's jeans have remained undone, though he's tucked his cock back in his boxers, presumably before applying the dildo to me.

I hesitate, and it's Anne's cue to lose her temper.

'What are you waiting for, child?' she says. 'Turn him around and then over.'

Part of me nearly chokes on the word 'child'. Part of me wants to turn around and punch her in the face for trying to make me feel small and stupid. But this impulse is counterbalanced by an extraordinary curiosity that has risen in me like a tide. What will it be like to take charge, to spank James?

I know that I'll kick myself later if I shirk the opportunity just because I was offended by a word.

Placing one hand, rather gingerly I admit, on James's shoulder, I steer him round. The fact that he's a willing conspirator means it's not difficult: I'm really only guiding rather than pushing him. There's no coercion involved.

As he moves into place, Anne speaks again, less harshly this time.

'Now pull his trousers down,' she commands, and I do so, tugging a bit weedily at first and then growing braver, yanking them and his boxers until his flesh appears. His arse is handsome: toned and firm and rounded, but not so rounded that it's womanly. It's an undeniably masculine arse. I bring a hand to one of the cheeks, overcome with the desire to touch him.

'No!' nearly bellows Anne, and I remove it quickly. I've transgressed, I realise, overstepped the mark. This is Anne's game and we play by her rules. Any sign of autonomous behaviour, no matter how minor, will be stamped out. I should have realised this by now.

'Spank him,' she goes on. I look at the paddle and then at James's arse. I feel ridiculous. They must know I've never done this before, that I don't even know where to start. I bring my arm back, take a deep breath and then swing it forwards.

James yelps, his head flying back towards his shoulder blades.

'Not so hard,' says Anne. 'Build it up, slowly. Come on, try again.'

I obey, swinging more lightly this time, increasing the strength of it infinitesimally each time.

'Much better,' Anne tells me, calmer now. 'Here . . .' She

reaches over to my free hand and places it on James's other buttock. It seems I'm allowed to do this now. I risk a stroke and, though James emits a welcoming groan, Anne doesn't object.

I keep stroking him as I increase the pace and pressure of the spanks. His moans grower louder and more insistent, telling me I'm on the right track. I wonder where we will go from here.

I'm just considering reaching around him and taking his prick in my fist to start wanking him, wondering if I can do that while maintaining the spanking motion – and whether Anne will allow it – when she extends a hand and takes the paddle from me. I relinquish hold, watching as she places it carefully back in her case then drops the lid and fastens the clasps with a decisive movement. That's when I know that it's over. She doesn't need to say a word this time.

James knows too: already he's sitting up and putting himself away, swinging his legs over the side of the bed. A little flustered and embarrassed now that the momentum has been interrupted, I pull my skirt down and reach for my knickers, bra and shirt. I'm disappointed again, only this time it's not because I didn't have James inside me, since I had a more than adequate substitute. It's not even because I didn't reach orgasm – not the be-all and end-all of a sexual encounter. No, it's because seeing – and hearing – James's delight in being spanked has sparked my interest: would I enjoy, as he does, the smack of hard wood against the soft flesh of my buttocks? All at once something that I have never dreamed of trying has become an ache within me. I know that I won't be satisfied until I've experienced it.

I give Anne a meaningful stare, hoping that she'll get the message by some kind of telepathic means, but she's gone all businesslike, tucking her case back under her arm, turning for the staircase without a word. I follow her, less because I seek her company than because I don't know what to say to James if we're left alone. My expensive education failed to instil in me the basic etiquette of spanking, left me clueless as to what to say to someone whose arse you've just pinked raw with a sculpted piece of wood.

When I reach the bottom of the stairs, Anne has already crossed the room to the console table by the door and is on the phone, calling a taxi. When she replaces the receiver, she turns to me.

'They'll be right here,' she says. 'Do you have everything?'

I nod.

'Good.' She opens the front door to the apartment and I follow her out. Neither of us bids James goodnight; he's still up in his room. Nor do we talk to each other in the lift, or in the cab on the way back to Bayswater. It's only as she's opening her own front door back on St Petersburgh Place that she addresses me.

'You can have the day off tomorrow,' she says.

Then she closes the door onto the dark street behind us, and I follow her up the hall and watch as she continues up the stairs without another word.

'Goodnight, Anne,' I venture, but she's already disappeared, and I'm left alone, my words evaporating into the silence that surrounds me.

5

Down Time

I wake to the rain against the panes of my attic-room windows, and for the longest time I can't bring myself to cast off my covers and get up. It's like when you're a kid and you wake up and you don't know where you are, only this is more serious and more disorientating: I know where I am, but for a few terrible moments I don't know who I am. And during those moments, a wave of desolation washes over me, and a kind of homesickness for the life I had not so long ago – my life with Nathaniel, safe and predictable, boring perhaps, but as comforting as the blanket I used to trail around with me as a kid, in and out of dirty puddles, through the house and up into bed with me, to ward off night terrors.

As if in a reflex action back to those long dark nights of childhood, I scrunch myself up into a ball, hugging the duvet to me, eyes closed tight. When I finally do sit up and face the light, the first thing I do is reach for my mobile and summon up Nate's number on the screen. I know that, if I sit here staring at it, I won't make the call though. I know that I'll talk myself out of it. So before I can do that I jab the green button with my thumb and listen to the ringing tone, wondering

what I'm going to say. It's not even as if I want him back: I'm
the one who ended it and I've never seriously thought, even
at my loneliest moments, that I made the wrong decision. I
guess I just want the reassurance of his voice, something to
bring me back to myself, or at least to the girl I was before all
this weirdness started.

The tone goes on and on, and I'm gearing myself up to
leaving a message – or probably to open my mouth to leave
one but then change my mind – when suddenly Nate picks
up.

'Gen,' he says, sounding surprised and a little wrong-
footed. It's been a while since we talked, and the last time
was pretty unpleasant. He was still very down about the split
and begged me to meet him to talk things through. Having
done that a couple of times before, I was adamant I wasn't
going to put myself through it again. Not only for my own
sake, but for his – seeing or talking to me, I realised, made
things worse for him, setting him back on the wrong track.
It raised his expectations only to disappoint them again, and
that wasn't fair. I told him all that, but he was enraged that
I refused to see him, that I had that power over him. I guess
that's why he sounds so dubious now. I shouldn't have called.

'Hello,' I say at last. 'I'm sorry – this is silly. I . . . I . . .'

'What's up?' he says. His voice has softened; he's concerned about me.

'I . . . I dunno. I just wanted to hear your voice.' It's the
truth, however unlikely or irrational it seems.

'Is something wrong?' he says, and there's a pain around
my heart, like a stitch. I have to resist the urge to curl back
up, foetus style.

'Not really,' I say, and my voice sounds false, too high, too
bright. I fight back the tears. I wish I could tell Nate all about

what's been happening to me, but apart from not knowing where to start, and the unlikeliness of it all, I know that I would lose him totally were he to find out what I've been up to. My first lover and one-time best friend is not the person to confide in about Anne and James.

He knows me though, and he knows not to push it. 'Well, it's good to hear yours,' he says gently. 'Your voice, I mean.'

'You too,' I manage, still quavery and hollow feeling. 'I'm sorry about . . . Last time we spoke, I was –'

He interrupts me, and I'm thankful, having had no idea what I was going to say. 'Harsh' is the word that comes to mind, but it was a harshness based, as I have said, on a sense of fairness. Which means that it wasn't really as negative as it sounds. There was a positiveness behind it, an attempt to move forwards.

'Don't worry about it,' he interjects. 'I understand. And, in any case . . .'

His words trail off, as if he's thought again, and suddenly I'm interested in how he was going to go on.

'In any case, what?'

'Oh, nothing. I shouldn't have . . . Oh, what the hell, you have to know sometime, I guess. It's just a bit –'

'Have to know what?'

'I didn't expect it to happen. It's still early days. But I've . . . Well, I've met someone else.'

There's a falling feeling inside me, as if a stone is plummeting down through me. When it stops, there's a horrible cold, dull sensation in the pit of my belly, and a vague nausea. I've lost him, I think bitterly. There's no going back. Whoever she is, it must be serious. He wouldn't mention it if it were just a shag.

'Who? When?' I stutter eventually.

'Her name's Anne-Mette. She's Danish.'

'Where did you meet her?'

He pauses, and I picture him smiling to himself as he recalls the moment he fell in love again and broke away from me, like a balloon becoming untethered and flying away into the sky. When the past he was clinging to became history, a photo album relegated to the bottom drawer. The day he stopped crying for me.

'In a deli,' he replies with a chuckle, after his moment of loving recollection.

I imagine him walking in and browsing the counter before his eyes alight on the blonde beside him and his belly lurches with desire, a desire that extinguishes everything we had together. I imagine him looking her up and down – surreptitiously, of course, but lingering on her large breasts emphasised by a close-fitting T-shirt. He always was a boob man, Nate; was always reminding me, as he slipped my bra straps from my shoulders and bent forwards to suckle at my nipples, erect for him, that that was what had first attracted him to me – my firm, well-rounded breasts, honey-hued and as soft as the skin of a newborn.

Then he clears his throat, readying himself for the conversational gambit that will let the blonde know he's interested without frightening her off.

Cut to his room, the room in the shared house in Brighton that I know so well, where my clothes used to hang beside Nate's in the wardrobe. It was there that we moved together after uni, after Nate got a graduate job in a software company. For a while we were happy, or thought we were. Looking back now, it's clear that things had started to go stale between us. The sex was petering out, and not only on my account. In fact, Nate cried off more than I did, claiming he was worn out from the early starts and the late nights, from struggling to make his mark and prove to his boss that he was indispensable. Arriving home, he'd reach for a cold beer before reaching for me, and then go on to polish off a bottle of wine to himself while watching a thousand inanities on the TV.

I was working part-time at a bookshop at the time, and supposedly trying to write the rest of the time. My aim was to break into women's mags as a money-earner, in doing so buying myself time to write the novel I talked so much about but could never get started. But it wasn't happening. Pitch after pitch was not so much rejected as stonily ignored, and my morale was ebbing. The days when I wasn't at the shop it was all I could do to bathe and dress. If I did, I walked along the seafront wallowing in self-pity. If I didn't, I'd sit at home drinking coffee and staring out of the window at the brick wall onto which our little studio faced. No wonder Nate stopped wanting to fuck me. We barely even talked.

We moved from the studio when a room became available with some colleagues of Nate's. He thought it would be good for us, would bring us out of ourselves and into the social life of Brighton. I guess I hoped so too. But it only tore us further apart, as Nate began going out with the boys, leaving me at home, staring at the four walls. That's when I realised our time was up. I was shocked when he resisted, when he fought for us to carry on. I was touched too, and gave it another six months. But, although he made an effort, I realised that the spark was gone. Not only the sexual spark, but the spark inside me. I had let my inner fire be extinguished by circumstances and I needed to get it back. That's why I moved to London.

And so Nate was left to his room, and for a while the scent of me must have hung in the air he breathed. My ghost must have haunted the place, making it hard for him to accept I was gone. It's always easier for the person who goes away, who leaves the shared place and starts afresh in a room or house unblemished by memories. Now, though, an exorcism has taken place. The Dane – statuesque, I imagine, with cropped hair and big green eyes and a fresh, wide, breezy smile that takes your breath away – has chased me out of the room for good, and out of Nate's heart.

'Are you still there?' comes Nate's voice down the line. His words break into my vision of the onset of their passion. She's responded to his advance in the deli, accepted his offer of a coffee at a little corner table overlooking one of the The Lanes with their cobblestones and chic boutiques. She's not in a hurry, having just finished her shift at the Scandinavian crafts gallery where she works – where I've decided she works.

They chat, and he decides that, in spite of the physical differences, there's something about her that reminds him a tiny bit of me – that that's what first attracted his attention. Only she's better than me: she's taller, she's leggier, her breasts are higher and bouncier, her eyes are bigger, warmer, softer. She's not got that irritating mole on her left cheek. Her hair is silkier, and blonde where mine is dark.

He leans in towards her, strokes it lightly. They've moved on from coffee to beer now; they're on their third and he's feeling daring. She doesn't react disfavourably; she's surprised, he can tell by the sudden stiffening of her body, but those eyes tell him it's OK, that he can carry on. His hand stays on the side of her head, moves round to her face, with its ruddily glowing pale skin stretched over a magnificently angular cheekbone and sweeping down to an enticingly square jaw. Her eyes twinkle, invite him to kiss her. He leans in further.

Before they know it, a little tipsy, they're falling into our – *his* – room, falling onto each other, not even making it as far as the bed before they start yanking each other's clothes off, their teeth clashing in the wildest and most yearning of kisses. And, as they do so, he's not even thinking of me, of the first time between us – more hesitant, for certain, after the long, slow build-up, but unquestionably memorable.

It wasn't just that it was the first time for both of us; perhaps it was the slow burn of it too, the way we'd driven each other half-mad with desire as we inched our way to sex. We'd met in the college bar, introduced by mutual friends, and I'd known from his furtive glances over the rim of his beer glass that he was interested. I was flattered: with his long dark fringe and boyish face, he reminded me a bit of Alex from Blur. When I found out he played guitar, that did it for me – I was an indie girl if ever there was one.

Music was our way into each other. I found out from friends what he was into, boned up on it in music mags that I read during boring lectures, and used that as a way of talking to him and getting to know him in a non-threatening way. I was awkward with the opposite sex: my single-sex private education had made boys into an alien species imbued with excitement and threat. I didn't know how to relate to them on a non-sexual level.

Of course, I'd had one or two boyfriends before uni, but I'd never really gelled with anyone, never gone beyond snogging. The minute I felt a hand begin to roam, make a snail-like path towards my breasts, I backed away. Thinking about it now, I guess I was afraid of my appetites, of what would happen when the dam opened. I knew that there'd be no going back, and so I held on. I wanted to be sure.

So Nate and I began slowly, edging into sex like blind people feeling their way into a room, relying on the walls to guide them, as well as their own instincts. Snogging turned into heavy petting, and that went on for a while, until the day came when it was no longer enough for me to massage his dick through the heavy fabric of his jeans and, looking into his eyes, I'd pulled down his zip and put my hand inside. My heart was in my throat as I did so, and my pussy was burning. I knew then that I was crossing the line, and I was ready to do so. I took hold of him assertively, marvelling at his smoothness against the palm of my hand as I wrapped it around him. I glanced down, at the snug fit of me on him. Then I began to move my hand over his shaft, looking back into his eyes for confirmation that I was going about it the right way. I was.

I was leaning over him, and he pulled my sweatshirt over my head then reached around me to unclasp my bra. It fell onto his chest. His eyes moved down to my breasts and then he brought his hands to them. As he grasped them, equally assertively, I arched my back and moaned. With the pads of his thumbs he began to massage my nipples, sending shivers through my whole body, and this time I threw back my head and cried out. I was beyond ready now. I was gagging for him.

Nate let go of me in order to fight his way out of his clothes like a wrestler on amphetamines. I stripped off my jeans and pants too, and as I threw them to the floor beside us was amazed by the wetness of my pants. So this is desire, I thought, and the P.J. Harvey lyrics came to mind: 'Said "I'm not scared"/Turned to her and smiled/Secrets in his eyes/ Sweetness of desire.'

As if tapping into my thoughts, Nate smiled up at me and whispered, 'I'm not scared.'

Taking it as a sign, I grabbed his hand, brought it to my pussy. He gasped as he realised how wet I was, how ready for him, and, bringing his other hand to my hip, he began to pull me down to him. I was shaking by now, the anticipation having become too much, the months of waiting stacked behind us, teetering over us, like buildings on the verge of collapse. It had to happen, and yet . . .

'Wait,' I said, and he froze. The look in his eyes was one of disbelief, terror even. *Don't do this to me*, they seemed to say. But I didn't want him to stop. In fact, that was the whole point. I wanted to draw this out for as long as possible, to savour it fully. I knew that this was one of the most important moments of my life, and I didn't want to let it go yet.

I clasped his hand where it had halted on my pussy and set it in motion again. As I did so, I opened my legs and straddled him more widely, so that I was fully open to him. He got the message, sliding two fingers inside me. I pressed myself down to meet them, letting my head fall back again. There was a strange gurgling noise emanating from my throat like something otherworldly, divorced from me. My whole body felt shot through with some kind of tingling, glittering matter. It was as if I was being lifted higher and higher, even as I tried to impale myself on my lover's hand.

And then I let go and folded myself back down onto him, revelling in the soft down of his chest against my bare breasts, the firm press of his skin against mine and the flutter of wispy hair against my nipples. He slipped another finger inside, and for a while I rode him, pushing to meet his hand as he moved it in then retracted it. With his other hand he had grasped his dick and brought it close to me and, sliding out his hand, he let it graze at my hole for a moment until we could both bear it no longer. He pushed himself inside me at the very moment that I was bringing myself down on him, taking him inside.

He yelled out, falling back against the bed with his arms outstretched above him, eyes closed, an expression of utter helplessness on his face as I began to ride him. I didn't have a clue what I was doing, but I followed my instinct, moving backwards and forwards, and then side to side, and finally in a circular motion over his hips. All the while, my hands on his shoulders, pinning him down, I watched his face for signs I was doing the right thing. At first he silently grimaced, as if in some kind of pain that couldn't be articulated in sound. Then his jaw unclenched and he opened his mouth wide and gasped. After a few moments his face slackened, and then he lay with his mouth open, his eyes rolling beneath closed lids. From which I knew that I was on the right track.

I closed my eyes again, and my hands moved to my breasts. Caressing them as Nate had done, both with my whole hands and the pads of my thumbs on my nipples, I carried on circling his pelvis with my hips, feeling him thick and hard inside me. It was an incredible sensation, and I wondered that I had been able to wait so long. I knew already that now that I had tasted this sweetness, it was something I wouldn't be able to live without, that it would be part of me as I had always known it would be.

Time slowed down as I gyrated on top of him, slowly, luxuriantly. What was the hurry, after all? We were young, without obligations or responsibilities. Essays could wait, lectures could wait, our friends could wait. It was spring, and before us stretched a whole summer of lazy fucking, in our rooms, in the long grass by the river, in any number of secret places. Now that we had started, the only limitation was our imaginations.

But the rhythm that had insinuated itself between us began to accelerate, as if of its own accord. Raising his arms and swinging them down over me, Nate opened his eyes, then he clenched my buttocks and swung me over onto the bed. For a moment he slipped out of me and I felt bereft. But he took hold of his dick and guided it back inside, and it was like welcoming back an old friend, one that I had come to rely on, couldn't live without. This time it was I who threw back my arms, at the same time spreading my legs further, encouraging him to go deeper and deeper into me. He was heavy on me and, as he moved up and down, his pace gradually increasing, his weight and the friction he exerted on my clit made my pussy begin to tingle and melt in a way I've never been able to put into words. It was as if I was expanding inside, and filling with warm honey, flowing with it like a river that has burst its banks.

Sensing my excitement mount, Nate struggled to contain his, but his thrusting motion seemed like something outside of him now, and he couldn't hold himself back. Crying out, he tightened his grip on my shoulders and collapsed on top of me as he came.

I was elated and let down at the same time, having felt myself to be on the verge. But Nate recovered himself quickly.

'I'm sorry,' he muttered, looking into my eyes, and hesitantly he brought one hand to my pussy. 'Can I?' he said.

I nodded. 'Of course,' I said, and then I swooned back as his fingers went inside me again.

Reaching down, I teased my lips apart a little, to show him what I needed. He understood and with the fingertips of his other hand he massaged my clit, first up and down and then with sweeping circular motions. The tingling sensation started up again, the feeling that I was expanding inside, opening up. I brought one hand to my mouth and bit the back of it so hard as I came that I drew blood.

'I'm sorry.' Nate's voice brings me hurtling back into the present. 'There wasn't any easy way to tell you about Anne-Mette. But it shouldn't –'

'It doesn't matter.' I'm shaking my head as I interrupt him, although I know he can't see me. 'I . . . I'm happy for you. Really. I want you to be happy.'

And there it is again: them falling into his room, falling through the door and onto the floor, fucking each other while still only half-naked, speechless with desire, unable to make it to the bed. I'm happy for him, and I'm jealous as hell, and I'm horny as hell too, thinking about him and me, and about him and her, and then, last of all, about James and me. That's why I called Nate in the first place – because of all this stuff with James. Because I needed to hear a familiar loving voice that will bring me back to normality.

Nate still loves me, as I still love him. But he's not there for me any more, not really, no matter what he says. Anne-Mette has turned his head, has opened up the future to him again, a future that excludes me. Oh, we'll swap emails from time to time, but they'll become less and less frequent, until finally they die away and we are nothing more to each other than memories of things long gone. Nothing more than trails of smoke on the horizon, from fires long burnt out.

'I have to go now, Nate,' I say, and I tell him again that I'm happy for him before hanging up quickly, before the sob that I can feel building up in my throat, clogging it, breaks out.

I'm still sitting on my bed, and the rain is still falling. I stand up. It's time to face the future, no matter what it holds.

A shower does me good: clears my head and freshens my spirits. I didn't want Nate back – that's not what the phone call was about – and I am genuinely happy for him that he's found someone new. But thinking about all the sex – me and Nate, Anne-Mette and Nate – has brought me back full circle to James and to my current situation, and before I know it I'm down in the living room in front of Anne's laptop, Googling Calla Lily, the 'secret place' James mentioned.

The website comes up, and at once I'm sucked into a seductive world of designer sex toys where the gaudy plastics of more downmarket options have no place. As well as wood and leather, the choice items here come in steel, crystal, ceramic, jade, pearl and even fourteen-carat solid gold. A gold-plated butterfly 'body piece' catches my eye – I'm not familiar with the idea but the blurb explains that it's an item of body jewellery worn around the neck and trailing down to the groin, where a 'clitoris clip' produces a stimulating sensation when you move. It sounds delicious, and I'm sorely tempted, but then I notice the £450 price tag and I think again.

I carry on browsing though, studying the anal beads and the Japanese silk bondage ropes and the embroidered masks, and thinking that I really haven't lived. There's a whole world of sex out there that I haven't even begun to explore, that I didn't know existed. A whole world of sex that both intrigues and frightens me. Do I want to be part of it or not? Am I missing out or better off keeping my distance? As with James – or should I say, with Anne and James – I am unable to gauge.

Thinking about James, I Google him next, wondering if the internet can remedy my ignorance as to his personal life. He has his own website, I find, but frustratingly his biography is strictly professional, listing his numerous fellowships and books and little besides. Wikipedia is equally uninformative. Irritated, I return to the Calla Lily site.

I keep checking over my shoulder, guilty, afraid that Anne might catch me 'in the act'. Not that I don't have any right to be using her laptop – she already told me I'm welcome to help myself. And of course it's through her that I know about Calla Lily at all, so it's not as if she could disapprove. But I feel, in some part of me, ashamed by what I'm doing, like a miscreant schoolgirl about to be found out and punished. There's something else too, something that I can't quite pinpoint but that has something to do with my not wanting Anne to know about my appetites. She knows too much already. Any more and she has a hold over me that wouldn't be tolerable.

Then I remind myself that she is my employer and that there's no way I should be sitting here doing this, that it is a sackable offence, and I go upstairs with the intention of knocking on her door and asking her if there's something I can be doing. So far, the only things I have done for Anne, beyond clearing the dresser, are of a sexual nature. And to believe that they are part of the job, that that is my role, is something I am unable to do. They are incidental to what I am here for.

But standing outside Anne's door, I can't bring myself to interrupt. I can hear the tap-tap of her keyboard inside, and I'm worried that if I break her concentration she'll be livid with me. I know I would, if I were a writer. And so I walk back downstairs, and after a moment's deliberation take my set of keys and head out of the front door.

For a while, aimless, I walk around Bayswater, telling myself I'm getting to know my new neighbourhood. But before long I'm walking down Queensway, looking at the shopfronts, and soon pleasantly surprised to find what I've been looking for: a branch of Ann Summers. Feeling a little thrill ripple through me at this first foray into a sex shop, I step up to the door and push it open.

This time I don't linger, don't browse. There's plenty to fascinate and to tempt, but I know what I'm here for, and so I head straight for the sex toys and cast my eyes over the selection. There are some bog-standard vibrators, but also all kinds of variation on the theme, from Rabbits to Lovebrushs – the latter a set of mini attachments that can be hooked up to an electric toothbrush. It's a hard decision, but I'm finally won over by a Rock Chick, which according to the literature is a unique hands-free clit and G-spot stimulator producing incredibly intense orgasms. And a mind-blowing orgasm is what I am burning for right now.

I let my card take the strain and leave in a hurry, eager to try it out. I'm so eager, in fact, that I doubt my ability to make it back to the house. But then I tell myself that it's best not to go back anyway, not just yet. Anne might be finished what she's doing and if she hears me return might find some task for me to do. It'd be a classic case of Sod's Law. Or I might make it upstairs to my room and be mid-wank when she comes knocking on my door, wanting me for something. No, I need pleasure and I need it now, no holds barred.

I cross the Bayswater Road and head into Kensington Gardens, casting my eyes around for a deserted spot. It's not so busy on this midweek afternoon, but I can't just do it right here in the open, where any old jogger or dog-walker can chance upon me. Heading east, I skirt the railings, looking for a clump of trees where I can take refuge. After a while I find what I need.

Casting my eyes about me once more, I lower myself

to the ground, clutching the plastic bag containing my purchase, my new toy, to my chest. The grass is springy and inviting beneath my hands. I lie back and hitch up my denim skirt, glancing around all the time. Then I place the bag beside me on the ground and fumble around inside it until I've removed the Rock Chick from its flimsy packaging. My breath is coming ragged with anticipation as I withdraw it from the colourful plastic and take my first proper look at it.

It's not like a vibrator, or any that I've seen before – it's not long and straight but curves round on itself, so that it can be inside you and stimulate your clitoris at the same time. I don't need to read the instructions to understand that the principle is presumably to rock oneself back and forth to get a double-whammy action alternating from inside to out and back again.

I reach between my legs, wet just from thinking about it, and pull my knickers to one side. But, as I bring the toy to me, I realise that the fabric will get in the way of the clitoral stimulation, and so I pull them down and off and push them into the plastic bag. Then I open my legs and push one end of the Rock Chick inside.

I gasp at the rush of pleasure as the other end settles against my clitoris and a wave of sensations both internal and external takes hold of me. It soon becomes apparent that I really don't need my hands and, as I take my lead from the tool and rock myself backwards and forwards, establishing a gentle but highly sensual tempo, my first instinct is to bring my free hands to my breasts and squeeze my erect nipples through my T-shirt. My jaw clenches as I do so, and my head grinds against the grass until I can feel the earth packed hard beneath it. But then I start to vary my movements, to experiment with a little swirling and tentative thrusting, and those combined with the vibrations running from tip to tip of the tool invoke a sort of dreamy languor in me, to the point that I actually feel myself relaxing. Letting go of my breasts, I throw my arms up over my shoulders and then let them fall back over me onto the grass. I smile and moan at once. I feel I could go on like this forever.

I think of no one as I let the toy work its slow magic: not James, not Nate. I'm lost to the feelings that are storming my senses, my organs, and not only my clit and my pussy. The soft grass against my arms and the backs of my legs, the warm sunlight on my face, the purr of traffic along the Bayswater Road alongside me – everything conspires to create a mood of abandon. I feel blissfully alone and untrammelled in the middle of the city, like some kind of nature spirit. I feel intoxicated and liberated and far from any other living being. No one could make me feel the way I feel now. This is pure me. Or should I say, pure impure me.

The sensations build up, however, almost without my realising: my moans grow louder and more frequent, my thrusting motions more forceful. I feel I'm on the cusp of something wonderful, some kind of revelation, and I'm rising to meet it at the same time as wanting to fend it off, to fully live these moments of crystalline pleasure. In a bid to head off my orgasm, I rise to my feet, still feeling dreamy and spacey, and lean back against a sturdy tree, facing the hedge so that I remain out of sight of any passers-by who might happen along the nearest pathway. Felicitously, the tree has a small jutting section at about the height of my buttocks, forming a handy ledge that I can use as a platform from which to instigate a sort of upwards thrusting motion. My hands come up to my breasts again and I squeeze them as the pleasure mounts like an inexorable tide. A cry escapes me.

My eyes pop open. Above the hedge, the top three or four storeys of a swanky-looking hotel are visible. A man is standing at one of the windows, staring down at me, a curious half-smile on his lips. As I spot him, he nods, as if to encourage me to go on. *Enjoy yourself*, he seems to be saying. But I don't need encouragement. The thought of being watched like this sends me over the edge; I thrust forcefully and unclench a climax so mighty that, afterwards, looking in the mirror back at the house, I find my back and my haunches scratched and grazed where I have driven myself up against the rough bark of the tree, oblivious to the carnage I was inflicting on my skin.

Then I fall forwards onto the grass and lie there panting. I don't look up, although the hedge would now obscure my view of the hotel window again. But I'd bet any money that my admirer is now jerking himself off, my image still blazing behind his closed eyelids.

When I've recovered, I push the toy back into the bag along with my knickers and walk back to St Petersburgh Place, still tingling inside. Anne might be denying me satisfaction, I think as I put my key into the lock, and James might continually exceed my reach, but I've found one hell of a way to ensure that I get satisfaction when she's not around.

6

The Toy Boy

I'm not long back and, ravenous from my exertions, am making some toast when Anne walks into the kitchen, smoke billowing out from one hand. Bringing her cigarette to her mouth to take brief but hungry drags that make her face seem even more pinched and bony than it is naturally, she's clearly worked up about something.

'Anything the matter?' I say, buttering my toast, glad of an excuse to avoid her gaze, although I know that she's not going to mention James and the events of last night. What I don't know is whether whatever it is that she's in a stew about is real or feigned, precisely in order that we can avoid talking about what is uppermost in our minds. Or uppermost in my mind, at least. You'd think it would be in Anne's too, but it's hard to tell. Is this kind of thing so commonplace in her life that she feels it warrants no discussion, not even a mention?

'That bloody woman,' she says bitterly, and I gather from the tumble of words and curses that follow that Anne's agent, the über-powerful Delphina Carmichael, has pissed her off in some way. I should be interested, and under normal circumstances I would be fascinated by this insight into

London literary life. But suddenly I'm replaying images from last night in my mind's eye, and my face is flaming crimson at the thought that Anne saw me naked, saw me losing control as James worked me with the dildo. Saw the strange, illicit pleasure it awakened in me to spank the bare arse of this virtual stranger, this man nearly four decades older than me. Anne knows things about me that no one else knows, that I don't even know myself, from being in her privileged position – present and involved yet distanced, poised, controlling things rather than losing her head. Remaining cool, she sees things that we don't as we are swept along. She sees who we are when we are taken out of ourselves.

Anne's still ranting and, finally, having spread my toast with Marmite and put the jar back in the cupboard, I have no choice but to turn and face her. It's easier than I think: she's lit a fresh cigarette and is huffing and puffing, eyes fixed on something beyond the kitchen window, outside in the small garden. Or perhaps on her own reflection in the glass. Perhaps, it strikes me, Anne is afflicted by a curse that may be a pitfall of being a novelist: that of always being an observer, unable to fully, unselfconsciously act because one is watching, noting, obsessively collecting data for one's fiction. And that must include data about themselves. Can Anne ever really join in, participate fully in life?

Suddenly she stops talking, and her face turns to mine. Our eyes meet. Mine search hers for some glimmer of recognition of what happened between James and me, between the three of us, last night. But all I see, still, is a kind of cold, hard quality, like that of the stars on a crisp, clear winter's night. There's a beauty to them, but also something frightening: a reminder of the vastness of the cosmic space that divides us, of infinity in all its indifference.

For a moment I am dumbstruck, lost. The things she has seen . . . But what was I expecting of her? Affection? Sex doesn't always lead to that. Nor does it begin with it. Why should affection enter into this at all? But it seems, as I stand there before her curiously blank gaze, that I would feel better about this if I knew that Anne cared for me, if at least a small dose of love entered into this.

I think of James and console myself with the conviction that some measure of affection does at least exist between the two of us, above and beyond what Anne says or does, perhaps even in spite of her. The courtesy and concern he shows me, the pleasure he calls forth in me, must spring from a caring source. Perhaps they are even the seeds of what might turn out to be love, if what exists between us was allowed to grow, to take its natural course. Certainly, I have more than a little fondness for him. I want him physically, but it goes deeper than that. I feel that something has happened to him somewhere along the line and that he needs a person who can understand him, who can act as a balm upon his wounds. Wanting to be that person is surely a form of love?

The silence goes on too long, and suddenly there's a change in Anne's eyes, and I feel that the coldness has been superseded by something calculating, perhaps even malevolent. Perhaps I'm paranoid, but it's as if she's assessing me, weighing up what she finds in order to plot anew, to take things in a fresh direction. I wonder if I'll be up to the challenge and, as the thought runs through my mind, I'm amazed at the change in me: already I'm so accepting of my place here, not even considering refusing to go along with whatever she is cooking up in her warped imagination.

'Is there . . . Is there anything I can be doing?' I manage at last. 'Filing or whatever?'

Anne shrugs, eyes still piercing mine. 'Not right away,' she says.

'But later? There must be –'

She doesn't let me finish. 'There's a student . . .' she begins, and then her eyes leave mine as she brings her cigarette to her lips and takes a long, contemplative drag. Again her gaze fixes on something in the garden, or on the reflective glass of the window pane. 'Come down at two o'clock. I want you to sit in and take notes.'

I watch her as she continues to smoke, having seemingly terminated the conversation. Her mind, it appears, is elsewhere, and I wonder if she's thinking of her new novel, if she's spilling over with inspiration and creative impulses. For a moment I'm jealous: how wonderful that must feel.

Then I frown. What does she mean by 'student'? She's not mentioned students before, and I can't imagine a novelist of her stature giving tuition, even if her reputation has slid in recent years. If she was struggling financially, surely the first thing to go would be this big house, which has more space than she needs, and a location that must give it a multi-million-pound price tag.

But I don't get chance to ask, because Anne has awoken from her reverie and is heading out of the kitchen. I look at my watch: it's one o'clock. It'll be an hour before I find out what this is all about. I decide to take a nap.

Upstairs, a little restless, I reach for the plastic bag containing my little purple friend and, after giving it a rinse, admire it, running my fingers along it, from one velvety end to the other. Then I can't resist it any longer and I hoik my skirt up, lie on my side and bring it to my pussy. It slides in smoothly, and the raised bump on the end fits up snugly against my

G-spot. My eyes water as I struggle with the urge to just let myself come right away. To help myself hold off, I roll over onto my belly and work at creating a measured pace that I can contain until I am ready to go the whole way.

When it begins to get difficult, because of the grinding of my clit by the other, ribbed, end, I raise myself onto my elbows and start to thrust. My hands, as before, are free, and this time I find myself reaching around and clutching my buttocks with my hands, prising them apart, driving my fingers and even my nails into my flesh. The sensation is further heightened. Letting go for a moment with one hand, I reach between my legs and activate the vibrating bullet. It's all systems go as the stimulation of my clit intensifies, and I come with a yell.

As I lie panting on my bed, I wonder if Anne is outside my door, but, even as I contemplate the idea, I realise that I don't care. So much has happened that I can't see what difference it would make. There's no privacy here: I've already become aware of and resigned to that. I'm in Anne's employ, living in Anne's house, and as such she has the right to do what she likes, as long as it's not illegal. This is the situation, and I either accept it or leave.

For a moment I let my mind toy with the idea of leaving, but I find no answers to the questions that are raised: What next? Where would I go? What would I do? Vron, ecstatic at having seen the back of me at last, would be adamant she wouldn't let me get another foothold on her place, and I can't think of anyone else who has the space or the goodwill to put me up for more than a couple of nights. I'd have to get my own place, and doing that in London would require me selling my soul, getting some high-paying job that would wear me down, putting paid to my writerly hopes and ambitions.

But I have to admit, as I ponder all this, that there's something else at work here too: Anne has me hooked. There's James, of course – bait if ever there was one, the carrot on the end of her stick. There's unfinished business with James, and I fear that Anne is my only means of access to him, meaning that leaving her would be to give up on him too, which I'm not ready to do.

There's more, though. This 'student' who I am shortly to meet – something tells me that this is not going to be a run-of-the-mill tutorial, that the teacher–pupil relationship I am going to witness is going to be skewed to some degree. It's amazing how little time it has taken me to judge Anne as someone who can never be straightforward in any of her dealings. Perhaps I am to be proven wrong.

To take my mind off the impending meeting, and also away from James and this whole complicated and perplexing situation, I pick up a novel and, before more than ten pages have been turned, start to fall into a doze. With the sun streaming through my mansard window onto the bed, cocooning me in warmth, I feel a welcome drowsiness, freeing me from care and confusion. I feel as if I could sleep for a hundred years. Only who would be the prince to come and kiss me awake? James Carnaby? Am I falling for this sugar daddy, this rich and well-known man who is so inexplicably single?

The dozy wash of thoughts through my head is arrested by the shrill sound of the doorbell. I sit up with a shock, smooth down my hair as I strain to listen. I glance at the time on my mobile. Whoever this mysterious student might be, he – or *she* – is very punctual. Which means that they are keen to learn whatever it is that Anne has to teach.

It's not a girl – I hear that as soon as I am out of my

bedroom and on the landing, harkening to the voices down in the hallway. There's Anne's, sounding softer and more welcoming than I am accustomed to. And then there's a male voice, quite hushed and tentative. The opposite of James's, with his assertive, forceful voice, essential for lecturing and making TV and radio appearances and doing book tours, for convincing people he knew more than anybody else about his particular field.

'Hello?' I hear Anne call, and I turn the top of the stairs on the first floor to find her looking up at me. 'Oh, there you are,' she says. 'Good. We can start.'

She turns on her heel, heads towards the living room. In the doorway I see a figure, tall, svelte. As Anne reaches him, he turns and precedes her into the room. She places a hand on his shoulder, appears to guide him. She's unexpectedly motherly in her gesture.

A few strides behind them, I reach the living room just as they're settling on the sofas, side-on to each other. The boy – he can't be as old as me – looks a little nervous but excited too. His cheeks are pinkish, contrasting with the auburn sheen of his hair. His eyes are roaming the room uncertainly, as if taking in details that he will wish to recall later. Immediately I know that he's never been here before. If he is a student, he's a new one.

His head swivels as he senses my movement; large blue eyes turn on me, electrifying me with their suggestion of a childlike innocence I know that no boy as beautiful as this can lay claim to. My breath catches, is held captive in my chest.

Anne speaks for me. 'This is my assistant,' she says to him, and I note that she doesn't mention his name either.

'Pleased to meet you,' I say, holding out one hand, which

he takes. The frisson is immediate, as if a supercharged current has passed between us. I think irresistibly of the Björk song 'Venus as a Boy', of the lines 'He's exploring the taste in her/Arousal/So accurate.' James has his charms, but they are complex charms that need to be decoded, unlocked. This boy is in-your-face, undeniable gorgeousness, like a vision of Cary Grant as he might have been at eighteen.

I tear myself away from him to find Anne studying me, openly curious about my reaction to the newcomer. I stare back at her, feeling brave. I know I have to be brave if I am to have any chance of getting what I want, and right now more than anything else I want some time with this amazing being.

What? her eyes seems to challenge me.

I open my mouth, almost choke on the words I want to say. 'What's the lesson?' I say instead.

She continues to look at me. 'Aesthetics,' she says slowly. 'Did you study anything about that at university?'

I shake my head. 'Not really,' I say, wondering where she's going with this.

'Shame,' she says, looking at the boy and then back at me. 'But of course, you didn't study philosophy, did you?'

'Not as such. Bits here and there, in passing.'

She shakes her head. 'Of course the French,' she says musingly, 'get a basic grounding in philosophy at school.'

I smile, trying to relax. 'Well, *of course*, you French are pretty much better than us at everything,' I say, half ironic, half serious. I'm a Francophile to a degree, but at the same time I'm wary of subscribing to racial clichés and stereotypes. I risk a glance at the boy. He's looking at Anne expectantly. He too hasn't a clue where this is leading. Does he hope it will take us to the same place as I do?

'Axiology,' says Anne, reaching for the little silver cigarette box on the low table in front of her. 'The study of quality or value, including aesthetics. Which is the study of the ways we see and perceive the world.'

The boy nods; I nod too. Then he looks at me, and I at him. For a moment we hold each other's gaze, and once again I savour the apparent innocence of those huge cobalt-blue eyes. Then we look at Anne as her words puncture the bubble in which we have sealed ourselves for a minute, making us oblivious to all else.

'Beauty,' she continues, exhaling a mouthful of smoke. 'Is it purely a cultural construct, or is there such a thing as objective beauty, a beauty that is evident to all?' She eyes the boy, almost mistrustfully it seems to me, as if his face might crack open like a mask, or dissolve into the air, and reveal something disappointing beneath. As if there's something false about his beauty, some trickery involved. There's perhaps even a little distaste in her expression, a refusal to be bamboozled by the physical.

The boy doesn't reply, but I don't feel that she really wants him to, that she's interested in what he has to say on the matter. And again I wonder if this is a tutorial, or something else masquerading as such. Why did the boy come here? What is he expecting? His open, unworldly face gives nothing away.

'Perhaps,' Anne says, 'it's just a question of the paucity of our vocabulary. After all, aside from the question of subjectivity, what makes a painting beautiful is very different from what makes a piece of music beautiful, or a poem.' She stubs out her cigarette, closes her eyes for a moment. 'Or a person.' I wonder what, or who, she is thinking of.

None of this talk is particularly new to me – having read

all of Anne's novels, I recognise beauty as a recurrent theme of hers. Her works endlessly run up against the big questions: the point of our existence, whether beauty is a distraction from the mundane and the mortal or instead the only thing that makes life worth living.

I take advantage of her having her eyes closed to look again at the boy, more questioningly this time. Is he a fan or a student of her work, here to learn more? I can't believe that he can be a writer himself, an acolyte, given how young he is. But why would Anne open her door to one student among the hundreds who must approach her each year, since some of her early works are on university syllabuses?

Then it comes to me: Anne is obsessed with beauty, and with its effects, and this boy is beautiful. She wants to observe his effect on me. Just as with James, I am a guinea pig, the litmus paper of Anne's own refracted desires. I sit forwards. I am willing to assume that role.

As if my thoughts have made themselves known to her, Anne looks at me and lifts her chin. Her eyes roll heavenwards. I stand up. I know where I am going, where we are going.

As I climb the stairs, I hear her speak in muffled tones to the boy, and am disappointed I can't hear what she is saying, nor his reply. I would love to know if he came here under false pretences or in the full knowledge of what was to be asked of him. Whether he would have come had he known, or whether he'd have been too afraid.

But when he comes into the first-floor bedroom, the one I was in just a couple of nights ago with James, there's no fear on his face – just lust. A film of sweat increases and enhances the natural shine of his beautifully toned and flawless skin. He truly is godlike, a male incarnation of Venus. Who could dispute his beauty? I do recognise that beauty is a cultural construct, but I can't imagine that there's a human being on any part of this Earth who would deny that this boy is astonishingly good-looking.

Suddenly I feel a little shy. Am I worthy of him? I know I'm not bad-looking by any stretch of the imagination. Men have always shown an interest in me, from wolf-whistling builders to some of my father's friends. I'm lucky enough to be slim without having to work out or watch my diet too closely, with a flat belly and firm breasts that vary between a C and a D cup. I'm of medium height but my legs look long, and my arse is shapely and rounded. My best facial feature is undoubtedly my mouth with its fleshy lips complete with Cupid's bow, but I have nice eyes too, or so they tell me. Smallish but expressive, with flecks of gold buried amidst the sea-green iris. My hair is dark brown tending towards black, contrasting with the ivory pallor of my skin.

No, I've always attracted attention from the opposite sex, without actively seeking it. I don't dress provocatively, although I'm happy to show off my best features, to wear skirts that end just shy of the knee, tops with a hint of cleavage. I know the importance of a good bra in the overall effect, which so many women don't. I like good shoes too. But my student budget has always severely curtailed my sartorial aspirations: I have the occasional more glamorous piece happened upon in a charity shop, but, before I moved in with Anne and started making a bit more effort, my day-to-day look tended towards the grungy – jeans, a T-shirt, battered Converse sneakers.

I look at the boy's clothes for the first time, as he comes to a halt in the bedroom, Anne hot on his heels. He's far from grungy: his pale-grey skinny-fit trousers are well cut, his shirt is casual but crisp, in a charcoal grey with light military styling. Rolled-up sleeves reveal strong forearms. My eyes travel down. In the low light of the bedroom with its closed curtains, his leather brogues gleam, freshly polished.

Seeing me size him up, he smiles shyly yet with – or at least it seems to me – a certain inner confidence in the fact that I am liking what I see. I think enviously of what his life must be, imagine him sauntering through university corridors on the way to lectures, turning heads as he does so, both female and male. Who could remain impervious to his charms? I wonder how many people he's slept with, whether he swings both ways. He's got the kind of looks that appeal to both boys and girls. And if he's up for this experience with Anne, with me, then won't he have been willing to experiment in other ways?

I'm jealous, imagining all this – his freedom, his openness. My university experience was so different because of my having got myself tied down so quickly with Nate. I wonder now if I did that because I was afraid, afraid of choice, of liberty, of going for what I really wanted. Why tie myself down so early, denying myself during one of the most sexually fruitful times of life, if not because I am terrified of my own urges?

Now, feeling those urges towards the boy, I am still terrified, but at the same time I realise that to deny them would be to deny my inner nature, my real self. Sure, it's risky, showing someone that you want them. You risk rejection, humiliation. But at least you'll have known, and not spend the rest of your life wondering about what could have been, if only you'd followed your instincts, if only you'd dared.

Standing here before him, I wish fervently that I could

wind time back and relive those university years without Nate by my side, like a comfort blanket, or a shield. Did I ever really love him, or was that just my excuse for taking the safe way out?

The boy's eyes flicker from mine to the bed, and he smiles. I smile too, and then we both look, knowing who's in charge here, at Anne. She is turning away from us, but it's only, it turns out, to take a seat in the corner of the room. Once she's settled, she looks at me with the mixture of haughty *froideur* and smouldering intensity that I am coming to know so well.

'Strip,' she rasps, breaking the almost unbearable silence.

I don't need to be told twice; my clothes are off in a matter of seconds. And despite my shyness in the face of this Adonis-like creature, I revel in my nakedness. I'm so up for this, I could scream.

'Now you,' says Anne. 'Boy. Strip.'

Looking bemused rather than humiliated by her curt and dismissive way of addressing him, her apparent desire to belittle him, he too undresses. But the way he does so is more slow and contained than me, as if he's keen to assert some kind of control here, or if not that then at least to let her know that he is no mere toy willing to bend to her in every way, like a sapling submitting to the force of the wind. I admire him for that, feel even more turned on. He seems to know who he is.

First comes his shirt, button by button. As he pulls it away from his hairless chest and his lightly muscular arms, he folds it and places it on the bedside cabinet. Likewise with his trousers, after sliding them down his slender hips and over his ankles and feet, having already untied his shoelaces and slipped off his expensive, handsome brogues. Last come his black stretch boxers, emblazoned with the word 'Spank' across the front of the waistband. I think for a moment of James, of the wooden paddle I applied to his arse, and of his obvious relish of my actions. Will Anne get her box of tricks out again now, and if so is spanking in store, or something else? Does this boy want to be spanked? Has he been spanked before? Do I want to spank him?

These are the questions that spring into my mind as I stand, proudly naked, almost triumphantly so, in front of them, thrilling to their eyes on me. The boy wants me – so much is clear from his expression. His eyes are bright and eager, his lips slightly apart, the bottom one snagged between his top and bottom teeth. Anne's face is harder to read. There's a distance in her eyes, as if, despite being the mistress of ceremonies, she is also retreating somewhere, going deeper inside herself, to some dark and hidden space to which no one but she can have access. I wonder what lurks there: memories, fantasies, images beyond the reach of words and reason?

She's like a spider, sitting there in her corner, patient after the long and laborious task of constructing a web. Which means that we are the flies – trapped, helpless, able only to wait her bidding, or the coup de grâce. The sinister image excites me even more. I feel as if my very destiny is in Anne's hands, inheres in what happens here, in this house, as long as I am brave enough to stay here and trust in her guiding star, even if it is a dark star.

My breasts are in my hands, my fingertips toying with my nipples. The boy is looking at me, questioning now. Perhaps he's growing impatient. I stare back, trying to tell him with my eyes that nothing here is down to me, that I am unable to act. Surely he's worked that out by now?

'Take him,' barks Anne, releasing us from the delicious pain of the wait.

I step forwards, exulting, the cat that got the cream. I push him down onto the bed and he yields, an invitation in his eyes.

7

The Diary

I am a puppet, I think as I step into the shower, with the smell of the boy, his sweat, his seed, still on me. Part of me wants to stay dirty, to retain him: who knows if I will have him again, if I will ever even see him again? I have absolutely no idea who he is or where he comes from. Have no idea where Anne found him or how she persuaded him to become involved in her game. I daren't hope that she might let me near him again, and I tell myself I should be grateful that, for the first time, she allowed me satisfaction. I know that orgasms aren't everything, that sex is as much about the build-up, but the way she has denied me up to this point has left me frustrated. Having come, and come hard, I feel a sort of release. I feel as if I might break free.

Fingering my pussy, the burn of the climax still there, or rather returning after the numbness that immediately followed it, I think about the boy. The sex was awesome, and I'd love to have him again. Not to want that would be very curious indeed. But there was something missing too. Despite his physical grace and beauty, or perhaps even because of it, and despite the mystery of his identity and the reasons for his involvement in Anne's schemes, I don't feel for him what I feel for James – the sense of an inner necessity, a drive towards him. Perhaps it's because, being so young, he's a sort of blank canvas. Whereas James has years and years, decades, of experience that I would like to know more about. James calls to me potently, like a map demanding to be read, an intricate network of pathways and roads that might lead me to places I never imagined even existed. Something glimmers in James.

And so I know that I can't break free, that I must stay here, in the hope that Anne allows me to pursue my obsession with James, lets me continue my exploration of this complex and beguiling character. Or at least lets me carry on to the point where I feel we don't need her any longer, where I feel comfortable making contact with him independently of her. For the moment that's not something I dare to do, not until I understand more fully the hold that she has over him, the intricacies of their relationship. I'm afraid that making an approach might bring the whole edifice of Anne's scheme, whatever it may be, crashing down around me, spoiling my chances for good. Until I know more about what's in it for James, and what he really thinks of me – whether I am really only a puppet, or a means to an end, for him too – then I daren't act. Anne holds me in the palm of her hand, and for the moment that is where I have to stay.

Sitting on my bed in my towel, I find myself overtaken by a need to write – about everything that's happened to me over the past couple of days, and how I've felt about it. I'm not sure where this urge springs from, but I imagine it's my way of making sense of things and of working out where to go from here. As such, it must be a healthy impulse rather than a need to dwell or a justification for self-indulgent outpourings.

I have a notebook – the one I used to take to cafés when I wanted so much to be a writer but couldn't think of anything to write about. But it's a mess, all smudged, full of doodles and little in the way of literature, like a chart of my wandering mind. I take it out of my bag and then cast it aside: it's depressing. I want a new book for a clean start, even if I am writing about something murky. It's a symbolic thing: a fresh chapter has begun in my life, and I should begin on page one of a pristine, virgin notebook. I start pulling on some clothes, thinking that I'll take a stroll over to Paperchase and treat myself.

Then I remember Anne's words about meeting at four to take some dictation, and I frown. Of course, I should be happy that at last she seems to be giving me some tasks to do – tasks outside the bedroom, that is. But I don't understand her need to dictate letters to me. These days, with word-processing applications, doesn't everyone just type their own correspondence directly onto their screen? To do otherwise seems only more time-consuming – time-wasting, in fact. But then Anne doesn't go about things in the same way that other people do.

I cast aside the jeans that I was about to pull on in favour of something a little more grown-up – a knee-skimming asymmetrical pencil skirt that I team with a baby-pink tulip-sleeve blouse. Both are from charity shops, but together they look quite smart without making me look like I've gone to too much trouble. As the sister of someone who works at Vogue House, I've not been able to escape the infection that is fashion-consciousness. I just haven't had the financial clout to let it really become a part of my life.

When I'm dressed, I apply a modest amount of make-up: my skin is sun-kissed from my walks in the park, so I need only a touch of rosy blush on my cheeks, a brief caress with the wand of my mascara brush, the merest hint of transparent lip gloss. It's a question of style, of not wanting to look like the dog's dinner or someone who cares too much. Something that the French, as it happens, are generally very good at. But it's also a question of Anne's perceptions of me. So far, she's seen only the frivolous side to me. No, frivolous is not the right word; I don't know what is. But she certainly hasn't seen me in any way that could make her take me seriously, as her assistant, as someone with aspirations to be part of the literary world in which she moves.

When I'm ready, I sit on my bed, unable to concentrate, and count down the minutes until I'm due to see her again. Time goes slowly and, despite my earlier doze, I find myself falling asleep again. My emotions are exhausting me. And all the sex, of course.

I wake suddenly. Anne is in the doorway; it must have been the door opening that roused me. She's smiling, but it's a pained smile – even, perhaps, a sadistic one. With one finger she's tapping the face of her watch.

I sit up, smooth down my hair, looking sheepishly back at her. 'What . . . What time is it?'

'Five past four,' she says. 'Did you forget we had an appointment?'

I shake my head, remembering again the times I was ordered to my headteacher's office to be scolded, told to buck up my ideas. Years ago, but the humiliation still scalds my cheeks.

'Well then –'

'I didn't forget. I . . . I . . .'

'You fell asleep, on my paid time. Not a good start.'

I stare at her. I want to tell her how ludicrous that sounds, when all I've done so far is drift around the house or the park, waiting for her summons. A summons that, when it comes, is nothing to do with assisting her – or not in any sense that was implied by the job ad. And also what's five minutes? It's almost as if she was waiting for an excuse to pounce, to reprimand me.

But I choke back the words, force a placating smile to my lips. 'I'm sorry.' I stand up and walk towards her.

She's side-on to me now, already turning to leave, but it soon becomes apparent that she's not expecting me to follow her, that she's changed her mind about the dictation – if she ever really had any to do. Her eyes are reproachful, her stance rigid.

'Don't disappoint me, Genevieve,' she says.

I swallow. This seems like an overreaction, but I can't tell her that. There are so many things I can't tell her. Can't tell her how much I want James, for instance, and that that's one of the reasons I'm still here, putting up with this shit.

So instead I keep my mouth shut and simply nod in response.

'Let's reschedule for tomorrow,' she says and, when I nod again, adds, 'Two o'clock.' She pauses, for effect it seems to me, then: 'Don't be late.' Then she is gone from the room before she can see the grimace on my face.

After she's gone I'm puzzled, and then I'm angry. How dare she talk to me like an errant child, I think, for such a minor transgression? Sure, what she said about me falling asleep on the job was fair enough – it's out of order. But it's hardly as if she'd laid out strict ground rules, made it known that punctuality was key. Quite the opposite: she was so free and easy, so undemanding, that I fell into a false sense of security.

After mulling all this over and still feeling hard done by, I'm overtaken once more by the impulse to write everything down in the hope that that might help me make sense of it. A change of scene will do me good too, so I wait until there are no sounds from the rest of the house and, hoping that Anne is locked away in her study and that our paths won't cross, head downstairs and then out of the door into the street.

It's still sunny, and I try to relax as I walk through Bayswater, letting my limbs be pervaded by warmth. Try to imagine that life is uncomplicated, that it's just another summer's day and I don't have a thing on my mind. Of course it's impossible to kid myself, but just being out of the house does provide some relief.

I choose a chic leather-bound notebook that I immediately dub my 'little black book' and, when I've paid for it and a sleek new pen, I head for a nearby café and flip through the blank pages, wondering how long it will take me to fill it, and what it will contain. The future gapes wide open, both beckoning and frightening. Appetites have been awakened in me that I didn't know existed. If someone had told me last week what was going to happen to me, the things I would experience, over the coming few days, I wouldn't have believed them. But they have, and now I must face the consequences.

I pick up my pen and, after reopening the notebook on the first page, begin to write all this down, a torrent of words issuing forth from my pen. The force of it shocks and delights me. It's as if a dam has been breached in me, and the rush is intense – almost as intense as the sex I've been discovering, the new ways of loving and being loved. For the first time in my life I'm not struggling to find the words or the subject matter but am borne along by a kind of delicious lucidity that is so foreign to me that it's as if I'm only an instrument, channelling something I barely comprehend. Suddenly I have a muse, and that muse is sex and longing. Things to which I devoted very little thought, that I took for granted, before Anne Tournier came into my life, or I came into hers.

For an hour I write solidly, and then I stop and have another latte and sit and watch the world go by from my window seat overlooking the bustle of Queensway. Where before I've paid little real heed to people, being always so bound up in my own world, now I find myself fascinated by just about everyone, wondering what they're really like, what they really get up to, behind their closed doors, in the secrecy of their homes, between the sheets. Suddenly everyone – the women in hijab, the Chinese waitresses on their way to work, even the street-sweepers – has the potential for hidden depths that I never considered before, because everything I did was surface.

Ideas start to come to me then, little vignettes and sketches for characters that might develop into something when I have more time. I scribble furiously, barely able to keep up with the mental flow that has been unleashed, and then I pack up my notebook and pen and head back to the house, feeling elated and liberated. As I suspected, writing up my feelings about Anne, James and the whole strange set-up at St Petersburgh Place has given me some perspective on it, made me feel more philosophical about it and more in control. I can say no, I realise, if Anne starts to think she can get away with more than is acceptable, or if she thinks she can order me around or treat me like shit just because she is paying my wages. I can let go of this if I want to. For the moment, though, I don't want to. I don't want to precisely because, for the first time in my life, the ideas and the words are coming thick and fast, and I know that this development has been precipitated by the events of the past few days.

And so I reach the house calmer than I left it, and, when I see Anne in the kitchen, I can be mellow and friendly. Sensing perhaps that I am less nervous in her presence, she is less agitated, a little warmer. She asks how I have spent the afternoon, and I tell her I've been writing and feel happy with the way it's gone. She tells me she's been doing the same, and we agree that there are few finer feelings than those of being productive and creative.

As she leaves the kitchen, a cup of coffee in her hand, she turns back in the doorway.

'Don't be shy,' she says, 'about showing me your stuff, when you are ready. I'm always happy to cast a critical eye.'

'That would be lovely,' I say, but my smile is really a wince. The last person I'd show what I've been writing today is Anne. She may have defrosted a tad, but I don't trust her one bit, and for that reason she won't ever know what I'm feeling about any of this.

8

The Maid

The next day I'm super-prompt, determined not to let Anne scold me again, for this time I'm not sure if I could hold my tongue. I've never been good with authority, or at least not the sort of authority where it seems as if somebody is abusing their position for dubious purposes, or to make themselves feel better. That was how it was at school – there was always something a little creepy about Mrs Scholes and the way she looked at me when she reprimanded me about something. She always had a slightly sadistic gleam in her unnerving pale-blue eyes, similar, I suddenly realise, to Anne's. The things I was being told off for never seemed to me to warrant that kind of reaction, just as they didn't with Anne yesterday.

Yet it worked – here I am, at one minute to two, outside her study door with one hand raised, ready to knock. But before I can, as if she's sensed my presence in spite of my silent approach, she opens the door and gestures for me to enter. I step inside. The thought that she knows I would be punctual makes me angry. But it's the first time I've been in her study, and of course, since she is one of my literary heroines, I'm bursting with curiosity about what it's like, so I suppress my pique.

The first thing I notice is that the curtains are drawn, blocking out what would be a pleasant view over the trees towards the rear of the house. I surmise that she must be one of those writers who brook no distraction by their surroundings, who would find that a pretty vista would get in the way of their internal musings. I guess I can understand that.

On the other hand, the walls are almost covered with things that could distract. One of them has a very large cork pinboard festooned with all kinds of things – postcards, scraps of paper that look like lists, old theatre and gallery tickets, photos of people I don't recognise. Another wall, the one side-on to Anne's bulky mahogany desk, is plastered with Stickies of various colours, some of them bearing a scrawl that is illegible from the distance at which I am standing, others bearing a single word, generally one that I've never seen or heard before: 'salsuginous', 'ullage', 'gadarene', 'yapness'.

It's odd that I see all this before I notice the erotic artwork that adorns the walls, for once I do I become aware that there is a great deal of it. For a moment I just stand looking round, taking it all in – it's an eclectic mix, ranging from Japanese-style woodblock prints through Renaissance prints of voluptuous bodies to lithographs by Picasso. Although it's clear that none of them is an original, Anne has quite a collection going here. It looks as if she has put serious time and effort and not an inconsiderable amount of money into pursuing this interest.

Anne is looking at me. 'Take a seat,' she says, and there's a flicker of irony in her voice, as if she's amused by the attention I'm paying her artworks.

I feel, again, the tug of resistance, the desire to respond to her, to protect myself. *Isn't that what they're there for*, I want to shout at her, *to be looked at?* It's as if she's mocking my appetites, or my discovery of them. There's something condescending about it all.

But I take a seat, holding my tongue. Beside me is a sturdy wooden bookcase in which I can see an array of Anne's novels, arranged in chronological order, all the way from her first, *Of Angels and Daemons*, to her latest, *Touching Fire*. All are in the original French, but on shelves below there are translations into English and other languages – Italian, Spanish and some others I don't recognise. Seeing them reminds me how lucky I am to be here, and how much I stand to learn, if only I am brave enough to see this through. To rise to the challenge of whatever is asked of me.

Anne is sitting down now too, looking through a pile of papers. She's lit a cigarette, which is wedged in the corner of her mouth, sending spirals of smoke up through the still air. Then she takes it out and rests it in the ashtray, turns to me, the papers on her lap, secured by her bony hands.

'You're probably wondering,' she says slowly, 'what is required of you here.'

I hold her gaze, not knowing what to reply, half dreading where this conversation is going to take us, half relieved to think that I might find some kind of resolution, or replies to at least some of the questions that are bubbling away in my mind, keeping me awake at night.

Seeing that I am not going to reply, she goes on, in the same measured tone: 'I don't want you to misunderstand, or to complain that you are here under false pretences. But the work that I require of you is neglible. Perhaps less than I originally thought.'

She looks at me and, when I raise my eyebrows, continues: 'You have to understand, Genevieve, that I live in what I call a state of creative chaos. I always have. And now that you're here, potentially to "cure" me, I find myself thrown into panic, wondering if I can live any other way.'

I sit up. 'Does that mean I'm sacked?' As I speak I realise that I don't know whether I want her to say yes or no. Release would bring relief, but perhaps only temporarily. I think of James. I should call him now. I should let him know how I feel and find out if it's possible for us to see each other without Anne's mediation.

'Certainly not,' she says. 'But I don't want you hanging around the house waiting for orders from me. Orders that aren't going to come.'

'Never?'

'Not never. There are things . . .' Here she trails off, pauses and stares up at one of the Picasso lithographs thoughtfully, as if she's never seen it before or properly looked at it. I look at it too. It's titled *Nu couché avec Picasso assis à ses pieds* and depicts the artist seated at the feet of one of his models, who is naked and recumbent beside a vase of flowers. She is looking at the flowers, or towards the viewer. His hand is on her arse. It seems very much that she is in control, in her poise and stillness. He looks like a bit of a dirty old man, although he must have been young at the time – the print is dated 1902–03.

'I do need you,' she says at last, but she's not torn her eyes from the Picasso. 'But in essence your time is your own. What I'm saying is that I don't want you to waste your time waiting for me to call on you. You want to be a writer, you say?'

'Y-yes.'

'Then you must take this opportunity to get out and experience life, find something worth writing about.'

'But you're paying me full-time.'

'So?'

'What . . . What's in it for you?'

'Let's just say I've made an expensive mistake and that more important for me than the money is honouring my arrangement with you.'

'But –'

'Please, Genevieve. It's not necessary to discuss it any more.'

'So you'll tell me in advance, when you have something for me to do, and the rest of the time I'm free?'

'That's correct.'

'Well, I don't know what to say. Except thank you.'

'You're welcome. Consider yourself my acolyte.'

I look at her. I know the word, and that it can be used in a lay context. But for me it has religious overtones – a whiff of ritual, and candle lighting, and incense swinging. Overtones that make it seem heavier than Anne's laissez-faire demeanour seems to imply. Heavier, perhaps even burdensome.

Sensing my discomfort, she adds, 'Or, if you prefer, I am your mentor.'

'Mentor', I know from my studies, comes from Greek mythology. Mentor was left in charge of Telemachus when the latter's father, Mentor's friend Odysseus, went to fight in the Trojan War. Which makes me a *telemachus* – more commonly known, in the modern world, as a protégé or apprentice. In the end, it all comes down to the same thing, whatever you choose to call it: I have the chance of a lifetime, and I mustn't blow it. Never in my wildest dreams did I think I'd be living in the house of one of my favourite writers of all time, being paid to learn how to write.

Anne is looking at me contemplatively. 'Having said all this,' she says, 'I would like you to help me out this afternoon.'

'Help you out?'

She's regarding me intently, and there's something in her eyes that both chills and thrills me.

She jerks her chin towards one corner of the room. I look over and see a decorative shoji screen embellished with cherry blossoms that could, from a distance, be mistaken for vivid splashes of blood. Beneath the spindly tree on which they bloom sit two geishas in traditional dress. I look back at Anne and she merely nods.

I stand up and walk towards it. Part of me feels like a sleepwalker, someone with no power over what they're doing. But my trembling legs anchor me firmly in the here and now of my physical existence, and the world has an almost hallucinatory clarity, as if everything has become hyperreal.

As I reach the screen, I'm still split in two. There's the girl who wants to run away, to turn around and throw all of this back in Anne's face, that undecipherable mask she wears, confounding all attempts to understand her, to get beneath the surface layer of cool. And then there's the girl, a very different girl to the one I always thought I was, who's desperate to know what's behind the screen. And this is the girl who wins out as I step behind it, breath held.

A small lantern flickers in the corner, lit from within by a simple tealight. There are three hangers dangling from the top of the screen. The first, padded in pink silk, holds an underwire bra in a French-maid style. It could be tacky, but even in the low light I can see that the material is of the highest quality. The bra itself is sheer. Two white lace frills run across the top of the cups, and where they meet in the middle is a large black silk bow.

Fingering it, I muse on its significance. Acolyte, I remind myself, derives from the Greek word for servant. Is this what Anne was referring to? Is this a role that I am willing to take on, if it means that I can stay here and benefit from her generous offer? And, if I do, what will be asked of me?

On another hanger is a matching pair of knickers, or rather – I see as I take it down – a thong. The fabric, again, is deliciously sheer; the lace, this time, is on the sides, arching up over the thighs. Lastly, there's what I recognise to be a suspender belt, although I've never worn one, again in sheer black with a white frill.

Holding the bra and knickers, feeling the fabric between my fingertips, I reflect that I've never worn underwear of this calibre. Anne has spent a lot of money – a lot of money on *me*, for the garments are clearly new. I sneak a look at the labels and she's got the sizes spot on. Clever Anne. Clever, clever Anne. Either she's guessed correctly or she's been in my room, checking.

But is she too clever for her own good? Is she really counting on me going along with this little charade? She must have money to burn if she's willing to take the chance. I think about all the artworks, and then of the books. Has Anne's writing made her rich, despite her waning reputation? She's certainly got a taste for life's more expensive frivolities.

I'm looking at the lingerie in my hand, and for the first time I'm utterly, utterly torn. I'd give anything for five minutes with my diary, my notebook, in order to try to work out what it is that I want, where I should go from here. My problems with authority, my schoolgirl rebelliousness, are bubbling beneath the surface, ready to come spurting out like scalding hot lava. But I don't want to blow it. Will Anne understand that if I explain?

I'm still deliberating when I hear the creak of the door. Anne's nipped out, I think, and it occurs to me I might be let off the hook. I could do a runner while she's gone, and find some way of explaining later – tell her I had a sudden cramp or headache or something, had to go for painkillers or a lie-down. But then I hear the clearing of a throat, indisputably male, and I realise that the sound of the door was someone coming in, not going out.

I freeze. Of course, this is what I should have expected. Anne doesn't work alone. Anne doesn't get her hands dirty. Anne's speciality is getting someone else to do her bidding. Who I am to encounter this time?

A thrill goes up through me as the question poses itself in my mind – a thrill of nervous anticipation. Fearful as I may be, Anne's provided me with nothing but the highest-quality males so far. I have a feeling she won't let me down this time either.

'Are you ready, girl?' I hear her rasp, and I start.

'Not . . . Not yet,' I stutter.

'Do hurry up,' she says. 'We're waiting.'

'OK.'

'You mean, "Yes, mistress."'

I pause midway through pulling my top over my head. *No, that is* not *what I meant*, I want to say. *That is certainly not what I meant.* But I don't. I want to know who is out there, and what I'm going to be doing with him. I'm not going to cheat myself of that – no way.

And so I bite my tongue and carry on stripping off, letting my clothes fall in a heap to the ground, any old how. I feel under pressure now, and it's adding to my nervousness. My hands shake as I unclasp the bra and bring it to my breasts, wrap it around me. It's a perfect fit – snug and, despite the flimsy look of the sheer fabric, extremely uplifting. Spying a full-length mirror a few steps away, I turn and admire myself. I look hot.

I step into the panties, which are equally well fitting and flattering, showing my slender, shapely thighs to full advantage. But I pause, again, at the suspender belt. To start with, I don't know how to wear it. But I baulk at it too. There's something old-fashioned and submissive about it, something that shrieks: *I am here to please and to pleasure you.* I suppose it's because it looks so uncomfortable, such a pain in the arse to get on and to get hooked up to the stockings. Such a palaver, when one could be wearing tights – unsexy, for certain, but practical and fuss free.

Then I say to myself: Fuck it, my role here is to please, to submit. If I don't accept that, then I must leave immediately, and leave Anne's house too for good. This is what is asked of me, what her money and generosity and hospitality are all about. This is what I am here for.

I take a deep breath, wrap the wide belt around my waist and hips and fasten it in the small of my back, watching myself in the mirror. In spite of my misgivings, it looks and feels good. I am increasingly horny, wet at the prospect of meeting the man who awaits me, doing his bidding. Suddenly the thought of being bossed around arouses me rather than irritates me.

I pick up the stockings, unfurl them, then raise one leg onto a chair and slip it inside. My skin prickles deliciously at the contact with the material. I slip on the other one, then turn and look at myself from behind. The stockings are back-seamed, with subtle heart motifs on the base of the garters.

Above them my bare arse cheeks, cut by the thin white-lace sliver of the thong, form an attractive heart shape too.

I turn around again. Though this is clichéd territory, a stereotype of naughtiness available in every Soho sex emporium, the overall look here is classy, rather than tacky. I don't feel diminished by it but empowered in some sense. And now that I have embraced my role, I am ready to play.

I reach one hand round the screen, grasp it before making my entry. Pausing, I feel like an actress about to make her debut on stage, filled with a kind of intoxicating giddiness.

'She's ready,' breathes Anne, dragging forcefully on the cigarette I heard her light a few minutes ago. She's excited, I think: her face won't show it, but this simple sound has betrayed her. I wonder if her companion has sensed that too. Already, I think, I am beginning to know her, despite the barricades that she has erected, the mental screen she tries to hide behind.

I step forwards, pause again: time to give them a tempting view of one calf in its black-stockinged loveliness. There's silence now, and I sense that the two people awaiting me are holding their breath too. I revel in being able to make an effect like this, in the theatricality of it all. I never knew that make-believe could be such fun.

Then Anne, perhaps feeling that I am too much in control, says sharply, 'Tell her. Tell her to come out. Here – summon her.'

A throat clears again, and there's the tinkle of a little bell. 'Come out,' comes a voice, a little uncertainly.

My hand clutches at the screen. It's James, I've realised in a flash. James is back, and it's James to whom I will submit. The roles have been reversed: where I spanked him last time we met, now it is he who gets to call the shots.

Only it's not, of course. Just as last time it wasn't I who was calling the shots but Anne, this time it's again my boss, my mentor, who is leading proceedings. Like a film director, or the novelist that she is, Anne is guiding us, taking us where she wants us to go. We are merely the actors in the drama that she is creating.

'Girl,' says Anne, and this time I step out, wondering if my displeasure is evident on my face. I loathe it when she says that word.

I am not *your toy*, I want to say, but I gag on the words, can't get them out. And anyway, I've caught sight of James's face, that face I thought I might never see again in the flesh, and my happiness at being in his presence defuses my anger, makes it as insubstantial as the smoke spiralling up from the cigarette in Anne's hand.

'At last,' says Anne, impatiently. She's so good at this, so convincing, that I wonder that she didn't become an actress, rather than a writer. She's so totally in role that not a chink of her shows through. She looks at James.

He, too, is slow in coming up to the mark. It must be frustrating for her, this failure for us to follow her directions without a time-lag, the space to think and to react. We need to get it together, I tell myself. Otherwise she'll get bored of us, and then it will be over.

I stand in front of them, but where my hands previously rested on my hips, defiant, now they are hanging down in front of me, crossed at the wrists, and my head is bowed.

'Madam called?' I say.

Anne rolls her eyes, exhales a long plume of smoke. She looks impatiently at James.

He takes up the baton, seeming a little more sure now that I have settled into my own role. 'Come here,' he says authoritatively, gesturing with one finger. 'Why so slow?'

I can't look him in the eye, I'm so excited to be near him again. I step forwards, legs like slush despite the taut binding of the stockings. A wet patch is blooming in my saucy little knickers.

'Sir?' I say, chin down, still not meeting his gaze.

'Why so slow?' he repeats, and I shake my head.

'I'm sorry, sir.'

'Sorry is not good enough.'

'Sorry,' I say again, unable to stop myself.

'Stop saying sorry,' he shouts but, when I look up, I can tell he's finding it hard not to laugh. The corners of his lovely mouth are twitching, and around his eyes his skin is crinkling. I cast my eyes back down, aware that if one of us succumbs to laughter then the other will too, and that will be it.

'What was it sir wanted of me?' I manage.

'I want you to polish my shoes,' he says, and I suppress another urge to laugh as he feels in his jacket pocket and pulls out a handkerchief, which he tends to me. 'Here,' he goes on. 'Make them shine.'

I kneel at his feet. His shoes are, as you'd expect of a man of his standing, very fine – of chocolate-brown leather, they look handmade. The handkerchief, too, is of the finest linen and smells faintly of lavender and something spicier, more exotic. It's crisp and neatly folded, perhaps even ironed, although my mind falters at the thought of James doing any ironing at all. Does he have a maid at home? I wonder. In my mind's eye I see a gorgeous brunette, dressed as I am now, standing before him, a teetering pile of freshly pressed shirts in her hand, a come-hither look in her eyes.

Not daring to raise my eyes, I bend forwards, rump in the air, and begin to rub at the supple leather with one hand, watching as its dullness slowly gives way to shine. I polish and polish, my own reflection becoming clearer, and then I switch to the second foot and repeat the process.

'How is that for sir?' I say at last.

He leans forwards as if to inspect them, but his eyes, I see, are fast on the cheeks of my arse, which is high up where I'm bent over his feet.

'Very nice indeed,' he says.

'Is there anything else I could do for sir?' I realise that the stress is dissipating and that I'm really rather beginning to enjoy this. I don't look at Anne, however, worried that doing so might break the spell, make me start feeling self-conscious again. Novice though I am, I'm already beginning to understand that I have to fully enter into the role if this is to work, shuck off my real self for a time, as much as I can.

'There certainly is,' says James, and my heart leaps as I hear the unzipping of his fly.

'More polishing?' I say, biting the inside of my cheek.

James groans.

I stand up, bend forwards over him, so that my hair trails down over him and my cleavage is on full display.

'If sir will allow me . . .' I rest one hand on his shoulder. With the other I reach inside his open fly and delve around. His cock springs into my hand and he lets out another moan.

'Jesus,' he emits.

Lifting one leg and then the other, I climb astride him, holding his prick in my fist through the opening of his trousers. Tugging gently but then ever more insistently, I look into his eyes.

'Is that all right for sir?' I ask. But the mischief in his eyes, the laughter he's been struggling to sublimate, has ebbed away, replaced by a seriousness. He's frowning, jaw set. He doesn't want to come yet; he knows he has to fight it but doesn't know how.

I cease my wanking motions, tuck him back in, tenderly.

'If sir doesn't mind me saying,' I tell him, 'this room needs a good going-over.' For some reason, my voice has taken on a bit of a Cockney, Eliza Doolittle twang.

I bend to pick up the handkerchief that I tossed to the floor, flashing him a full-on view of my arse in all its heart-shaped glory. Then I start to prance around, dabbing at the bookshelves and the various work surfaces, half-heartedly, not at all seriously, just enjoying the effect that I must be having on James in this outfit.

Of course, there are two pairs of eyes on me as I do this, but I can honestly say, as I reflect on this later in my room, that at this moment I'm not thinking of Anne at all, am barely even aware of her presence. Everything is directed towards James, and for a few minutes at least I am able to pretend to myself that this is between him and me, that we are autonomous beings.

I rise up on tiptoe and contort, reaching high, bending low, ensuring that he gets alluring views of me from all manner of angles. Anne has one of those small ladders that you see in some bookshops, and I step up onto that, reach for the uppermost shelves, swishing the hankie around. Then I climb down, sit on the steps with legs akimbo as I attend to a heavy glass paperweight, rubbing the cloth over it intently.

After a while I start to get lost in my actions, half-believing in myself, in the scene that I have been creating. But then James coughs lightly, and I look up.

'Good work,' he says. 'You're very thorough.'

'I take pride in my work. I like to give satisfaction. Is there . . . Is there something else I could be doing for sir?'

He points down and past me. 'There are some shelves,' he says, 'that I think you've missed. I can still see some dust.'

I pretend to look where he's pointing. 'Oh, I'm so sorry about that, sir. I'll tend to it immediately.'

'If you would.'

I turn round and, as I do so, I hear him stand up. The floorboards creak as he moves across the room towards me. At the feel of his hands on my bare shoulders, I shiver with desire.

'There, down there,' he says, starting to ease me down. I sink slowly to my knees beneath the feather weight of his touch. With my hands I grope for the steps, bring myself down to them and drape myself over them. My arse is up in the air again.

I feel James's hands rest on my cheeks, enclose them with damp palms. He wants me, I think victoriously.

With one thumb he reaches in between my cheeks and pulls aside the ribbon of the thong. His thumb pad rests on my sphincter. I push back and spread my legs wider, wanting him inside me.

'I can still see the dust.' I hear Anne's voice, and her presence comes rushing back into the room like a storm rolling in across the sea. 'Come on, girl.'

I shake out the handkerchief, which has been crumpled in one of my clenched fists, and stretch it towards one of the lower shelves. James is still grasping at my arse cheeks, his hold harder and harder, his thumb taunting my little pink rosebud. As I swoosh the hankie around, I hear Anne rasping orders: 'Harder, faster. Come on, *come on*. It's still not clean. What's with you today?'

'I'm trying my hardest,' I hiss, unable to keep the silent deference required of a maid. My act is breaking down, my mask slipping, as my desire for James begins to overwhelm me. I want Anne out of here, I want this costume off. I just want to be with James now, the real, unmediated James. I want to stop pretending and for this to be for real.

But Anne keeps pushing. 'The floor,' she barks. 'It's filthy. Polish it.'

She gets up and stamps across the room. Spit spatters against the floorboards beside my hand. 'A bit of elbow grease wouldn't go amiss,' she says. 'Come *on*, girl. Or do I have to do it myself?'

I scrub furiously at the floor where she spat, watching as the hankie turns brown with the wood stain. My bum is jiggling wildly. I chance a look over my shoulder and see that James has his cock in his hand and is bringing it towards me. My pussy throbs.

He enters me, but Anne allows me no respite, standing there beside me, chiding me to do it better, more thoroughly, pointing out bits I have missed. All the while that James is fucking me, the satinesque baton of his prick gliding in and out of me, I have to carry on, doing Anne's bidding, submitting to her ridiculous demands. I'm appalled and yet oddly stirred by the situation, as if it calls to some fundamental duality in me.

As James's thrusts become faster, deeper, more intense, I cease the play-acting. I just can't hold it together, whatever Anne may think of me. Sensing me flag and lose heart, James eases himself out of my pussy, then wraps his arms around me and turns me over. I sit on the top rung of the little ladder and he kneels between my legs. I look at Anne, pleadingly.

Let me have him, my eyes say to hers. I have no more shame, no more pride. I just want him.

Her smile is thin, ungenerous, like pale milk, but she

nods her assent, as if she knows that I'm on the brink, that I won't go on with this if my own desires are consistently deferred. And it's then that I realise that maybe Anne's not as in control of this as I thought she was. Perhaps, just perhaps, Anne is starting to need me as much as I need her – need her in order to be with James. What lies beneath her need, its underpinnings, are unclear to me, but suddenly I smell fear on her, the fear that I might turn round and throw all of this back in her face. I may be the maid, the acolyte, but sometimes the apparent underdog has more power than he or she realises.

I think of the film *The Servant*, with Dirk Bogarde. And then I think of *The Maids*, a play with which Anne must be familiar, being French. It's a long time since I've read it, but I remember the basic plot: two housemaids, sisters, ritualistically killing their employer while she is out, taking it in turns to play her. Does Anne realise that I felt like killing her just now, when it seemed as if she wasn't going to let me have my way? I wouldn't have, of course, but I would have killed this little set-up stone dead, would have walked away this time.

She stands back, and now she's only an observer, as James drives himself into me to the hilt. I lean back against the crammed bookshelves, arms spread out on either side of me to steady myself. As he thrusts and thrusts, he pulls down my bra, liberating my breasts, and buries his face in them. I feel the exquisite chafing of his pubic bone against my clit, and I hold the bookcase tighter until my knuckles are bloodless. For a few minutes we continue like this, and then I push James up and off me, assertive now. I force him down onto the top step and impale myself on his prick where it strains up for me, my freed tits in his face. Now he's resting back against the shelves, his arms similarly outspread. His eyes are closed, as if in prayer or supplication. There's a sort of beatification on his fine, chiselled features. I want to kiss him, but I daren't, despite my newly acquired assertiveness. I'm afraid of letting Anne into our intimacy.

Or am I deluded? Can there be any intimacy in a set-up such as ours? James and I exist only in this strange little universe created by Anne. Outside it he and I, as a couple, don't exist. What I feel to be intimacy is only a fantasy, a dream of life as it could be. In my real life, I would never have met James, never have spoken to him. Our lives were so far apart, we might as well have lived on different planets. We are thrown together by chance and circumstance, by Anne's mighty will and the fantasies that fuel it. Without her there'd be none of this.

James's hips are bucking beneath me, his rhythm losing itself as he grows close to the edge. I watch his face and, seeing his eyeballs roll beneath his lids, his mouth fall open, I feel so incredibly hot that I know I'll come soon too. I bring my hand down to my clit, press hard and then start massaging it. Leaning back and away from James, one forearm lassoed around his shoulder and neck for support, I ride him helplessly, sobs issuing forth from my throat as I start to come, my whole body shuddering on top of him. As he comes too, with a roar that frightens me even as it excites me even more, I turn my head – I'm still not sure whether I meant to or if it was a reflex – and open my eyes.

Anne is watching us – of course she's watching us. But as I sit up and fall forwards onto James, wrapping both arms around his neck, she's already turning away, as if something else has caught her attention. For a moment she stands stock-still, as if lost in contemplation, or as if she's lost the thread of her thoughts, and then she walks over to her desk, takes hold of her mouse and calls her computer screen back to life. She sits down, peering at the screen, then she speaks at last, absently, as if called away to more urgent matters.

'You may dress,' she says. 'And then you may leave, quietly.'

She turns her head towards us then, but her eyes are empty. 'You are dismissed,' she says.

Out on the landing, it takes me a few moments to realise that we are alone, James and I. Of course, Anne could be behind the door, listening, but something tells me that she has, for some reason known only to herself – or perhaps not even to her – loosened her hold. I think she's still at her desk, gazing at her computer screen, sucked back into the inner world where she goes to make her fiction.

But I'm taking no chances, and neither is James: we walk down the stairs in silence, jumping at every squeak of the boards, as if we were misbehaved children trying to make a getaway. Only at the very bottom of the stairs, in the ground-floor hallway, does one of us break the silence. To my surprise, it's me: I'm overflowing with desires and questions and the need to express myself.

'I have to see you,' I whisper urgently.

James smiles secretively. 'You're seeing me,' he says, spreading his arms. 'I'm here, right in front of your very eyes.'

I step into his arms, bury my head in his shoulder. His linen jacket smells manly but clean. I think I perceive notes of vetiver.

'You know what I mean.' My voice has a wounded tone to it. Why won't he take me seriously?

Above my head I feel his head shake, his chin grazing the top of my head.

'What?' I step back and look up at him, tears already pricking my eyes. I blink them away. What was it I said about keeping a check on my emotions?

He shakes his head again. 'It simply won't do,' he says.

'Why not?'

'Anne . . .' He trails off.

'But what can she do? She can't stop us seeing each other.'

'She could fire you.'

'I don't care. I would be with you.'

This third shake of his head is vehement where the others were gentle.

'I'm sorry, Genevieve,' he says, looking into my eyes kindly. 'It's beyond me.'

He's making for the door, and my thoughts are racing. What can I do to make him change his mind? Without knowing what all this means to him, how and why he got involved, I can't appeal to his reason. But I'm mystified as to why he is so resistant to the prospect of us being alone together. Nothing during the encounters we have had has suggested that the primary interest for him is 'performing' in front of someone else. No, that's not how he gets his rocks off. Is it all about subservience then, submitting to Anne's orders? If so, then it's not really about me and I should forget about him.

He opens the door and steps out into the still-bright day. I want to follow him, ask him to walk in the park with me, to talk to me of his dreams and his fears. I want him to tell me how he came to be where he is, alone yet implicated in Anne's web. Talking might make him realise that this is not the only way, that there is an alternative.

But before I can formulate the words, he's pulling the

door closed behind him, and I'm left standing in the hallway, suddenly gloomy now the light's been shut out.

The house is quiet around me, as if I were the only one here. I make myself a cup of tea in the kitchen, walk slowly upstairs. Passing Anne's study I hear the clicking of her keyboard. I feel a stab of irritation, and of envy. How dare she manage to switch off from what's just happened, tune in to her fiction? And why must I remain so enmeshed, so unable to crawl out of the mire?

Upstairs I stretch out on my bed and relive the whole incident in my mind, from the moment Anne summoned me inside her study to my hearing James's voice as I stood behind the screen. Then I start to giggle as I remember kneeling forwards, arse in the air, to polish James's shoes. Giggle to think of the way he shook slightly as he struggled not to laugh. The fun we had, for a while. The absurdity of it all. It seems like something from a raunchy film.

Then my mind spins forwards to his parting shot: 'It's beyond me.' Why does Anne have such power over him, and me none? He seems closed to persuasion, and I am hurt by that, after what we've been through together. It's not just sex that we've been having after all. It's an intimate dialogue that takes us somewhere deep, somewhere deeper than I've ever been before. I can't speak for James, but I don't think it's all about sex for him either.

I pick up my notebook. Yesterday I covered several pages with my musings about Anne, James and the boy – about everything, in short, that's happened to me since I've lived here. Then there were the pages of notes inspired by the people I saw passing the window as I sat nursing a latte in the coffee shop. I run my eyes over them and am heartened by what I read. There are some good ideas there, it seems to me. One or two things that even suggest themselves as short stories. I put little asterisks by them. Suddenly I feel better, taken out of myself into a new realm of possibilities, a realm where I have ultimate control. What fun, I think, to be a writer. No wonder Anne is so hooked on control.

I look back down. I'm thinking of starting a short story. But first I want to empty my head of everything that's happened today. Call it a kind of cleansing, a spring clean.

I grip my pen and begin writing.

9

Girl Alone . . . ?

The next morning I wake feeling good, despite James's refusal to see me outside of the bizarre threesome that exists between him, Anne and me. I wrote in my diary for a good couple of hours yesterday, describing events in as much detail as I could to give some context, then exploring my feelings. I tried to see events from everyone's perspective, to give myself more distance from them – Anne's and James's motives are, of course, obscure to me, but then so are my own sometimes. Yet getting it all out of my system helped enormously, granting me some sort of catharsis.

Afterwards, the words kept flowing, this time in the form of a little vignette that started to take shape, the beginnings of which might turn out to be a short story – or perhaps even something longer. Certainly, the character intrigues me. She's a version of myself, of course, but someone more daring than me, someone who knows what she wants and isn't afraid to go get it. Which gets her into all kinds of hot water. I haven't gone further than a couple of pages so far, but I'm excited to have started at all. I feel like I'm on the threshold of something big, something that may determine how the rest of my life unfolds. Perhaps, after all, I will be a writer.

Sitting up and stretching, I welcome the day and whatever it may bring. James might be beyond my control, in thrall to Anne, but I am a free agent and I need to take advantage of my enviable position, my stroke of luck – being paid to basically do bugger all the whole day long.

I dress and head out to the same coffee shop as before. Over a buttery *pain au chocolat* and a large latte, I scan the pages of the *Time Out* I bought on the way, trying to decide how to fill my day. As usual, I get overwhelmed by the sheer choice of things to do in London. It's almost paralysing. By the time you've deliberated on all the options, there's no time left to do anything.

I'm ashamed to say that I'm not so familiar with this city, despite calling it home. When I was at Vron's, I saw ridiculously little of it. OK, I was broke, but I knew even then how many things are free here – the Tate galleries, the British Museum and countless other venues. Yet still I didn't go, stupidly. I don't think I'm the only one, though – I guess when you actually live in a city you put things off, promise yourself you'll go sometime but never do, whereas a tourist jams it all into a week, and so paradoxically sees more than the person who lives there.

Giving myself a mental kick up the arse, telling myself that now is the time to see all this, I slap closed the magazine, drain the dregs of my coffee and head out onto Queensway. Anne is right, of course, when she says a novelist needs to get out, experience the world. How could I have expected to find anything to write about when all I did was mope about at Vron's or sit in cafés? I wasn't nourishing myself as a writer.

I'm planning to go to the Tate Modern and wondering

whether to take the Tube or the bus, when suddenly I see Anne walking along the Bayswater Road at its junction with Queensway. Unable to stop myself, I walk in the same direction and see her come to a halt at the bus stop. Thoughts of the Tate forgotten, I stand with my back to the stop, feigning interest in the contents of a travel agent's window. When a bus comes and she boards, I wait a few minutes and then get on too. I'm lucky in that she headed up the stairs; I take a seat on the lower deck, at the back, and grab a discarded copy of *Metro* that I can use to shield my face when she comes down.

I laugh inwardly at the silliness of it all, but part of me is deadly serious. This too seems paradoxical, but happening on Anne outside of the house that we share may offer me a glimpse into who she really is. Perhaps she is meeting someone, or doing some research. Perhaps she is even going to see James, and I will get chance to eavesdrop on their conversation and find out what this is all about.

Part of me squirms as I think that. What might they say to each other about me, when I'm not there? Do they laugh about what an easy lay I was, how quickly I allowed myself to get caught in the web, like an indolent fly, drunk on summer heat and sweet things, heedless to the danger? Do they discuss, in detail, the things that James and I did to each other's body, give me marks out of ten for technique?

The bus rattles along the Bayswater Road and into Oxford Street, and I keep my eyes fixed on the bottom of the staircase lest I miss Anne coming down. Suddenly I'm boiling with hatred for her and the way she has co-opted me, without regard for my feelings. The way she is taking advantage of my need for money and my ambition to write. She holds this in front of me like the juiciest of carrots, and I am helpless to escape. Is it worth it though?

We're nearing Selfridges when Anne appears at the bottom of the stairs and glances towards the back of the bus. I jerk the newspaper up in front of my face. The doors open as we reach the stop and she steps out, rather jauntily I think. She seems to be in a good mood. I am wondering if she's going shopping. Maybe she's heading for Selfridges' lingerie department, looking for something new for me. Now that would be a laugh, spying on her as she leafs through the rails, imagining me in this or that flighty little number.

I hop off too, and follow her as she takes a side street alongside the department store and continues to a place called Manchester Square. I've never been here before, but I soon find out that it's home to the Wallace Collection, an art museum housed in a glorious townhouse overlooking the square. Anne breezes inside, seemingly very familiar with the place: she heads straight up the stairs to the first floor with barely a glance around her.

I keep on behind her, feeling foolish, wondering what I think I am doing. There I was, bemoaning Anne's attempted transformation of me into an acolyte, a follower, and here I am literally following her, like some spook. A stalker, that's what I am, what she's made me into. So much for going out seeking writerly inspiration.

Anne heads straight into a room called the Boudoir. It's tiny, and empty, and so I have to linger outside, otherwise I'll reveal myself. Anne spends a good ten minutes inside but, from my oblique view through the doorway, seems to focus her attention on one particular piece. She studies it for a while then takes a small pad from her shoulder bag and writes some notes. When she's finished she crosses into the next room.

I shoot into the Boudoir, so named, I learn from one of

the wall panels, because it was the first of Lady Wallace's private apartments. There's certainly nothing illicit on show here – the paintings look as if they probably date from the eighteenth century and depict mainly classical and moral themes. There are also several imposing writing desks and secretaries.

I go straight to the canvas in front of which Anne tarried. It's called *Innocence*, and it's by Jean-Baptiste Greuze. I frown at it. The innocence in question, that of a young girl with her robes falling down from her shoulders to reveal peachy flesh, seems precarious, perhaps even feigned. Or is that the point?

I don't have time to ponder it too much, aware that I might be losing Anne. I peep round the doorway into the next room in time to see her making her way into a larger gallery. Here it's some miniatures that hold her attention; again, I hold back, curious but not daring to get any closer. Only when she enters the next gallery do I step inside the large one and inspect the works. They're all, I notice, by a French artist called Charlier, and nearly all mythological in theme: *The Birth of Venus*, *The Toilet of Venus*, *A Muse and a Cupid*, *Venus and Cupid in the Clouds* and *Pan and Syrinx*. There's lots of pink flesh on display. I wonder if Anne's novel is somehow linked with mythological themes.

Just as I'm looking at the last work, unfamiliar with the myth, a very familiar voice rasps in my ear, and I almost leap out of my skin.

'Do you know the story of Pan and Syrinx?' it says, and I whirl around, my face puce.

'Anne!' I exclaim. 'What a coinci–'

Her knowing smile arrests me in my charade. She touches me lightly on the forearm, as if to reassure me that it doesn't matter – that she knows I've followed her here, that I was spying on her and that she doesn't care. That it doesn't even surprise her.

I wonder at what point she became aware of me, and think of the moment on the bus when she looked towards the rear and I whipped up my newspaper. As I do, I become convinced that she noticed me then, and that I've been making a total fool of myself.

'It's a fascinating story,' she says, and I wonder what she's talking about. She gestures back at the miniature. 'Pan and Syrinx,' she reminds me.

I shake my head. 'I don't know it.'

She smiles, but she's not looking at me. Her eyes are on the picture, and her voice seems to come from far away. 'Ovid's *Metamorphoses*,' she says. 'You obviously haven't read it.'

'Greek mythology wasn't my thing at uni. Or Roman, whatever it is.'

'Greek and Roman, actually . . . Anyway, the story has it that Syrinx, a nymph, was pursued by Pan to the Ladon River.' She pauses. 'I presume you know who Pan was . . .'

'Er, some kind of nature spirit.'

She sighs, as if saddened by my unending ignorance, and shakes her head. 'You're getting confused with pantheism, which *is* Greek but means "God is all". As in, God is the same thing as Nature, the Universe, or however you want to describe it, rather than a personal deity.' She pauses, then continues: 'Pan is the god of fields and forests, and so symbolises human lust and savagery in Man. You usually see him with goats' features. Anyway, Syrinx begged her sisters, the river nymphs, to help her escape Pan and his lascivious advances, and they turned her into reeds, from which the god later made his famous pipes. You've heard of those at least?'

She looks at me in silence for a moment. 'In case you think I'm having a jolly day off,' she says coolly, at last, 'I'm actually doing research.'

'For your next novel?'

'That's right.'

'Am I allowed to know what it's about?'

'Allowed? You are my assistant. It would be hard to keep secrets from you.'

I laugh inwardly, and more than a little bitterly. Anne is one big secret to me, an utter mystery. It's me who's become transparent: having shown her my body, how it gives and receives pleasure, I feel that I have exposed my soul too. I am wholly vulnerable, where she is an impenetrable fortress, or a sheer wall of rock with no footholds.

She shoots a glance at her watch. 'I'm ravenous,' she says. 'How about lunch in the restaurant? On me, of course.'

'I'd like that,' I say, and I mean it. I'm apprehensive, for obvious reasons, but I'm also thrilled at the chance to have this face to face with Anne, to get to know the woman beneath that diamond-hard surface.

The restaurant she referred to, it turns out, is a French brasserie in the museum's gorgeous ground-floor conservatory. We find it empty bar two sets of couples: men and women facing each other, staring into each other's eyes, fingers entwined. It's the kind of romantic place where a man might bring his lover to propose to her, or where one might initiate a clandestine affair. Anne and I are the odd couple. No one in their right mind would take us for lovers, and we're not – not really. Or only via the intermediary of James. No, they would much sooner take us for mother and daughter.

As the thought flickers through my mind, I wonder if there's not something of that to our relationship after all.

Anne is hardly the most motherly of women, and there's surely some significance in the fact that she's never had children. But as I sit down across the table from her, it strikes me that the way I look to her as some kind of model, this reverence I have towards her work and the aspiration to write similar novels, makes me, in a way, her successor. Her daughter.

She's saying something to me now, and I sit up in my seat. If I'm to live up to Anne, make the most of this mentorship, I must pay attention. Must take it seriously, and not get lost in dreams and fantasies.

She's recommending the oysters from the raw bar, asking me if I've ever tried them before, and my thoughts turn inevitably to Sarah Waters and to girl-on-girl action. Anne isn't a lesbian. I know that from her work, from her preoccupation with relationships between the different sexes. But does she swing both ways when it suits her? She seems to have a voracious sexual curiosity that makes that entirely possible. And she's certainly not averse to watching girls in action. Could all of this turn out to be some kind of preamble to seduction? Is Anne Tournier trying to get into my pants?

I look her squarely in the eye. 'I don't like oysters. I don't like the idea of them.'

Her face doesn't register any emotion as she continues to peruse the menu. 'Well, I'm tempted by the steak tartare,' she says. 'Like many of the French, I'm a die-hard carnivore. The rawer the better, that's my motto.'

I look down at my own menu, choose fairly randomly. 'Think I'll go for a Niçoise salad,' I say.

'And some wine?'

I shake my head. I don't want to let down my guard, just in case she does have something fruity in mind. In the wake of recent events, I'm worried about my ability to say no. I have less self-restraint than I thought I had.

After we've ordered, Anne leans back in her chair. Without a cigarette in her hand or the corner of her mouth, she looks a little lost, a little incomplete. She regards me, and her expression is slightly inquisitive, as if it's she who's trying to figure me out now and not the other way round.

Unable to bear the scrutiny, I return to the subject of her book. 'So your novel . . . it's about Greek mythology? That's a bit of a departure for you, isn't it?'

She shakes her head as the waiter places a glass of red wine on the table in front of her. '*Merci*,' she says, and there's a twinkle in her eye as she looks up at him. He's a good-looking bloke, as is often the case with French waiters in classy places like this. I wonder what she's thinking, if she's imagining him naked, fucking her, or fucking me. I think of the boy and wonder again where Anne picked him up. Perhaps in a restaurant just like this one? Perhaps – the thought crosses my mind for the first time, scalding me with its implications – she even paid him for his time. Which makes him . . . Which makes me . . . My mind reels. I wish I'd ordered some wine after all.

'It's not *about* Greek or Roman mythology,' she says, picking up the thread of our conversation. 'But it draws heavily on them for inspiration. It's . . . I hate to summarise a book in a few words or sentences. It does it so little justice, makes it sound naive and simplistic. But let's just say it's about change – hence Ovid's *Metamorphoses*.'

'Change?'

'The human ability to evolve, according to circumstances. My characters – well, let's just say, my aim is to throw them into difficult circumstances and see how they adapt. To investigate change as a survival instinct, if you like.'

'Is it set in the modern day?'

'Very much so. In modern-day London.' She takes another swig of her wine, hungrily eyeing the glistening pyramid of raw beef that the waiter has just set before her, studded with capers and topped by a raw egg. She takes up her cutlery.

'I suppose I've always, through all my books, been fascinated by the idea of how much we can change ourselves, and how much remains innate and static. And by the question of how much we can change other people. They say, don't they, that you can't change other people, lovers, for instance? But is that really the case? On the contrary, I think that people are very open to persuasion, very . . . *corruptible*.'

As she lays her stress on the final word, she's looking not at me but at the handsome young waiter. Brazenly, he's holding her stare, as if challenging her. What does he think she wants of him, a woman of her age, with her looks? She's not ugly, but she's time-worn, a little tired. The smoking and the skinniness have done her no favours. Certainly, she's not on his level. Yet she's got his attention. He's flattered, or intrigued. Maybe it's just adding a bit of spice to a boring shift.

I watch her, and I watch him, and I think about the paintings that Anne sought out upstairs. First *Innocence*, and then Pan's lusty pursuit of Syrinx, ending in her transformation into reeds. Reeds that he later, in turn, changed into a pipe. I'm dying to read her work in progress, find out how all this fits into that. But it's really the Greuze painting that my mind keeps running up against, like a wall. The 'innocence' depicted there is an innocence that is begging to be defiled, to be corrupted. The model seems to be 'asking for it'. Which makes her the very antithesis of innocence.

I push my salad leaves around my plate as I mull all of this over. I wasn't innocent to start with, but I was unworldly. Thinking back to my interview with Anne and her unconventional avenues of questioning, I'm starting to ask myself if she didn't choose me for the job precisely because of my relative lack of experience. Am I some kind of experiment, a guinea pig on whom she's trying out her theories of change and corruptibility?

The waiter is attending to one of the couples at the other tables now, and I realise that Anne is watching me as I play with my food.

'Is it not good?' she says.

'It's . . . It's fine. I'm just not that hungry.'

'What are your plans for today?'

'I was going to go to the Tate Modern, but –'

I halt as I realise that I'm about to drop myself in it. Anne must have guessed that I followed her, that our meeting here was far from a bizarre coincidence, but the last thing I want to do is admit that to her.

'Yes,' she says. 'There's only so much art one can take in one day.'

She gestures across the room for the bill and, when the waiter places it beside her on a little silver platter, puts a sheaf of notes down. I notice that she leaves a healthy tip.

We move towards the exit.

'Do you need a lift back?' says Anne. 'I'm getting a cab.'

I shake my head. 'I think I'll have a look around Selfridges. Unless you want me for anything, that is?'

'No, that's fine.'

We're outside now, and she's swivelling her head, trying to spot a vacant taxi. I thank her for lunch, and she smiles, looking at me intently.

'Next time I'll try to talk you into oysters,' she says, and there's a curious note to her voice, a brittleness, like ice on a winter pond. It's as if suddenly her voice might shatter into thousands of tiny fragments. 'Did you say you'd never tried them? Well, you must, you must. Remember –' A cab pulls up beside her and she steps up to the passenger door, leans in to instruct the driver where to go, then opens the rear door and lifts one foot. 'Remember what I told you – a novelist must embrace life and all the experiences it offers. *All* of them.'

And with that she leaves me standing on the pavement, bemused, fearful and exhilarated all at once. It's a crazy mix of emotions, and I realise I'm exhausted by it all, that I do want to go home after all. I head back to Oxford Street and the bus stop.

The house is quiet, almost eerily so. I make some tea and head upstairs, past Anne's office. No sound emanates from it, but I'm certain she's in there, staring at the screen or researching something in a book, or perhaps simply sitting in her armchair thinking, trying to weave together the various strands of her narrative, meld the mythological elements with the contemporary. As usual, I'm jealous, thinking of her embarking on this great creative adventure. How satisfying and exciting it must be to write a whole book. To create something from, basically, nothing.

Carrying on up to my room, I console myself with the thought that I am a little bit further along that road than I was this time a week ago. Then I'd barely gone past the starting line. At least now there may be a story on the way, and I've filled several pages of my journal. The shell has cracked, and I've begun to fight my way out, into the light, and follow my dream.

Although I don't really feel like it, I force myself to open my notebook and, after a slow start, I manage to write several more pages – not of the story, but of my diary. I describe the fiasco with Anne, the botched spying attempt, the peculiar lunch, the looks exchanged with the handsome waiter. And when I've done that, without any real forethought, I find myself writing about the waiter – a fantasy of what might have happened had I been alone with him, the last customer in the restaurant late at night, sipping a brandy while he polished glasses and cutlery, readying the tables for the next day's lunch service.

And he comes over to me. In the flicker of candlelight from my table, his complexion seems darker than I'd thought, perhaps Mediterranean. A rich olive brown. I think of the beaches of St-Tropez, of Cannes – of rows of bodies slick with oil, toasting to the dark gold of demerara sugar beneath the blazing August sun. He'd be at home there, with his honed, muscular body; at home in a pair of tight lime-green Speedos that accentuate the firm handful folded within, which turns so many heads on the sand – of both sexes.

'I suppose you're coming to throw me out?' I say. 'You do have a home to go to.'

He smiles, and there's mischief in his eyes. 'There's nothing says I have to go home just yet,' he replies softly. There's a gentle provocation to his tone. He takes hold of the back of the chair opposite mine. 'Do you mind?' he says, but he's already pulled it back before I reply.

'Be my guest.'

When he sits down he reaches over and, without taking his eyes from mine, pulls my glass towards him, lifts it and takes a hefty swig. Then he puts the glass back down.

'So how come you're dining alone?' he asks. His English is idiomatic but his accent gives it a sexy French overlay that makes me melt.

'Sometimes alone is good.' I smile in what I hope is a subtly alluring, mysterious way.

He smiles. 'They do say that, don't they? That to be known, you must first know yourself. And the same with love. You must learn to love yourself before you can expect anyone to love you.'

Beneath the table I'm rubbing myself through my dress and my knickers. There's such an invitation in his eyes, but in line with his words it's an invitation that's not necessarily bound up with him, with the expectation of my taking this encounter over the line into something physical.

'Is that good?' he says, and I realise that he can see the movement of my arm and has guessed that I'm playing with my pussy beneath the table.

My mouth opens but I can barely release a word, so inflamed am I now. Of course, I wanted and intended him to be aware of what I am doing, but now that I am sure that he is, I'm feeling almost freakishly excited. I'm unable to speak, so quickly am I losing myself to the sensations I'm calling forth in myself.

Beneath the table I slip off my high heels, so that with my feet I can gain better purchase on the floor. Then, pulling up my dress, I push my hand inside my knickers. The froth of my pubic hair against my hand thrills me further; I feel wanton and illicit. Then I realise that the waiter, too, has slipped off his shoes, or at least one of them, for I feel bare flesh against the tender flesh of my inner thigh. I release my hand from my pussy and grab the foot, pull it up towards me. Wriggling his toes, the waiter begins to probe my wetness.

Throwing my head back, I strum at my clit while he continues to move his toes around my lips and my hole, dipping in and out with *his big toe. My hands are on my breasts now, squeezing, tweaking, as ecstasy takes hold. I spread myself wider, push myself onto the waiter's foot, my eyes closed, unable to see the look on his face.*

I open them at last, as I ride the cusp of my climax, in time to see the chef standing in the doorway, still wearing his toque. Only then, as he takes it off, do I realise that this chef is a woman. A very attractive one too, with a swathe of dark hair, almost black, that cascades down her back like silk, and almost ferociously blue eyes. I was already coming, but the fact of our eyes meeting across the room at such a critical moment pushes me over the edge, so that I'm crying out, unabashed in my joy, my hands clenching around the sides of the table.

As I flop back in my seat, still not taking my eyes from her blazing blue ones, I hear the waiter say, 'Ah, Sandrine, there you are. Are you going to join us for a nightcap?'

I sit bolt upright and . . .

I have to stop writing there, I'm getting so wet. I can't carry on, can't concentrate on the words any more; they're fluttering around like butterflies, failing to alight on the page, dancing and shimmering and impossible to catch. I'm losing control of them as my excitement mounts.

I bound over to my bed, lie on my side and, pulling my knickers aside, start fingering myself. I'm absolutely dripping down there. I stretch for the bedside table and take out my Rock Chick, then I kneel up, open my legs and feed it into myself. I set the vibrator mechanism for extra clitoral stimulation and I'm away with the fairies, thrusting and grinding and swivelling my hips. When I start to tire, I roll over onto my back and continue the same basic motions. Soon I'm biting the back of my hand as I try not to scream out when I hit jackpot.

Afterwards I lie there spent, idly fingering my pussy, still damp but a little numb now. It's a kind of warm, drowsy numbness that I love. I feel I could fuck myself some more, in a little while, but that first I might like to lie in a swoon, dream, think about James, and the boy, and my fantasy waiter. And the chef, that sultry raven-haired beauty who made such a surprise appearance towards the end of my piece.

Of course I could have gone on writing, could have brought her over to our table, allowed her to get involved in our game. What stopped me? I said I was getting too excited to carry on, but was I being disingenuous? Was I perhaps just afraid, afraid of what might happen if I let her enter the scene? Am I blocking out some of my desires through fear, to the point where I don't even recognise them as mine?

Confused, I get up, take a shower and head downstairs. I make a cup of coffee and then head into the living room and settle down on a floor cushion by Anne's shelf of photography books. I flip through a few, unable to find what I want, then I come across a bunch of images by Man Ray. One of them, *Juliet et Margaret*, is a solarised photograph of two women entwined, bare breasted. Patterns are drawn on their faces: leaves, flowers. I find the image exotic, beautiful, alluring. I was a big fan of the Surrealists during my studies. I wished so hard I could travel back in time and be one of them. They seemed to fear nothing, be open to boundless experimentation.

I look again at the girls in the photo. What would it be like to be with a girl? It's a question I've never consciously posed myself, but looking at the image, I wonder why not. Suddenly it seems not only that there's a whole world of experience out there that I have been denying myself, without any real grounds, but also that I've been barricading myself in, erecting defences about things without due cause. What's the worst that could happen if I tried it out with a girl? I could hate it, and so I would stop. I could be terrible at it, and she would make me stop. Or I could like it, love it even, and then what? I would carry on, want to do it some more. Would that make me a lesbian? It would depend how good it was. But, if it did, it would be because it was really good and I'd want to do it again and again and again.

So there's nothing at all to be afraid of. Either I'll like it or I won't. Only if I like it a huge amount will I be forced into making any major decisions or any great life changes. But I'll cross that bridge when I come to it.

I reshelve the books and head into the kitchen for a snack. I'm just heading out with a peanut butter and jam sandwich to take up to my room when I run into Anne.

'Peckish?' she says.

I smile sheepishly.

'Well, you didn't eat much lunch,' she says. 'And one needs to keep one's strength up.'

Remembering that she paid for my largely uneaten food I start to apologise, but she holds up her hand. 'You just weren't in the mood,' she says.

She passes me by, goes into the kitchen. I hear her mutter something and, not knowing if she was talking to me, say, 'Sorry? Did you say something?'

Still with her back to me, she says, 'Oh, nothing really. Just that – I thought maybe you should have tried the oysters after all.'

I narrow my eyes. It's as if she's been reading my mind, or spying on me. Not that I could complain, after my stalking antics of this morning. But I decide to be brave this time, that it's time to start asserting myself.

Sensing this, knowing that I haven't gone upstairs, Anne turns around and meets my gaze.

'I was just thinking the same.' My whole body tingles. 'I was just thinking that perhaps I'd like to try oysters after all.'

Anne smiles. 'I was hoping you'd say that.'

We're upstairs in Anne's study, looking at pictures on the internet, pictures of girls. Not pornos – just pictures of actresses and models, most of them fully clothed if not entirely naturally posed and at ease. Anne's trying, she says, to find out what kind of women I like.

'How about her?' she asks, stopping at a girl who looks a little like the French actress Emmanuelle Béart.

'Too –' I stop. I don't know what I feel about her.

'Too innocent?' suggests Anne, leaning in for a closer look at the screen. 'She's beautiful, that can't be disputed. Or should I say, beautiful according to Western conventions. But some people might find her too childlike, too doll-like, with those huge eyes, the full lips. The strange symmetry of the face. The scrubbed aspect to her. Too clean. ' She clicks back to Google.

'So you say you've never had a girl?' she says, and suddenly I feel like yelling at her: *I've told you that already, twice in fact! Why do you keep making a big deal about it? How many women actually have slept with another woman, if only once? Have you?*

The way she's setting about finding me a woman, as if it's some kind of project or mission, has me wondering about Anne all over again. This sex at arm's length she seems to get off on – what's that all about? She seems surprised that I haven't ever done it with a girl, but at least I'm doing it at all. Anne's sex life doesn't seem to have any substance, to be all watching and no joining in.

Sensing, perhaps, my exasperation, Anne doesn't wait for an answer but keeps clicking on links, bringing up pictures for me, asking me whether this girl or that girl does it for me. You'd have thought doing this together might bring us closer, might make us co-conspirators. You might imagine doing this with some people over a few glasses of wine, as a laugh, giggling and taking the piss out of each other. But not with Anne. The atmosphere is leaden, ponderous. I can't help but think that Anne is taking this too seriously. But I daren't challenge that, daren't try to lighten things up. She, as ever, is in charge, even if I took some sort of initiative for once.

In fact, thinking back to a few moments ago and the conversation in the kitchen, I wonder if Anne hadn't already laid some trap, which makes a joke of my so-called initiative. Sure, it was me who had the fantasy of the waiter and the female chef, which seems a little absurd to me now: I wonder whether I'll ever finish the story. But it was Anne who sowed the whole lesbian idea in my mind, and she who prompted me in the kitchen, by continuing with her oyster innuendo. So I can't be said to have reached this decision by my own volition.

Sensing that I might be getting cold feet, Anne turns away from her screen. She's canny enough to know that, if she pushes me too far, too fast, I might panic, and then she'll lose me. The last thing she wants to do is to scare me away.

'I ought to be getting on with the novel,' she says, and her tone is a little regretful, although I can't tell if it's real or put on. Perhaps she has grown bored of my dilly-dallying, my non-committal attitude. Or perhaps she's had a sudden inspiration for her novel and needs to get on with it before it's evaporated.

I stand up, knowing that I'll outstay my welcome if I don't go now.

She looks up at me, and there's a sort of scrutiny in her eyes, as if this time it's she who is trying to figure me out.

'You could always carry on alone,' she says, 'if it makes it any easier.'

At my raised eyebrows, she continues: 'It's not easy, disentangling what one likes from what one's been led to believe one likes. What one *thinks* one should like. What is acceptable. You have to strip away all those social conventions and expectations. Who knows? You might find you like bull dykes in dungarees. Or big busty porny blondes, at the other end of the spectrum. Or maybe demure girl-next-door types do it for you. Here –'

She scribbles something down on a piece of paper and thrusts it into my hand. 'That might help.'

I look down. It's a URL. 'Thanks,' I mutter, unsurely.

'Just take your time,' she says. 'There's no hurry.'

I turn away, wondering what's in store for me when I log on to the site. As I'm closing the door behind me, leaving my mentor to her work, I hear her say, 'Happy hunting.'

'Thanks,' I mutter, although she spoke so low, she could almost have been talking to herself.

Downstairs I sit in front of the laptop but find myself staring out of the French windows at the back of the house over the rather overgrown garden, full of withered herbs in pots and long moribund grass. A cat strolls past and gives me a cursory look. I wonder if I should offer to help sort out the garden. It would be good to spend some time outdoors, with a purpose. I feel as if I am accomplishing nothing.

I look back at the computer, call up the internet browser

and type in the URL that Anne wrote down for me. It's a site, as I might have imagined, devoted to nude women. But it's all very tasteful – there are artworks by various international artists, some pretty trashy but others rather good. One of the first things that catches my attention is a series of photos of nude sculptures found in Denmark – Copenhagen, specifically. Some are outdoors, in parks, while others are in museums. Among the latter, an image of a woman bending forwards, arms clasped behind her and restrained by a rope in the small of her back, above curvaceous stone-white buttocks, unexpectedly intrigues me. Is she bound against her will, or assenting to the restraints? The photograph is taken from behind the statue, so it's impossible to see the expression on her face, if indeed she even has a face.

I'm frustrated by the lack of detail regarding the work – what it is, who it's by and where it is, should I choose to go and see it. I suppose I could always email the photographer, if I really wanted to know, or even the Copenhagen Tourist Board. But it's not that important. Instead I navigate my way back to the homepage and start looking at the photographs.

All at once I feel like a kid in a sweet shop. There are thousands of women here, of all colours and shapes, from skinny to voluptuous, from Black African to Scandinavian. Many of them are simply breathtaking. I feel a pulse of stress, a headache taking root in my temples. How am I supposed to know what I want? How is anyone ever supposed to know what they want, when there is so much choice out there? Making a choice necessarily means limiting oneself, narrowing the field of possibilities.

And what is Anne asking of me here? She wants me to tell her my type, so that she can furnish me with a woman I like. That's not been said explicitly, of course, but it's what lurks below the surface. Anne is helping me to find myself, helping me to open up to the world of experience that I have been denying myself by denying my unconscious urges, and in doing so helping me to become a writer. Again I ask myself what's in it for her, beyond a voyeuristic thrill. Is that enough? Can't she get all this from the internet, from films and artworks?

I look back at the screen. This is a challenge, I tell myself, and I have to prove myself equal to it. It takes self-discipline, concentration. Stripping away the layers, the self-consciousness, takes effort, as Anne has warned me.

I look at one of the girls. She's blond, Swedish perhaps, with large green eyes. She reminds me of a girl at school, someone who was a year ahead of me. I'd never really noticed her until I was in the lower sixth form and she in the upper sixth. I still can't really explain how I felt at the time, but I developed a sort of excessive interest in her. At the time I thought it was just envy: the desire to be like her. She was cool, with cropped hair, daringly boyish, and slanting, catlike, sea-green eyes. She wore jumble-sale macs over hippyish skirts and Doc Martens. She smoked and drank. Lots of boys liked her but she disdained them, said they were boring and stupid and uncultured. She wrote poetry, talked about avant-garde Polish films.

Yes, I did want to be like her, but, looking back now, I think that it may have been more than that. I think it may have been what's called a crush. Of course, there was a lot of that going on at an all-girls school. Another girl in the upper sixth was said to have an unhealthy fascination with our French teacher, or rather our French *assistante* – a girl from Paris, taking a year out of her degree to get teaching experience. The girl, Alice let's call her, worshipped this *assistante*, but it was rumoured to be more than that – little can remain secret when lots of girls are closeted in a dorm together, and the word in the school corridors was that someone had been in Alice's bedside drawer, sneaking a peek at the diary that was hidden beneath her undies, and found lots of doodles and scribbles suggesting erotic yearnings for the Parisian. The girl who slept next to Alice claimed to have heard her wanking one night, sighing and moaning beneath the sheets, in the darkness of the dorm. She said she wouldn't swear on it, but she was convinced that Alice had muttered, 'Sylvie, Sylvie,' as she'd come.

Did I merely admire Roberta, the blonde, or did I want her? As I sit here in Anne's living room looking at the girl on the screen, I have to wonder. This one definitely stirs me, makes me want to get to know her. There's something in the look in her eyes that gets to me, and it's a feeling similar to the one I got when Roberta graced me with a passing glance – a lurch in the belly, a dizzy spell followed by the inability to concentrate on whatever it was I was doing at the time.

I ponder on it all: it's difficult to know, when we girls see another girl we find attractive, whether we want them or whether we would just like to *be* them. I imagine there are plenty of girls thinking they are lesbians when in truth they are just admirers of particular women and their looks or clothes sense – Kate Moss, Juliette Binoche, Angelina Jolie. And plenty of others who think they are merely appreciating someone's looks when in truth what they really want to do is get under the sheets with the object of their admiration.

It's a tough call, requiring strict self-scrutiny and the ability to be honest with oneself. Which is just what I am trying to do now. I edge my chair closer to the table, cast Roberta from my mind and focus on the girl in the picture and my feelings about her. The image is not pornographic so much as erotic. The girl is sitting side-on to the photographer, on a simple wooden chair against a stark white background. I try to analyse what it is that appeals to me about her, beyond her looks and the resemblance to my former classmate. There's nothing really outstanding about her – she's neither skinny nor fat, with medium-sized boobs, perky but not in-your-face. As Anne suggested, maybe I just go for girl-next-door types.

I go back to the index. Maybe I'm not being honest with myself here either. Maybe by sticking to the known, the familiar, the everyday and unthreatening, I'm denying a whole side of myself. Anne is encouraging me to take risks, to broaden my perspective. Otherwise there'll be no point to all of this and I might as well walk out of the door now.

I click on a thumbnail image labelled 'Keira'. Keira turns out to be a dark-haired Irish girl with a brazen 'fuck-me-if-you-dare' stare. She's wearing thigh-high patent boots and is holding a whip. Her bush is a silky sliver, her lips meaty and prominent, her breasts too large to be entirely real. She looks far too dangerous to be the girl next door. She looks like trouble.

One hand creeps between my legs even as I'm telling myself that she's not my type. For a while I content myself with rubbing my yearning pussy through my jeans, but as I continue to look I quickly find myself wanting more, so I unzip myself and slip my hands down the front of my knickers. My clit is fat, protruding, as if on a quest for pleasure. I moisten a finger in my mouth and then apply it to my clit. It's like an electric pulse goes through my entire body. A warm nectar floods my pants. I slide my finger down through my wetness and into my hole. Then, still staring at the screen, I pull my jeans down to my knees with one hand, first on one side, then the other, and then down and over my ankles, discarding them at my feet. When I'm freed, I lift my legs to the table, spreading myself, one foot on either side of the keyboard and the screen.

I plunge three fingers inside, then one hand, while with the tips of several fingers of the other hand and then the heel of it I attend to my burning clit. My throat is dry and I'm feeling dizzy. Anne could walk down at any minute. Or a window cleaner could appear at the French doors. The thought of being disturbed, discovered, only excites me more. Anne seems to have awakened a taste in me for being watched.

I force myself to focus on the screen, to look into Keira's eyes. Keira's watching me, I tell myself. This is Keira's hand on my clit, Keira's fingers inside me. It's not convincing. She remains an image on a screen. I close my eyes and she floods my brain. I move to the floor, one hand on a breast, the other still inside me. With my eyes closed I am more able to persuade myself that she's here with me, that it's her fingers on my nipple, her hand reconnoitring my sopping core.

Images dance behind my closed eyelids: Keira leaning over me, searching my face for indications of pleasure, of what is really getting to me and how she should go on, but also images of Roberta, my schoolmate, like split-second subliminal shots in films. She's fighting to get back up from the cutting-room floor, the girl next door. She's refusing to be relegated to the bin. I welcome her back in and now there are two of them tending to me, running their hands over my limbs, tweaking and sucking my nipples, stroking my clit and exploring me from within. Two of them bringing me higher, higher, so that I feel I'm floating up from the floor.

And then Keira's standing astride me. She's forced Roberta aside, is looking down at me, brandishing her leather whip. There's a black glint in her eyes. She knows she's dangerous and she relishes the dark thrill she can unleash in me. I throw my arms back over my head onto the floor, slave to her, under her spell. Let her do her worst. I am entering new territories.

The doorbell interrupts my wild reverie and I leap up, pull on my jeans and stuff my damp knickers into my back pocket. Smoothing down my hair and trying to steady my breathing, which is coming in saccades, I hurry down the hallway and open the front door. It's a courier for Anne, a large white puffy envelope handed over by a girl in leather and a motorbike helmet. She smiles at me through the visor as she hands over her clipboard with the document I need to sign acknowledging receipt. Her dark eyes shine and I go weak at the knees. When I close the door I have to lean back against it, I feel so dizzy.

It takes several minutes for me to recover myself sufficiently to take the parcel up to Anne.

I stand outside Anne's door for a while, wondering what I am going to say to her. I've found out so much about myself in the last hour or so, but none of it is really very conclusive. In fact, what I've found out, beyond the fact that, yes, some girls do turn me on and I would like to sleep with one and find out what it's like, is that I'm a bundle of contradictions. Demure girl-next-door types do attract me, but so do dangerous ones in thigh-length boots wielding whips.

After a while, as if sensing that I am there and growing impatient at my hesitation, Anne opens the door.

'Come in,' she says. The usual harshness is gone from her voice, replaced by what may even be gentleness. I wouldn't swear on it, but it's as if she can sense that I've put myself through the mill, that all of this soul-searching is taking its toll on my brain as much as my body.

I step inside, hand over the parcel. She takes it and looks at the label.

'Ah good,' she says. 'I've been waiting for this.' But she places it on her desk unopened, turns back to me, eyebrows raised. 'Well?' she says.

I smile a little helplessly, shrug. 'It's – I don't know – it's . . .' I don't know how to say it, or even, really, what I'm going to say.

She pats my arm, and again I sense something almost maternal in her gesture.

'It's not easy,' she says, 'finding out who you really are, beneath all the layers, the hard crust that has built up over the years.' She stares beyond me, as if quite taken by her analogy. 'It is,' she says, 'now I come to think of it, rather like a volcanic eruption. You fight so hard to repress all those untidy urges, and when you do start letting them out, it's like a surge of hot lava – exhilarating and liberating but frightening too.'

Her eyes come back to me, and suddenly I am scared. Her pupils are huge in the low light, and I feel as if I am being sucked into a black hole. Anne, I think, has bewitched me. I've been a fool to think she is doing me a favour: this is all about her and her need for control. Bored of her life, her solitary writer's life, she has been seeking an outlet for her frustration, looking for sport. And something in the way I responded to her questioning in the interview told her that I would play along with her.

And yet, and yet . . . Much as the void in her eyes scares me, her amorality, I feel that I am on the brink of something important and that to back away from the precipice would be to shirk my duty to myself, now that I have started out on this route. Of course, there's nothing to say I can't pick up a girl myself – go to a lesbian bar and score with some chick. But I'd have to get wildly drunk first, just to have the nerve, and what's the point of that? What would be the point of a drunken shag that I wouldn't be able to remember? How would I know if I wanted to do it again?

I look at Anne. Whatever her motivations and true feelings towards me, or lack of them, she can be useful to me. I have to keep reminding myself of that fact. She illuminates a path that I simply would not have the guts to follow myself. In fact she illuminates two different paths: the one that leads to my being a writer, and the path to erotic self-discovery. How the two are linked is not yet clear to me: they may intersect at some point, or run parallel for a time, or join at their endpoint. But that they are linked has become obvious to me. To try to follow one without being aware of the other would mean failure.

'I've . . . I've been looking,' I manage at last, 'at girls.'

Anne's lips twist into a wry smile. 'And?'

'And – I don't know. Different things, really. I'm not sure.'

'You're still not sure, is that it?'

'No, it's not that. I . . . I think I should. I mean, I really want to. Only . . .'

'Spit it out, girl.'

There she goes again, with the 'girl' thing, the schoolmistressy condescension. I have to take a deep breath to stop myself from reacting, from throwing it all back in her face. I avert my eyes from her scornful face, fix them on one of the Picasso lithographs.

'I want to,' I say. 'I'll show you.'

*

Up in my room, I take solace in my diary, writing pages and pages. Much of it is vitriol aimed at Anne, to whom I feel somewhat enslaved and more than a little bitter. But once I've got all that out of my system, once I've brain-dumped onto the once-pristine white paper, staining it with my bile, I am free to write about my feelings towards Roberta and the other women I fantasised about. Before long I'm feeling all hot and bothered again and having a session on my bed with my Rock Chick, visions of Keira in my mind.

I'm nervous about tonight, of course, and astonished that Anne thinks she can pull it off at short notice. I wonder where she is going to go to procure me the woman of my dreams. That woman, of course, is Keira. I decided it was just too complicated to tell Anne of my ambivalence, of my yearning for two very different kinds of women. So to make life simpler, I called up the erotic website on the computer in her study and clicked on Keira's picture. I didn't look at Anne's face as I did so, afraid that she'd be smirking at my choice. Afraid that she'd have an 'I knew it' look on her face. Sometimes I feel that Anne knows me better than I know myself.

When I've come, I slumber for a while, conserving my energy. I didn't have a wild sex life with Nate, and all of these exertions are wearing me out. Tonight is a big night – a life-changing one – and I want to be up to it.

10

The Woman

Anne and I are sitting in the living room, drinking a sherry together. She doesn't know that I've already had a couple of swigs from the vodka bottle she keeps in her drinks cabinet. Much as I said to myself I wanted to go into this sober, open-eyed and with all cylinders firing, my nerves got the better of me as the minutes ticked by, and my hands were trembling so much when I came downstairs that I had to have something to strengthen my nerves.

We're not talking, but it's a companionable rather than an embarrassed silence. A thoughtful silence, as if we are both mindful of the significance of what is to come. Anne doesn't look nervous, but then why should she? She won't be directly involved, although without even consciously thinking about it, I have accepted without questioning that she is to be present, in her usual observing role. Now that I do think about it, I wonder that I am so seemingly unfazed by it, and then I wonder if in fact Anne's presence is helping me this time, if I'm not actually using her as a crutch to face a situation that I might not be able to countenance all by myself.

At the squeak of the front gate I jump up, nerves ajangle. Terror-stricken, I look at Anne, but she stares back calmly, and in her eyes I think I see something mocking again. *Going to wimp out?* they seem to say to me. *Can't go through with it?* And in turn I think, Fuck you. I am going to do this. I won't give you the satisfaction of seeing me fail.

The footfalls on the stone path have ceased and are followed by a knock on the door – loud, assertive, unabashed. I rush for the door. Facing up to things is easier, I'm discovering, than holding back. All I want to do, really, is run upstairs and hide under the duvet, alone. A night with my Rock Chick would do me just fine. But I will hate myself in the morning for having taken the easy way out.

Through the patterned glass panes of the front door I can see an outline, the shape of a figure dressed in black. With detachment I watch my hand reach for the latch, and it's as if it belongs to someone else.

The door opens in slow motion. A face appears, unsmiling, a little severe. She's like, I think, a younger version of Anne: dark bob, angular face, inscrutable eyes. She's wearing a belted overcoat with a chic French air to it. She says nothing.

'Come in,' I say at last.

She steps inside, looks around appraisingly as she starts to shrug off her coat, then hands it to me. Beneath it she's wearing the sort of body-conscious stretch black dress, entirely featureless, that you used to see in the 1980s. Think Emmanuelle Seigner dancing with Harrison Ford in *Frantic* – one of the great nightclub scenes in film history. Slinky, seamless, ultra short. Underneath it she has seamed stockings, and on her feet are a pair of almost vicious-looking black stiletto boots. She's like a gorgeous cat, stealthy, mysterious and amoral, inhabiting a world of her own. I can't imagine where Anne knows her from – or, perhaps, where she found her.

She walks ahead of me, and I can tell by her slight hesitation between the living room and the kitchen doors that she's not been to the house before. Which makes the latter option more likely. Again, I wonder how one goes about that – how a forty-something woman in London procures another woman for her female acolyte. Is it a matter of just picking up the phone, calling in some favours, plumbing one's social network? Or did Anne perhaps contact an escort agency, describe her requirements and hand over her credit card details? If so, and this is a commercial transaction, does it make the experience any the less real?

The girl presents herself to Anne, and the pair nod to each other in greeting, which doesn't help me to establish whether they have met before or whether they have some kind of relationship, however tenuous – are friends of friends, perhaps. Then Anne gestures towards the drinks cabinet in the corner.

'Can I serve you anything?' she says.

The girl nods. 'A brandy would be good,' she replies.

Her voice is warm and husky, and I start to tremble again. I don't want them to sit drinking and chatting; I just want to get on with this. I head over to the corner and, as Anne turns away to proffer the girl her drink, I serve myself a generous slug and down it in one. Then I turn to them.

'Shall we go upstairs?' I'm astonished by my forcefulness, but I can't hold out any longer. I am going to meet my destiny, am walking towards my future.

Two pairs of raised eyebrows meet my words, but nobody protests. I place my glass down and head out of the room, confident that they will follow. On the stairs a moment of doubt is followed by a sense of intoxication as I see them come out of the living room and begin to ascend too. I know that my control is illusory, momentary, but asserting myself makes me feel less at the mercy of whatever it is that Anne has set in motion. Which is something that I assented to her putting in motion, of course, and that I want as much as I fear.

Once inside the guest room I sit down on the end of the bed and slip off my shoes. The girl strides in ahead of Anne and stands in front of me, draining the glass that she's carried up with her, one hand on her hip. Then she puts one foot up on the bed, her knee bent, and pushes me back.

Surprised, I try to struggle up, but already she's crouched over me, tugging at my jeans, undressing me. I look towards Anne for a reaction, taken aback that things are happening so fast, wondering if this is what she has instructed the girl to do or whether the latter is acting of her own volition. But Anne isn't even looking: she's busy rearranging the cushions on her armchair, tidying her little nest in the corner.

The girl continues being forceful, stripping me with impatient tugs and yanks of my clothing. Naked I lie in front of her as she surveys me, her regard cool and appraising. I reach for her, try to pull up the hem of her dress, but she brushes my hand away, then takes hold of me and turns me over. I gain only glimpses of her over my shoulder as she holds my wrists together and binds them with something that feels like rope.

I avoid looking at Anne, the architect of my humiliation. I don't want her to see how this is both appalling and arousing me, calling forth as it does memories of those sixth-form days when I lusted after Roberta while steaming at yet another reprimand from Mrs Scholes. A confusing time that has never really resolved itself in my mind. Perhaps that's why I am here now. Perhaps all of that – single-sex public school, a Sapphic crush, and a sadistic and possibly even lesbian headteacher – was bound, at some point, to lead to this.

'I hear you've been a naughty girl,' comes the husky voice I've heard only once thus far. It's followed by a clicking sound from the corner of the room. I look over and see that Anne's box of tricks has materialised from somewhere. It's on her knee now, and she's waving a hand around inside it. When it retreats, she's holding a slender leather crop with a handle that looks as if it's made from crystals. Like the paddle I used on James, it looks expensive. Anne doesn't stint when it comes to sex toys.

'Thanks.' The girl reaches over and takes it from Anne, and the pair exchange a look. I wonder again at the lack of conversation between them since the girl arrived. Did they talk about this beforehand, plot it all out, or are they playing it by ear?

I stop wondering as the tip of the crop rests on one of my buttocks, sending a buzz through me. My whole body tenses in readiness for the whipping that is due to me.

'Yes, I have been a naughty girl.' My voice sounds strange to me. Never in a million years would I have admitted that to Mrs Scholes – not even when the scolding was founded. Even when I had committed a misdemeanour, I made it a point of honour not to react to her rantings, but instead to stare out of the window, over the beeches in the school grounds to the fields beyond, where freedom lay. Now I realise that that may have been why she kept calling me back – my refusal to submit.

Yes, I guess I had a problem with authority, and it's time to accept my punishment, to admit that I've been a bad girl. I hitch my bum higher, thrusting my cheeks upwards and backwards towards the girl.

'Hurt me,' I whisper, and my voice seems even more alien than before.

'What did you say?' demands the girl, although I'm sure she heard. 'Speak louder.' Her own voice is cold, as harsh as a frosty winter's day.

'Hurt me.' I close my eyes as I obey her, tasting the bitter-sweet flavour of submission. For someone with attitude problems the scale of mine, this is hard-going.

'Again,' she says. As she prods me with her words, she drives the tip of the quirt into the flesh of my arse cheeks. 'Louder.'

'Hurt me,' I almost shout. I can't bear this any longer, this painful and yet delicious wait. Can't bear the excitement that is building up inside me, in my belly and my pussy and throat and my brain, exploding like fireworks behind my eyes. Who'd have guessed I'd be asking for it, *begging* for it, like this? If Nate could see me now . . .

But she doesn't hurt me, the girl. She teases me some more, first whipping the pillow in front of my head, then tracing the quirt, oh so slowly, so very slowly, over the nape of my neck and around to the sides of my throat, then down, down, over my shoulders and my lower back, so that I'm wondering if I'm going to lose consciousness and miss out on what's in store, what's coming with some kind of elemental force, like a cyclone.

She leans forwards over me, and for a moment I feel the sheer material of her slinky dress against my back and the crush of her breasts. She reaches round me with one arm, grazes my clit with her fingertips but then removes them at once, uses her arm to lever me over so that I'm prone on the bed, looking up at her in surprise. But she seems to studiously avoid eye contact with me, concentrating first on untying the restraint around my wrists and then on the whip and its subtle manoeuvres. She's a professional, that's clear, and I wonder again where Anne found her. Did she just Google 'London dominatrices', or was she already in contact with this girl? Has she, even, used her before?

My musings cede to the smack of the tip of the whip against one of the girl's palms. 'Pay attention,' she barks, and I swallow, horrified and exhilarated at once. This is beyond what I have imagined pleasure could be, beyond all fantasy and speculation.

I watch, wide-eyed, as she lowers the tip of the instrument to my skin – first my throat, then sweeping down over and around my breasts, encircling my nipples until I'm crying out, twisting and rocking on the bed, the sheets pulled up in my clenched fists.

She carries on, down over my belly towards my bush and the moist opening that lies within my thatch. For a moment, again, she pauses at my clit, strokes it with the nub of the quirt. It leaps into life, like a little pink flame seeking pleasure, ardent. But it is denied satisfaction as she carries on down to the silken flesh of my inner thighs. I feel myself leaking nectar, drizzling the whip as it moves between my open legs. I want her to put it inside me.

'Turn over,' she commands, and I do her bidding, willingly. I close my eyes again in readiness for the whipping to commence.

For a few seconds there is silence and stillness, and it's at this moment that I remember Anne. I glance over towards her, but she isn't looking in our direction. She's looking down at her hands demurely folded in her lap, and I have the fleeting absurd conviction that she has fallen asleep, right there in her chair, with all this going on. But of course she hasn't – I see the slow, measured batting of her eyelashes and realise that she's gathering her thoughts before the storm that is about to be unleashed.

She looks up, and I hear the whoosh of the crop through the air before I feel it on my buttocks. Anne, I realise, was giving the orders there. By raising her eyes, she was giving the signal. There's a chain of command here and she's at the top of it. Of course I knew that all along, since she's the instigator and probably also the paymaster. But I suppose I didn't realise to what level she'd be directing the course of events.

My flesh stings madly as the crop strikes, and I jerk forwards, teeth clenched, eyes closed tight. 'Aaaaaah,' I manage, although I know that I am only on the first rung of the ladder of pain. How far are we going to go? Does it depend on me, on my assent, or is this in the girl's hands now – or rather, in Anne's?

Suddenly I'm scared. I'm in too deep, I think, and this could get out of control. I clutch the sheets even tighter in my fists. A splash of crimson liquid onto the bed beneath me alerts me to the fact that I've bitten my lower lip so hard I've drawn blood. I watch as it spreads, forming a tear-shaped stain. As if that's my cue, I allow my tears to come. They cool my blazing cheeks and also bring some relief to the tension I'm feeling.

'Again.' I wonder who it is inside me that is talking now. There's another fearsome swoosh and then a biting, searing sensation that burns and burns. I scream, but there's a sort of jubilation in it, a welcoming.

'More. Harder.'

The girl does what I say, and I feel a mental rush at having wrested control. Sure, I'm here because of Anne, *for* Anne in some ways. But I did ask for this, and now that it's happening I'm asking for more, and getting it. I'm not a mere puppet.

The crop comes down and down. The pain gets more and more intense, yet at the same time I seem to be developing some kind of immunity to it. It's as if, in a way, I'm soaring up and out from my body, leaving it behind as I float somewhere high up. Just as when you orgasm, there's the paradoxical feeling of being taken out of yourself right at the moment of the greatest physicality.

I'm close to coming, of course, but I won't unless I can reach my clit with my fingers, which is impossible at the moment, given that I'm leaning face down on my elbows. In any case, I'd like the girl to do it. I'd like her to roll me over again and tease me with the end of the crop, brush my clit with it until it stands to attention like the tiny phallus that it is, then bring her mouth to me so that she can taste my sweet juices as I open and close like a flower in fast-motion, over and over.

I reach behind me, grab the crop and halt its motion. I'm looking over my shoulder as I do so, and I see the girl look questioningly at Anne. The latter nods, then she looks at me.

'That's enough,' she says, and I can't help but let out a whimper of dissatisfaction.

'That's *enough*,' she repeats, even more sternly. 'You may retire to your room.'

What if I don't want to? I want to scream at her. *What if I don't fucking want to? And what if* she *doesn't want me to?* But I don't say that, of course. To do so would be a mistake, an error of strategy. For this is a game surely. For the moment I am Anne's pawn, but I'm beginning to suspect that it won't always remain that way. Anne may not realise it, may not have thought this through properly, but the more self-awareness

I gain, the more powerful I am going to become. It may not show right away, but it's inevitable.

I climb off the bed, gather my clothes in my arms and head for the door without looking at either of them. Already to do that seems like a small victory. Anne, I suspect, wanted me to plead with her to let us carry on. But I won't. That's one thing she won't get out of me – or not unless I think I have something to gain by doing so.

I close the door quietly behind me. There's no drama here, no sulking or tantrums. I will bide my time, study Anne's moves until I can begin to anticipate them and in doing so gain some measure of dominion.

Walking up the stairs to my attic room, I wonder what is happening in the guest room now that I am gone. Are they talking, discussing what happened, how I reacted? Is Anne handing over some money to the girl, thanking her? Or are they chatting like the friends that they are? I'm unable to know, but it's a measure of how far I've come that I have to suppress a chuckle as I run through the options.

Lying on my bed, I finger the tender oyster flesh of my buttocks. It's sore, to be sure, but the skin hasn't been broken. I wonder how hard you have to be whipped to bleed and then to scar, and I flinch inwardly. I reached my own pain barrier downstairs in the guest room tonight. I can't imagine being taken any further than that, or why one would want to. Those are depths I will not sound.

I reach for my diary, start scribbling in an attempt to untangle the knot of my thoughts, decipher my very mixed feelings about what I have just been through – what I put myself through of my own volition. Never in my wildest dreams would I have imagined submitting myself to the ministrations of a dominatrix, but I did, and now I have to understand that.

The words and phrases come disjointed, staccato, but through them there begins to emerge some kind of picture involving my feelings towards older women in positions of authority – my mother, Mrs Scholes, Anne. As a little kid, I remember, I was almost instinctively naughty, unerringly doing the wrong thing. My mother was a cold woman, emotionally distant and disengaged. I haven't thought about all this in years, because she died when I was in my mid-teens, by which stage I'd been in boarding school for several years anyway, and so could scarcely miss her. But now I wonder if she might have suffered from post-natal depression. Certainly, there was little bonding between us. Again, looking at events with hindsight, I wonder if my persistently bad behaviour might have been a cry for attention, a way of trying to get her to take notice of me?

And that carried on into school. Rather than apologising to Mrs Scholes, I kept her interest up in me by ignoring her reprimands, staring out of the window. It was flattering, in a way I couldn't articulate at the time, even to myself, to be called in to see her so often. As well as giving me a cool status among my classmates, it made me feel important, *noticed*.

I put down my pen, get up and go to my window, staring out into the darkness beyond. Is this what I am reliving with Anne, these ancient wounds? Is that why I found the girl and her crop so compelling?

I lie down again, letting the tears come. It's like an unbottling, an uncorking of stale air and bad memories. Immense sadness overwhelms me, and yet at the same time I feel relief to have recognised all this at last. For only in recognising it can I hope to overcome it.

I curl up on the bed. After a few minutes I let one hand trail down to my buttocks. I skim the sore flesh with my fingertips. I won't, I think, be whipped again. I don't regret it. I even enjoyed it – a lot. But it's done, and it's not part of me any more. I'm moving forwards. I've been punished enough.

As if in response to my thoughts, there's a gentle rap on the door, like a caressing of the wood, so soft that I'm not even sure that it happened at all.

'Come in,' I hazard.

The door opens slowly. A girl stands there, in jeans and a sweatshirt. Cropped blond hair, green slanting eyes. She smiles shyly. It's Roberta, I think. Roberta and the girl on the internet, the one who looked like her. She's come – they have come – to give me solace.

She steps up to the bed without a word, and her smile is like that of an angel. I tell myself I must have dozed off, but, when her hand rests on my buttock, I know it can't be a dream. I quiver inside, like a violin being properly tuned for the first time. Her touch is sure, good, real. I moan, fling my hands back over my head. I open my legs.

'Feel me,' I whisper. 'How wet I am.'

The girl goes down on me and I almost pass out with pleasure. Her tongue jabs at my clit, over and over, and then she begins to nibble it with her small, regular teeth. I hold the sides of her face, her satinesque cheeks, and raising my own head and shoulders look down at her. This is a gift, I think. A gift from Anne. A reward after the punishment I underwent.

But how could Anne know about Roberta? It was only downstairs that I began thinking about her, after I left Anne's room. And I said nothing to my mentor about my schoolgirl crush when I went back up to her room with the parcel. I showed her only the dangerous-looking girl, Keira.

Then I remember what sparked off the whole reminiscence about Roberta – the picture of the girl on the internet, the one who reminded me of Roberta. For Anne to know about them, she must have been spying on me somehow. I'm pretty sure she wouldn't have made it all the way downstairs without my hearing her, which must mean that her computer upstairs must somehow be linked to the downstairs laptop, giving her access to what I was looking at.

But I don't care. It doesn't seem important now, here, with this girl between my legs, casting all my worries aside, making them dissolve like smoke in the rain. Bringing my hands away from her lovely elfin face, I try to prise myself still further apart, wanting her inside me. She looks up, smiles at me with what seems like utter sincerity, and then watches herself push two, three, fingers inside me.

My hands clamp the sides of her head again, and I begin to thrust my crotch up and down, meeting the movement of her hand as it pushes in and then withdraws a little. With the thumb of her free hand she's massaging the eager little bead of my clit. I'm going crazy, but I want to touch her too. I've had enough of being on the receiving end tonight.

Sitting half up, without upsetting the girl's motions, I reach for her sweatshirt and start to tug it up over her neck. Beneath it she's naked, bra-less. Her tits are magnificent: medium-sized, fleshy, downy as peaches. She's lightly tanned, with rashes of freckles on her forearms and below her clavicle. I could eat her, I really could. I hope she'll let me.

She rolls back, undoes her flies and starts to shimmy her jeans off, little by little, revealing long brown legs covered with little blond hairs that shimmer in the low light. She's beautiful, but in an ordinary, unthreatening way. Unlike with the dominatrix, I feel that I am in the presence of an equal, and that that means I can have some fun. What happened with the other girl may have been enjoyable in a dark way, but fun it was not. Or not my idea of fun.

As if she's reading my mind, the girl reaches one hand around my head and pulls me into her, pushes her tongue inside my mouth and wraps it around mine. It's my first snog with a girl and I feel shy but enraptured as we probe each other's mouth, growing braver by the minute. Her breath is minty and fresh. She's like a great big gust of country air after the grime of the city. I close my eyes and we're rolling around in a summer meadow together, crushing wildflowers as we frolic like lambs.

After a while I dare to reach between her legs. Here, again, she's unshaven but not unkempt, her bush a tiny little powderpuff of burnt-sugar hair. She leans right back and I bury my face in it, inhale its candyfloss sweetness as I look up towards her breasts. In front of them I see her nipples, pink and hard, like new rosebuds. As I place my tongue against the nub of her clit, I lift my hands to her globes and savour their glorious perkiness.

She's moved up the bed during all of this, and her shoulders and head are now tipped over the end of it, so that I can't see her face any more. But I can hear her moaning, and I know I'm doing the right thing. Then suddenly it strikes me that there's been no sign of Anne, and that that's odd. I look towards the door. It's still half-open from when the girl came in, but there's no sign of my mentor. I'm glad, but at the same time I'm surprised, mystified and worried. What does it mean, that she's sent me this girl but doesn't want to watch? Has the game come to an end? Is this my prize?

With effort I tell myself to forget it, to just let myself get lost in the moment. I think too much, although as a would-be writer I can't see that that's a bad thing. How can I render all this in prose if I don't analyse it, dissect it?

As if sensing my ardour diminish as I distance myself from what's going on, the girl sits up and places herself in front of me. For a moment we sit face to face, regarding each other. Although we are dissimilar in appearance, for a moment I have the disconcerting sensation that I am in front of a looking glass, seeing a mirror image of myself. This is a girl like me, an ordinary girl. What is there to draw me to her? How can you want what you are?

Her eyes are understanding, tolerant, non-confrontational. They are kind eyes, but they can't take me anywhere I haven't been, I realise. Not like the dominatrix. So what's the point?

She brings her hand back down to my pussy, slides her fingers through my slick lips to my hole. They slide inside me easily, and I let myself fall back. With one arm outstretched, I reach for my bedside drawer, pull it open and feel for my Rock Chick. I bring it to my mouth, put one end of it in and coat it with my saliva. Then I bring it down to the girl's pussy where she's sitting astride me. She looks at me with wide questioning eyes.

'Is it good?' she says, and I realise these are the first words she has spoken to me since she arrived.

I nod. 'You'll like it.' I push the tip inside her. Then I click on the vibrator option, ensuring that the other end is aligned with her clit. As if she's a pro, she begins to push herself backwards and forwards. I hold on to her hips and it's as if she's riding me, as if she's fucking me. Her hand inside me, meanwhile, apes the motions of her body, until we are both moaning harder and harder, on the verge of coming.

I clamp her buttocks between my hands, aware that my nails are cutting into her skin but unable to let go, like a cat with its prey. There's a savagery inside me, like a desire to bite and maim what I love – that inexplicable desire we sometimes feel as children. I pull her down and down and she collapses over me as she comes. I let go of her with one hand and rub my clit ferociously as she cries out, and within seconds I'm crying out too, and our voices are mingling, until you can no longer tell us apart. In extremis we have become one person, one body jacking in pleasure, and as I lie beneath her limp body, drenched with the sweat of her, I think that this may be love.

When I awake she's gone, and it's as if I've had the most beautiful dream. As with most beautiful dreams, an unutterable sadness takes hold of me at the realisation that it won't ever be true. But then I notice that the door is ajar, and, when I see Anne standing there looking at me, I know that it was true.

'How was it?' she says through cigarette smoke. Her eyes are narrowed, as if she is weighing me up.

'I . . . You didn't come.' I'm aware that I'm completely naked, my body still anointed with the girl's liquids – her saliva, her sweat, the juices from her sex – but I'm not ashamed. Anne knows me: my body, what I do with it, how I am in the throes of pleasure. I have nothing to hide from her any more.

She shakes her head.

'Why not?' I push. 'Was it not part of the . . . the test?'

She shakes her head again. 'This is not a test,' she says.

'Then, what?'

I'm sitting up now, looking at her squarely. I have nothing to lose by asking her this. She can't take away from me what I have done, what I have discovered about myself. And feeling that I must be reaching the end of my journey, I don't fear incurring her wrath. But I don't believe she will be angry anyway. Suddenly we have reached a point where it seems possible to talk sensibly to each other. Maybe it's all to do with the whip. The naughty schoolgirl in me has been punished and now I'm a grown-up, on an equal footing with Anne. Or as equal a footing as one can be on with one's heroine.

She's stepped towards me now, taken a seat on the end of the bed. With her hand she strokes the sheet where it is rumpled from our exertions. But she seems absent, far away from me. I'm not sure whether it is the light in here, but suddenly Anne looks very old and very tired.

Realising she's not going to answer, I swing my legs over the side of the bed and reach for my clothes. 'Will I see her again?' I ask.

She shrugs. 'Do you want to?'

'I . . . I liked it a lot.'

'I can arrange it.'

My brow furrows. The girl was divine, the sex extraordinary in spite of her ordinariness. But, if I were to see her again, it would have to be on my own terms. 'I don't suppose you are going to tell me who she is?'

Anne looks at me now, that gemstone hardness in her eyes. 'I can't,' she says.

'The rules of the game?'

'There is no game.'

I begin to lose patience. I'm fed up of cat-and-mouse, donkey-and-carrot, all the jumping through hoops. I wanted James for myself, and couldn't have him. I want the girl and can't have her. I'm all for gaining life experience, but this is beginning to cause me pain. Attachments seem to want to form, in spite of me, in spite of Anne, and I can't cope with having things ripped from out of my reach. The test, or the game, or whatever Anne wants to call it, must end here.

She stands up, walks slowly from the room, head down. She, too, seems depressed, at the end of it all. Maybe it's for the best. I won't have hard feelings. She has taught me so much – indirectly, of course.

'Goodnight,' I say as she exits the room.

She turns in the doorway, raises a hand. 'Goodnight, Genevieve,' she says quietly, and then she closes the door behind her.

11

And the Little One Said . . .

It's hard to get up the next morning, knowing that I must leave but not having a clue where to go. There's Vron's, of course, but something tells me I won't be welcomed there with open arms. The last thing I need at the moment is to feel unwanted, an intruder in someone else's home, even if that someone is my sister.

Other than that, I can't think. So I lie in bed telling myself to get up and pack my case but not actually doing anything about it. My mind is occupied by James and the girl from last night. If only I could go to them, I'd feel better, but James has warned me away, and I've no idea where – or even *who* – the girl is. My situation is hopeless.

An hour later, no closer to a solution, I pad downstairs for breakfast. I'm hoping I won't run into Anne, but Sod's Law is at work again and she's in there, flicking through a journal as she waits for the kettle to boil. From the living room I hear the sound of Hettie vacuuming.

Anne raises her head when she sees me, eyes me warily, as if she knows something's up.

'You look peaky,' she ventures. 'Didn't you sleep well?'

I pull back one of the chairs and sit down. I put my head in my hands, and then suddenly I'm doing what I promised myself I'd never do in front of Anne – I burst into tears. I sit there shaking and sobbing and making an unholy display of my feelings. I'm just trying to collect myself enough to get out of the room and upstairs, intent on packing my bags and getting the hell out of there even without a clue where I'm going, when I feel Anne's hands on my shoulders. Slowly she starts to pull me up and for a moment I think she's going to hug me. But no, Anne remains Anne, as cool as a cucumber. Instead of hugging me she keeps hold of my shoulders but steers me through into the living room, guiding me down to the sofa, ushering Hettie out with instructions to leave us alone for half an hour. Then she disappears, before returning a few moments later with a steaming cup of tea. She places it on the coffee table in front of me.

'I put a sugar in it,' she says. 'For comfort.'

Anne makes tea with milk. It's one of her few concessions to Englishness, aside from living in this country. She still writes in French and dresses in a French way. I imagine she thinks and dreams in French. I wonder if she fucks in French. I wonder if she fucks at all. James must know. Perhaps James even fucks Anne, and that's why he doesn't want me. At this rate I don't suppose I will ever know. Anne is keeping schtumm, and James has disappeared off the scene.

Anne has crossed over to the mantelpiece, lit a cigarette. Leaning back against it, blowing rings of smoke out into the room, she looks self-consciously dramatic, or like a character from a novel.

'Don't go,' she says at last, without looking at me. She clears her throat. 'I know you're thinking of leaving and I think it would be a mistake.'

'Why?'

'Because we're not finished yet. You're not finished. There are things you still have to learn.'

'Like what?'

She screws up her faces, looks waspish. 'If it was a simple matter of putting things into words,' she begins. 'But it's not. There are some things that can't be taught. Some things you can only learn for yourself.'

'Then why do I need to stay here?'

Her eyes turn on me, as icy and empty as a polar wilderness. 'Because,' she says, enunciating each syllable as if I'm a halfwit, 'I can facilitate these things for you.'

'And what,' I say, hardly able to believe that I'm asking the question at last, after so long, 'is in it for you?'

She waves one hand. 'I have no stake,' she says. 'I just want to help.'

I chuckle but without amusement. 'You like watching. That's it, isn't it? You're a voyeur.'

She continues to direct her cold blue stare at me. 'You simplify *everything*,' she says, then shrugs and looks away. 'I suppose it's inevitable. You're young. But I thought that this, at least, would have shown you that life is much more complicated than you think.'

I open my mouth to reply, although I'm not sure what I'm going to say, when she sweeps from the room, having evidently decided that the conversation is over. And, although part of me hates her for having bossed me around, for having told me what I can and cannot do and made me feel small, I know that she's right. I'm not done here, and I still have things to learn, things for which I need Anne. Unfinished business.

*

In my room, later that day, after a long walk in the park, I sit down with my diary and list ten things that I've learned about myself since I met Anne:

1. *That I find older men attractive.*
2. *That I find younger men attractive.*
3. *That I get a thrill from being watched when I have sex.*
4. *That I like spanking people, or at least spanking James.*
5. *That I like to be whipped, although I'm not sure I'd do it again.*
6. *That I like girls.*
7. *That I like different kinds of girl.*
8. *That I've been denying my appetites in the past, and that that was unhealthy.*
9. *That I do have things to write about.*
10. *That I'm lonely.*

It's an odd, disparate, ragbag list, and one from which I can draw no real conclusions except that my journey so far, the journey that I began when I moved in with Anne, has been worthwhile, in the sense that it has advanced me as a writer and a person. The last entry, though, floors me. It's something I've never consciously thought and, now that I have, I'm devastated. All this gain, and yet ultimately I'm very very alone. Anne, potentially a mother figure, is cold and distant, a user. James won't allow me to build a bridge to him. And the girl – the blonde girl – might as well be a figment of my imagination, so insubstantial is she. Our encounter – fleeting, ethereal, ungraspable – has all the qualities of a dream. Suddenly I find myself wondering whether it would have been better to stay with Nate after all. Stagnant though our relationship, our sex life, might have been, surely it was preferable to this ache, to this terrible, biting loneliness?

I wonder that I only feel this on a conscious level now, although I must have been lonely at Vron's. I guess I must have been blocking it out then. There were always people, Vron's friends and colleagues, drifting through her flat, hanging out, on their way to or from this party or that hip new club. I fell in with the crowd sometimes, without ever really being part of it. I guess that must have masked my essential solitude. That I haven't seen any of them, or even my sister, since leaving her place proves that to me.

There was one night, just one, when I felt as if I might belong, or begin to belong. I'd been living there a good month and a half, perhaps even two, sleeping on the sofa and hanging out in cafés by day. One night Vron came in at about 2 a.m. with a bunch of friends, among them an amazing Somali guy, with skin like burnished ebony. I was still up, watching some crappy film. Vron turned off the TV and switched on some music, a Kruder & Dorfmeister CD. Still wired from the club, she and her friends drank some more and started dancing.

I watched the Somali guy for a while. He moved like nobody I had ever seen before – fluidly, as if the music was moving through his limbs, had become part of him. He had his head thrown back, his eyes half closed. He was losing himself. I was envious. I always felt so damn self-conscious, even when I was just sitting in a café, trying to write. In fact, looking back now, I think a lot of the problem with becoming a writer was to do with this pose, this affecting to be a writer without having become one.

After a while, recovering himself a little, he saw me watching him and, smiling, came over to me. Extending a hand, he drew me up from the sofa and pulled me into the centre of the room. Wrapping one arm around my waist, he began to gyrate again, gradually expanding his movements until it felt to me that he was losing himself again. Only he wasn't. Through his hipster jeans I could feel the press of his dick, and he was hard. He wanted me.

It was the first time since Nate that someone wanted me. Or at least that I was fully aware of. Blokes did give me the eye in the street, often, but that meant nothing – you never knew whether it was you or if they looked at every girl that way. Looking at Nadif, as his name turned out to be, I felt giddy with desire and possibilities. Remember, Nate was the only guy I'd been with at this point.

I pressed myself against him, suddenly brazen. I wished I'd had something to drink, but I daren't pull away and go to fortify myself with a glass of wine or vodka for fear of breaking the mood. His hands tightened on my hips, mine on his shoulders. My breasts tingled. Even sober, I felt drunk. What was this boy, this man, doing to me? I was losing control and I loved it. I wanted the world around us to disappear, all these people to bugger off home and Vron to go to bed so that I could drag Nadif over to my sofabed and hump him senseless.

I could see Vron staring at me, and I thought I saw a sneer of disapproval on her face. She didn't seem too keen on me being in with her crowd; I think having her baby sister around cramped her style. I looked away, determined not to let her spoil my fun. Why should she be the only party girl?

Someone brought some vodka shots out, and the music was turned down and we all congregated around the coffee table, on Vron's large suede floor cushions. Someone starting talking to Nadif, and the rapport that had grown between us was broken. A girl on my other side started talking to me, and when I finally managed to break free of the conversation, I found that Nadif had disappeared, along with several others among the party-goers. From across the table, Vron was looking at me with what looked to be triumph. She was happy, it seemed, that I had been disappointed. I almost suspected her of engineering it somehow. But of course Nadif was a free agent. If he'd really wanted me, he would have stayed. What we'd had was a momentary flirtation that he'd forgotten about within moments. When someone suggested moving on, he'd forgotten me altogether.

Naturally, I masturbated on my sofabed that night, after everyone finally left, as dawn was streaking the sky outside the window. It was Nadif I thought of as I prised myself apart with my fingers, drenched with my own juices; Nadif's firm dark prick that had sought me through the denim of his jeans. I hoped I would see him again, but he wasn't one of Vron's usual crowd, and I had reason to suspect that she didn't want him to associate with me for whatever reason.

It was a month or so before I understood her reaction, when I came home one day and saw Nadif emerge semi-clad from the bathroom and head for her bedroom. His dark limbs gleamed, and beneath the towel wrapped around his waist I imagined the silky smooth baton of his dick, a magic wand of dark wood. I felt a pang then, for what could have been. Vron and I are pretty similar, looks wise, although, since she works in fashion, she is more glamorous and groomed. Nadif *had* fancied me, had wanted me that night, but she'd put her foot down because she planned to move in on him herself. I was pissed off, of course, but I told myself that it was fair enough, really – he was her friend, and she had first dibs on him.

So I was lonely at that time, but without really realising it. I was kind of trundling along on autopilot, treading water, not really thinking about my life. To someone like Vron, so ambitious, so driven, I was probably a bit of an embarrassment. A lost cause. The little sister who'd split up with her first boyfriend and was adrift in London, without a job, a man or a hip circle of friends like her. She must have pitied me, in her cold fashionista heart, disdained me, and thanked the stars that she wasn't me.

Tears prick my eyes as I sit on my bed at Anne's thinking about all this, and about how meeting James and the girl has brought these feelings out into the open. It's clear to me that I'm lost in London, always have been. I never found my footing in those three months at Vron's, and then I went straight on to Anne and the very ground fell away beneath me. I need to find terra firma. But how? By leaving Anne, or by staying? By getting out of London entirely?

Confirming what I have been discovering of late, writing all this down soothes me, gives me some kind of respite from the swirl of thoughts in my head. It simplifies things, I find – or rather, it shows things to be simpler than they seem in the clamour of my head and heart, which seem to be telling me different things for much of the time. Or alternating in their advice, which is disconcerting.

I wonder if it doesn't simply come down to the fact that I have nowhere else to go, and no one to go to, that I am still here. Anne, frosty as she may be inside, is the first person to show interest in me in a long time. Nadif, it turned out, was equally happy with my sister. Not that it lasted long between them – he was around for about a week, in various states of undress: in his boxers in the kitchen, making coffee to take back to Vron in bed; on the sofa in her bathrobe, flicking through her magazines; on his way back and forth from the bathroom. And then he ceded his place to someone else.

Vron is as ruthless in matters of the heart, or the loins, as she is in her professional life. She seems to suck her lovers dry and discard their husks without a second thought. From one beautiful boy to another she skips, never allowing feelings to intrude. Like Anne, she seems to have been hewn from a block of ice.

Perhaps, I write in my diary, that's where I have gone wrong – by allowing myself to start feeling, first for James and then, latterly, for the girl. I should have remained detached, aloof, as if this were a scientific experiment – which it is, in some ways. I should have remained on the surface, looking in from the outside, observing myself as if I were a character in a film. I've lost all perspective by getting in too deep. I should have run away as soon as I realised that I stood no chance of getting James to myself. Now it's too late.

But yes, I feel better just by noting all of this down on paper, and resolved to see it out. I feel that something decisive is imminent, that Anne has something very particular in mind and, judging that it can't be any more extreme than what I have already experienced, I decide that I owe it to myself to follow this through. Knowing myself, to my very core, has become a necessity, as essential as breathing, as food and water. Before, I wasn't fully alive. It's time to start living.

A note under the door is the sign from Anne that things are moving forwards. It's simple and to the point, unlike my mentor herself:

Claridge's, Suite 216, 8 p.m. Anne.

I shiver with anticipation. She has given me so many things, so many facets of myself that I didn't know existed.

I shouldn't waiver from my route to self-discovery, even though I'm naturally nervous.

I wonder what to wear, but having no idea what's in store, who I am to meet and be with, what scenario Anne has in mind, I am at a loss. I look through the meagre contents of my wardrobe then decide to go shopping. The high-street chains are within a short stroll. I'm being paid for what amounts to very little. I should treat myself.

In Top Shop, rifling through the rails, I realise how much I've changed in my relationship towards my body. Suddenly I find myself gravitating towards much more close-fitting, extrovert styles than I would have chosen before, from skinny jeans to slinky, thigh-skimming dresses. My body, I have discovered, is a source of immense pleasure and undreamt-of sensations, and suddenly I want to celebrate that.

When I've picked out a few items to try on in the changing room, I head for the lingerie section. Here again, I find myself attracted by styles that I wouldn't have considered before all of this: thongs, knickers with little cut-outs revealing intimate parts, quarter-cup bras, sheer fabrics that leave nothing to the imagination. And finally – I can't resist it, plucking it from the rail like some longed-for treasure – a shell-pink sheer baby doll with ribbon ties and matching knickers that it will barely cover. It's ridiculously feminine, and picking it out proves to me that I've become a woman.

I head for the changing room with my booty, feeling intoxicated and extravagant. If this is so unlike me, then why am I so excited? The reason is plain: this *is* me, the me that I've been hiding from for so long. With self-recognition comes relief, release and euphoria.

Inside one of the spacious cubicles, I undress slowly, almost ritualistically, savouring the gradual revelation of this body both familiar and, in its new pleasures, alien to me. I study my long legs, my breasts, my bush in turn, as they are stripped free of clothing. They delight me, both aesthetically and in terms of the memories they hold – memories that include more distant times with Nate but that focus on the past week in London. I feel proud of my body, and empowered – empowered by its existence as an object of desire. Suddenly the eyes that flicker over me and then return to rest on me in the street seem not a threat or an embarrassment but a confirmation of myself as a sexual being. And there's nothing wrong, I now understand, in being a sexual being. We are all sexual beings. The problems come when we don't recognise that.

I stand naked before my reflection, taking it all in – the sheen and smoothness of my flesh, the sweep of my breasts, the flatness of my belly. I'm no supermodel, but then would I want to be? They make great clothes horses, but without their glad rags skinny women can look pretty dire.

Around me I hear the clatter of clothes hangers and the occasional low exchange of words.

'Sal, does this suit me?'

'What do you think, Mum? Is it all right for Ally's wedding?'

'Does my bum like big in this?'

Even as I listen, smiling to myself, the voices fade to a background hum, a kind of static, as pleasure takes hold of me. My hand, which lingered for a moment too long as I admired myself, moves between my legs. I rest a finger on my clit, already finding it hard not to moan out loud. The thought of being heard only excites me more, rather than proving a deterrent. I'd like them to see me, see what I can do to myself, how I can make myself feel, what I look like when I'm losing myself to pleasure.

As I start to judder my way to climax, I lean back against the flimsy partition wall to afford myself some degree of support. Looking into the mirror, I realise I can get a better view of myself this way – see how my glinting fingers dip in and out of me, through my lips and into my pussy. How my thumb brushes my clit, knowing the exact degree of pressure that is needed to drive me wild. How my free hand clutches at one breast, feverishly. I imagine James sitting on the little bench, watching me, his cock out of his flies and in his hand, being worked at furiously as my excitement inflames his. Then I think of the girl, the blonde girl, beside him, naked, also playing with herself as she watches me come. The combination of all of this sends me over the edge, and within seconds I'm coming vociferously, eyes closed, lost to everything but what's happening inside.

Afterwards, too wet and too sweaty to try anything on, I hurry out. I'll buy what looks as if it'll suit me and try it on at home. If something's not right, I can always bring it back.

As I push open the cubicle door and head back along the corridor to the shop itself, two of the assistants are watching me, and I can tell that they're suppressing giggles. For a moment I feel mortified, but then I think, Sod it. I'm not ashamed of my body – quite the contrary. And, before I can think better, before I can censor myself, I flash them a complicit smile, tip them a wink and then I open my mouth slightly and run the tip of my tongue around my lips.

Their heavily mascaraed eyes become round with shock, and I laugh and hand over a few items I've decided not to buy, then saunter out of the changing rooms and towards the till, feeling both financially and mentally reckless. It's a great feeling.

*

I walk home and have some toast and Marmite and a coffee before going upstairs to get ready. My mood has dampened slightly, and though I'm excited about tonight and my rendezvous with Anne at the hotel, I'm pretty nervous too. I guess I'm worried that I won't be up to what is expected of me. After coming this far, I suspect that Anne will be posing me a significant challenge, testing my limits to the max. Anne, I feel, has her endgame in sight, and the prospect daunts as well as intrigues me.

I try on my baby doll and love myself in it. Never before have I felt so feminine, so unbridled, so free and self-expressive. I stand in front of the mirror for ages, gazing at myself – not in a vain way, but in sheer astonishment that I have come so far from the rather prudish and certainly unadventurous girl who turned up at Anne's for a job interview that was to lead her into such uncharted territory. And I *was* unimaginative – what Anne has tapped into and opened up and allowed to flourish is my imagination, the thing that a writer must have before anything else can happen. I was profoundly lacking in imagination before all of this happened, entirely lacking in a fantasy life. Now I understand that it's fantasies that will fuel most of the fiction I will produce. Some of it will be autobiographical – there's no avoiding that. But the well of fact will run dry quite soon, despite the injection of excitement and passion that has happened of late. And that's when fantasy will come into play. If writing is a muscle that has to be flexed, then so is the faculty for fantasy.

I glance towards my bedside table, where my vibrator resides. I'm horny again, but I don't have time for another wank if I'm to be on time. So rather reluctantly I strip off my baby doll and put it into a bag to take with me. Then I slip on some of the other new lingerie – a polka-dot thong and a matching nude bra with scalloped edging over the crest of the cups – and sit down in front of the mirror to do my face.

The contents of my make-up bag are scant. On ordinary days the most I manage is a quick whisk of my lashes with a mascara brush. But, rooting around, I find a sample sachet of light-diffusing foundation I must have kept from a magazine, a little pot of pink powder blush and a tiny nub of kohl that must have been lurking there for years. I apply them in turn, carefully, watching a different face emerge in the glass.

It's amazing, I reflect, what one can do with a little time and effort, with application. One's identity, it seems, is endlessly fluid. I have reinvented myself – with more than a little help from Anne – and I can reinvent myself again at will. Which means that when I say I'm 'finding myself', I understand that there's no one self to find, that we are mutable, evolving beings. So perhaps I should say that I'm excavating aspects of myself, of a possible me.

It's time to dress. I eye my purchases strewn across the bed. I don't want to get too dressed up and look idiotic, but the hotel I've been summoned to is posh, so I'll feel out of place if I don't make an effort. What I don't want to do is look tarty. I don't want to be mistaken for a hooker and ejected from the building before I reach the suite indicated on Anne's note. Among the items I picked out are a 1930s-style black dress with a lace panel above the cleavage; a printed dress from Top Shop's Kate Moss collection, with a frilled neckline; and a tiered miniskirt embellished with sequins, which I would pair with a plain black vest top. None is right. I lift up the dresses and beneath them lies my wild card: a black one-shoulder all-in-one playsuit. It's unusual and sexy yet chic.

It says 'classy' rather than 'tarty'. With the black stilettos I picked up, it has the makings of a killer outfit.

Trying it on for the first time, I'm thrilled by my purchase. It's something I would never in a million years have seen myself in, and yet it looks the business. *I* look the business. It accentuates my long legs, making me look taller, while the fabric-falling detail across the chest is flattering to my boobs.

Feeling psyched up for my meeting, I fumble in my make-up bag again, find an old, barely used lipstick tube and apply a slash of dark mauve to my mouth. Blowing myself a kiss in the mirror, I grab my bag and leave the room.

The house is quiet. Anne must have left already. It would have been sensible to share a taxi, but that would have lessened the drama of this meeting. So far, everything that has gone on has taken place, rather claustrophobically, within the confines of Anne's house. The only other venue was James's flat, and that was equally claustrophobic. To be allowed out like this is exciting. I don't know what it signifies, but I hope it's a sign that Anne is loosening control. I want to be set free now, like a bird being launched up into the sky. It's time to fly solo.

I walk out of the house and up the street onto the Bayswater Road, where I hail a taxi. The hotel is actually within reasonable walking distance, just beyond Park Lane in Mayfair, but I'm in an extravagant mood. And anyway these ridiculous shoes are already beginning to pinch.

As I climb into the cab and recline against the seat, I imagine my grand entrance: the taxi swinging theatrically up to the front door, a doorman stepping forwards to open the door and help me out. The driver will be expecting a hefty tip given the prestigious address. I wonder if, despite my outfit, he's taken me for a hooker. Or should I say, a high-class call girl. He must see all sorts in the back of his cab – all sorts of people making all sorts of illicit transactions.

We're at the hotel within minutes. I pay the driver, bunging him a couple of quid on top of the fare, and try not to fall flat on my face as the doorman helps me out. Of all the hotels in London, this has always seemed the most fairy-tale like to me, although I've never been inside. It's always in the gossip rags, linked with various celebs, from Madonna to Courtney Love. I'm not actually much impressed by all that. I just love the art deco interiors, along with the wonderful snippets of history I've read, such as that Winston Churchill designated one of the suites Yugoslav territory when the exiled King Peter stayed there.

I head for the cocktail bar for something for my growing nerves. After spunking a further tenner on a Polish martini, I admire the silver-leaf ceiling and other glam decor while I drink. One of the barmen eyes me and I look away, unsure whether he finds me attractive or has taken me for a call girl. Realising I'm getting paranoid, I head for the lift.

On the way upstairs, through the burn of the alcohol inside me, I wonder about the prices in a place like this. I've never been anywhere like it, so I can't begin to guess, but something tells me that we're talking in excess of a grand per night for a suite. How can Anne afford that, even as an occasional blow-out? Or is someone else footing the bill?

I exit the lift and the door to the suite is a few paces away. My heart is thudding away by now, so that for a moment I have to stand still and clutch my chest with my hand, wondering if I'm going to fall over. When I've steadied my breathing, it's another few minutes before I can bring myself to knock. I feel like I'm on the threshold of something – a cliff might be the best analogy. I'm wearing a parachute but

I have no idea if it will open or if I'll be dashed to pieces on the rocks below. Yet I don't want to go through the rest of my life asking myself 'What if?'

I knock, and am greeted by silence and stillness. I knock again, more assertively, and then again. The door opens and an unfamiliar face appears, an arm gestures for me to come inside. From the uniform I judge him to be a butler. He relieves me of my jacket and bag and takes them to the wardrobe, giving me a moment to look around and get my bearings.

The entrance hall leads on to a sitting room decorated with lilac fabrics, from the silken and sheer curtains to the leather of the sofas. The look, in keeping with the hotel in general, is art deco. A table bears an ice bucket from which the neck of a bottle of champagne protrudes invitingly – I'm dying for another drink. Beside it are some canapés, a bowl of fruit, a plate of fancy chocolates and a spray of fresh flowers in an opulent vase. Through and beyond the sitting room I can glimpse the bedroom. I wonder what romps will be taking place there later tonight, and I start to tremble a little.

'Madam?' The butler, or whatever he is, is looking at me, and I realise I've been miles away.

'A glass of champagne, madam?' he says, and when I nod he goes and uncorks the bottle with professional restraint, pours me a flute-full.

I take it, and it's all I can do not to down it in one. Although I'm no connoisseur, I know it's a prestigious brand, and it looks delicious – straw gold and cold and fresh with lots of tiny bubbles like stars shooting up through the glass. I sit down and sip it in a genteel fashion, watching the butler take his leave. As soon as he's gone, I scarf it. It's as gorgeously refreshing as it looks and, being champagne, it's too damn easy to drink. I pour and polish off another glass, then another. For a moment I feel guilty, and then I think, Bollocks to it. On the scale of whatever this lovely suite costs, a bottle of champagne isn't worth thinking about. Whoever's paying won't bat an eyelid.

I kick off my heels and go for a walk around the suite, eyeing up the beautiful furniture glinting in the low light. I walk into the bedroom and try out the bed for size and comfort, and find it excellent in both respects. I check out the bathroom and am pleased by the sumptuous marble and the Asprey toiletries. This is the kind of luxury I could get accustomed to. It flashes across my mind that being a high-class call girl might be fun after all. How different is it, after all, to what I am doing now? I'm basically being paid to dress up and put out, only it's Anne who's the client in this skewed relationship that we have.

Speaking of Anne, I hear the main door snick shut and I turn and see her standing in the hallway with the room swipe still in her hand. She's dressed in an elegant but muted way, in black linen trousers and a turtleneck topped by a dark cape. Her bob is sharp and faultless. She looks every bit the famous writer. In her other hand she's holding sunglasses and I realise that she's probably made efforts to arrive incognito. She's still a 'face', despite her waning reputation. I'll wager that the suite is booked under an assumed name.

Our eyes meet, and there's the usual *froideur* to Anne's demeanour. As she gestures for me to sit down, she looks me up and down in my playsuit, and I sense her approval by the way her eyes gleam. I'm still not convinced she actually fancies me, that that's her reason for watching me in all of these scenarios that she's devised. But it seems I've hit the nail on the head in terms of what she expects of me tonight, and

I'm pleased to have pleased her. I think again of my mother and her disinterest in me, and I wonder if I'm destined always to strive for the approval of older women.

I arrange myself on the sofa, to best advantage: side-on to her, knees bent, delicately bringing the champagne glass to my lips, no longer slugging it back like some dipsomaniac. I watch Anne for a sign of what is to come, and my faculties are all sharpened in anticipation: surely someone is about to arrive, the other actors in this little mise en scène of Anne's.

Anne sits down opposite me, lights a cigarette. For a few moments there's the usual silence, and I'm happy with that. It's become like a ritual. If Anne thinks she can intimidate, even break me, this way, she's very wrong.

But then, to my surprise, she clears her throat, leans forwards across the low table between us, and speaks. 'What would you say,' she asks, 'if I told you you could have anything you want? Anyone you want.'

I stare at her. 'I . . . I wouldn't know where . . .'

I take a swig of champagne, wondering where she's steering me. Is she talking about heartthrobs, about famous but unattainable people? Is she talking about sex on tropical beaches with an incredible sunset as a backdrop and a cocktail at hand, or is she talking about the reality of my life? Anne is no fairy godmother with a magic wand. Her powers are limited.

She looks at me, and there's no kindness or mercy in her eyes. How could I have ever thought her motherly? But then, of course, with a mother like mine, my expectations were low.

'So you haven't learnt anything,' she says, 'over this past week? You don't know anything about who you are, what you want? Have I been wasting my time?'

'I do know, only . . .'

I think of the list I wrote in my notebook. The things I have found out seem contradictory. I like older men, I like younger men. I like men, I like women. I like extreme women, women who punish me, and I like soft, uncomplicated girl-next-door types. I like being watched when I'm wanking or fucking, and yet I would do anything to have James or the girl alone, to have a little privacy in which my true feelings towards them can bloom and we can get to know each other on a natural, unforced basis.

'Only what?'

I look at Anne, and for a moment I truly hate her and want to throw it all back in her face, walk out. When she gets snippy with me, I feel utterly humiliated to be here with her, at her behest.

'Only, I don't know. It seems the things I want are so different that they cancel each other out. I like men, still, but I like women too.'

'They're not mutually exclusive.'

'No, but I don't even consider myself bisexual.'

'Then what?'

'Then – I don't know. I suppose I just fancy a woman every now and again. As a change, I suppose. Or if it's someone who blows me away. At heart, it's blokes I like.'

Anne smiles in that cold, disengaged way of hers. 'Now we're getting somewhere,' she says. 'So if I could get you anyone now, anyone you wanted, it would be a man?'

I hesitate. I want to say 'Yes.' I'm thinking of James. Anne has a hotline to him, has some kind of hold over him, and it would take one nod from me and he could be here within minutes. So what's stopping me? I think of my last meeting with him, when I begged him to see me alone and he refused, for reasons that weren't 100 per cent transparent at the time.

I was cross with him, and still am. But that's not enough to stop me from saying his name, from making him my choice.

I think of the girl – the second girl, not the dom. Soft as butter she melted against me. With her came Sunday-morning ease, a feeling of relaxation even as we drove each other into a frenzy. A feeling of falling into each other that I'd never had with any man. I knew her body because I knew my own, and vice versa. From there it was so easy to please and be pleased. I want James, but I want her too.

I look at Anne. Dare I? Is it too much to ask? She's asking me what I want, and that is what I want: James *and* the girl, together, in bed with me, the best of both worlds. Or is that just too greedy?

She's looking back at me, a little combatively, as if she's daring me to speak my wants and needs. I can tell that she thinks I'm not up to her, but however hard it is to ask, I won't give her the satisfaction of knowing that I've failed, that I didn't dare.

'James,' I say, my voice quavering.

She continues to look at me, steadily. 'So little,' she says, 'to ask.'

'Not just James. James and the blonde.'

She smiles, and for a moment I don't understand the glitter of something like exultation in her pale-blue eyes. But then, as she steps up to a door that I hadn't noticed, one that leads to a second bedroom I didn't know existed, I realise why she looks so pleased with herself. She's second-guessed me.

She opens the door to reveal James and the girl, sitting on the edge of the bed drinking champagne together. Anne, it seems, knows me better than I know myself.

For a moment I'm enraged. I hate it that she knew, even

before I knew, what I most wanted. But then James and the girl both smile at me, warm genuine smiles of welcome quite unlike Anne's, and I melt inside. I am in for some real fun.

Using all my inner resources to talk myself up, reminding myself how great I look, I slip my shoes back on and stand in the doorway, hands on my hips, smiling back. I feel like a kid in a sweet shop. Where do I begin? Where does all this begin?

James, sensing that I am struggling, extends a hand. 'Genevieve,' he says kindly. 'Come in. I believe you and Celine know each other.'

I nod, a bit embarrassed. The blond girl stands up, comes towards me and kisses me on both cheeks, her hands on my shoulders.

'Lovely to see you again,' she breathes in my ear, and I feel giddy at the memory of our lovemaking. I sincerely thought I'd never see her again, that she'd remain forever a beautiful memory, elusive as a dream from which one awakes too soon.

She takes me by one hand now, guides me into the room. I'm glad that she is taking the lead. The confidence I summoned in myself has evaporated. I don't know what the hell I'm doing.

Celine hands me over to James, like a gift, then retreats, to sit in an armchair in the corner. For the moment that's fine: I love to be watched, and who better to watch me than Celine? I glance around. Anne is in the doorway. There's something stealthy to her, catlike, as she comes further into the room and takes an armchair in the opposite corner to Celine. The two women exchange a look, something complicitous. I try not to feel paranoid again. This is no natural situation, and I must accept that these people have met without me, talked about me, plotted and schemed and deliberated. In a way, I should even be flattered by it. None of them stands to gain anything by it, financially at least. Not unless Anne is paying them, and I don't believe that dosh is behind all this. She may have reimbursed the dom, but not these guys. This is something that goes beyond money.

James looks me up and down. 'You look great,' he says in a half-whisper that we both know the others can hear. I flush with excitement and longing, with the knowledge that James does want me, even if it's not possible without Anne's presence or consent. And with the knowledge that it is not only James's eyes that are on me. Is Celine getting turned on too?

The playsuit has a halter-neck top, and I reach up and around to my nape to loosen the tie. The fabric slips away from me, revealing my new bra, from which I removed the detachable shoulder straps when dressing. James watches appreciatively, lips pursed. He seems thoughtful, and I'd pay any money to know what's going on in his head.

Taking the initiative, I bend forwards, my hair swooshing down against James's face and shoulders. He pulls down the cups of my bra and brings his mouth to my nipples. I begin to shake but manage to maintain my focus, unbuttoning his shirt and slipping it from his shoulders. His chest is magnificent – strong, tanned, carpeted with soft hairs, a mixture of chestnut brown and grey. I run the palms of my hands against it, appreciating the delicious smoothness of his skin and his hair, then I bring my fingertips to his nipples, tweak gently. He moans, and I tighten my grip a little, remembering the spanking I gave him, how he liked a certain degree of pain.

He's still sitting up, and I bring one knee onto the bed beside him and then the other, so that I'm straddling him. Feeling powerful and in charge, I press one hand against his naked chest and push him back onto the bed. He gasps, and his eyes tell me he's burning for me. His hands spring to my hips, try to pull me harder onto the bulge of his cock inside his designer jeans. I resist, much as I want to fuck him, to ride him hard.

My breasts spill forth from the bra where he pulled the cups down. The top half of the playsuit is bunched around my waist. The trouser bottoms are still in place. I look behind me, wondering what Anne has in her armoury today.

As if anticipating my move, she's picked up her wooden box from the floor and placed it on her knee. She looks at me expectantly. But I'm not getting down from James. I gesture her over, astonished at my audacity.

She looks surprised too, but she stands up, comes over to us with the box in her arms, then tends it to me. I look inside.

'Those,' I say, pointing out some leather cuffs. 'And that.' The second item is a whip that looks to be made of human hair, auburn in hue. 'But first –' I look down at James beneath me; he's gazing up curiously, probably trying to guess what I have in store for him. 'First that.'

Anne puts a hand inside, brings out an eye mask in moulded gold leather. She hands it to me. It's butter soft – so much so that it could be skin. James watches me as I run my fingers over the surface of it. His eyes glint in a mixture of apprehension and longing. I make him wait, continuing to caress it with my fingertips. Then I hang down over him and position it over his nose and eyes, reaching round to tie it at the back of his head. He becomes very quiet, his lips parted, his breath held. His entire body has stiffened in anticipation.

I look back at Anne. Suddenly I'm self-conscious and don't know what to do, and I'm glad she's here. She holds responsibility for all of this, so I have no shame in appealing to her.

In turn, she shifts to face the girl, points back towards the sitting room. The girl seems to understand, rises and leaves the bedroom. For a few moments Anne stands looking down at James, and I understand that we are to wait. Then she says, 'Rise,' and James sits up and casts about for my hand. I take it and together we leave the bedroom.

I don't see Celine when we enter the sitting room, but more flutes brim with champagne on the coffee table. Then she appears, and in place of her chinos and shirt she's wearing a maid-style skirt with a frilly apron front, seamed stockings and a black corset. She bows her head a little when she sees me. On one upturned hand she holds the platter of canapés.

'Madam?' she says, and I take one and bite into it, through unctuous black olive tapenade to the crisp toast beneath.

The half that I don't eat I bring to James's mouth. At first he recoils, not having expected it, then not knowing what it is. I press it to his lips again, whispering 'Trust me,' and he nods and parts them, lets the crisp bread and silky topping slip inside his mouth. Biting into it, he nods again, as if in recognition. I realise that the word 'trust' was like a trigger, reminding him that we know each other, that we mean each other no harm – quite the contrary.

I gesture over towards the coffee table with my chin. Understanding, Celine steps towards it, picks up a glass and hands it to me. I take it, bring the fizzy straw-coloured liquid to James's lips. He greets it with a swig, then another. His hand moves towards my wrist so that I can't take the champagne away, and it's now that I remember the restraints.

I look at Celine. 'In the other room. The cuffs.'

It's hard not to say 'please', to be so rude, but I need to

stay in the role, otherwise this whole staged scenario will break down. If anyone steps out of their role, that will be the end of it.

Of course, we all know we're playing a part – there's no escaping that. But we all want this to carry on, and for that it is crucial to keep up the charade. Like actors on a stage, we have to maintain the pretence until the curtain goes down.

Celine scurries away with a duly deferent 'Yes, madam,'

I turn back to James. 'You've been a very bad boy.'

'I know,' he says, and there's a faint undertone of mirth that I know he's trying so very hard to contain.

'You do know you'll have to be punished?' I go on, also struggling against the laughter that's threatening to rise like the bubbles in the glasses of champagne.

'I should be,' he says. 'I should be punished.'

Celine appears by my side. As well as the cuffs she's holding the whip.

'Put them on him,' I say, and she steps forwards.

'How would madam like it?' she asks.

'Behind his back.' I realise I'm grinding the spiked heel of one stiletto into the carpet. I really am getting into role here.

I watch as she turns James around, so that he's facing away from me. Celine handles him a little roughly, and I sense that she is struggling to remain within the confines of her role, that she is spilling out a little. She wants to be in my place, the ringleader. But I'm not willing to cede it – not yet, at least.

She places the cuffs on each of James's wrists, buckling them slowly then attaching them with the bronze link. James is bent slightly forwards, his head drooping. He seems to have gone all floppy, as if all will and decisiveness have gone from him, his acceptance of his submission being total. And yet with his back and torso naked, his trousers still on, his wrists cuffed behind his back, he looks so sexy I'm creaming my pants. But I will wait for the satisfaction of my itch. There are other things to attend to.

'The whip,' I command Celine, and I take it from her. The ribbed handle is supple yet firm in my hand, but when I run the auburn hair through my clenched fist, it's silky soft and feather light. Lifting it away from me, I bring it down against my palm. It tingles rather than hurts.

'Get him ready,' I say, and Celine takes James by the elbow and draws him over to the sofa. There, she pushes him down, so that he's on all fours on the sofa itself, and slowly pulls down his jeans and then his crisp white boxers. I look with relish at his arse, this arse that I paddled only a few days ago. An arse honed and yet well rounded. An arse just waiting to be reddened with my whip.

I step up to him. 'Say you're sorry,' I bark, and before he can speak I bring the tail of the hair crashing down on him. He jerks: it must sting, like the paddle, like the crop that the dom used on me. It's up to me to gauge how far he wants to go by his reactions. I raise my arm and bring it down again, then again, harder and harder. He begins to make guttural little noises that bespeak pain and pleasure, or perhaps an inextricable melding of the two. I lose myself in the rhythm of my strokes, heedless now to the presence of either Celine or Anne.

After a while I'm sweating. James is showing no signs of wanting me to stop: he must be used to much worse than this. I climb down from my stilettos and slide the bottom half of my playsuit down, then step out of. Slipping my shoes back on, I stand there in my nude polka-dot undies, whip in my hand, feeling like the queen of the world but unsure where to take it from here.

Celine appears at my side. 'If madam would permit,' she says, and she takes the whip from my hand.

Moving round me, she stands behind me and places one arm around my waist, hand flat against my belly. Then she brings the other hand around and starts moving the whip between my thighs, so that the trail of auburn hair sweeps my inner thighs deliciously, tickling and teasing me. Slowly her other hand moves down my lower abdomen and into my knickers.

For a minute or two her fingers flicker at my clit, around my lips, so that my head falls back and my mouth falls open in an 'O' of pleasure. Then she pulls the panties down around my thighs and lets the hair of the whip play around my pussy, moving first around my clit and lips, as her fingers did, and then dipping through my legs along my perineum to my sphincter. There it flickers, turning me to jelly, continuing its exquisite torture.

But I don't want to lose control just yet. I want to maintain it. In some dark part of me I'm enjoying this master-and-servant relationship, and I don't want it to be reversed. Far from being the cuddly, cute, sweetly fuckable girl-next-door, Celine is turning out to be quite the little vixen. But she's not taking over my show.

I snatch the whip from her hand, turn it on her. 'Madam does *not* permit,' I say, and there's savagery in my voice, despite the role-playing. 'And for your cheek, you'll receive forty strokes as well. Bend over.'

She does as I command, without resistance, all too ready and willing, it seems, to submit and to be punished. Turning her back to me, she pushes out her bottom, which peeks out from the back of her apron-style skirt, and throws me a look over her shoulder – a look of invitation. Wildly excited, I lash her with the spray of mahogany hair. She shrieks playfully.

'More, mistress,' she cries out. 'I've been so terribly bad.'

Her arse flesh is softer, less aged and paler than James's. The hair, silken as it may be, soon begins to leave visible marks. They will fade quickly, but seeing them appear drives me on to more. Celine is not complaining. What is it in her own life that makes her accept this, even seek it?

James has rolled over onto his face on the sofa, and I can tell from the way the bottom half of his face is twitching, from his moans, that it is killing him not to be able to see this. I turn my attention back to him, sitting beside him and rubbing his arse with my hands.

'I'm thirsty, mistress,' he says.

'Oh, are you? Then what do you say?'

'Please, mistress?'

'And what else? What else can you do for me?'

He's quiet for a moment, and then his lips quiver in an attempt not to smile. 'I could . . . I could lick your shoes, mistress.'

I glance down at my shiny patent stilettos and see my made-up face staring back up at me. I look like an alien being, like someone I've never met before, and for a moment I feel lost, freed from my moorings. There's liberation in there, but there's fear too. How far I have come from who I am, or who I thought I was.

'On your knees,' I say to James, although to myself my voice lacks self-assurance. He doesn't seem to notice, acquiescing. As he bends forwards, I look at the back of his head, with his close-cropped grey hair, and I want to grab it, take it in my hands and pull him up and cover his hair and face with kisses. Want to make love to him, in the boring, old-fashioned way. But that would mean moving back into my comfort zone, which would be a retrograde act. I must see this through, if only to learn that I am, at heart, a conventional girl after all.

He's prostrate before me now, his lips swollen in a pout, approaching my shoes. I push my feet forwards a bit to meet them, and he presses his mouth to the pointed tips of my stilettos, one at a time. Then his tongue inches its way out and he begins to lick first one shoe then the other. I'm still sitting down, and I open my legs and begin to massage my pussy through my pants. I'm very wet, and ready to be royally fucked. But I must resist, must keep resisting the desire for satiety, the push towards orgasm. Must learn to slow the tempo right down, in order to savour every sweet moment to its core.

I lie back a bit, still feeling between my legs, my eyes half closed. A bounce beside me on the sofa announces the fact that Celine has sat down. I turn my gaze on her. She smiles, takes a chocolate from the plate that she's holding and brings it to my lips. I close my mouth around it, bring it whole onto my tongue and feel it melt inside me as it reaches body temperature. Something sweet leaks out of its centre – cherry liqueur, I'd guess. I close my eyes fully. The Aztecs, I remember, thought chocolate to be an aphrodisiac. In modern scientific jargon, it's claimed to have 'mood-lifting agents' that mimic the effects of falling in love. I struggle to remember the name of them, and then give up.

James's face appears at my knees, still masked. He's finished cleaning my shoes with his tongue, and though I can't feel too guilty – they were brand new, after all, and I caught a cab to the hotel so they didn't pick up many street germs – I pluck a chocolate from the plate and feed it to him, as if he were a little dog. Again he hesitates, instinctively, until he's reassured that it's not something nasty. Not that he doesn't trust me, but he can't even see that it's me who's giving him the chocolate.

'I'll get some more champagne,' says Celine, as she trickles the remnants of the first bottle into our glasses. She heads over to the phone to call room service.

Meanwhile, I lean forwards, take James's lovely face between my hands, kiss him passionately on the mouth. I've slipped out of role, but I'm burning for him now, unsure how much longer I can keep all this up. He kisses me back, pushing himself up from the floor, clumsily, since his hands are still bound. I fall back, with him on top of me, still blind beneath his mask but very definitely reciprocating the kiss. The scenario is threatening to break down, but I don't care. I just want James on me, around me, inside me. I want him to envelop me and inhabit me and subsume me. I've even forgotten the girl at this point. As for Anne, I've become completely oblivious to her presence. Just as actors must forget, I suppose, their audience, if only for a while.

But she's back now, Celine. Room service must have arrived, for she's holding a fresh bottle of champagne, still corked, and a platter of oysters – twelve beautifully slick critters pooled in their half-shells, their juices winking in the low light. Now I do look at Anne, who is sitting impassively on the opposite sofa. I'm reminded of our conversation about liking and not liking oysters, and my eventual admission that I would, after all, like to try them. Anne gazes back at me, her lips upturned in the beginnings of a smile. She nods at me. I glance at Celine, remembering our brief time together. Afterwards I had thought it was love, was desperate to see her again but certain I never would. I mustn't squander this opportunity.

I'm still lying under James, looking up at Celine and over

at Anne. Wriggling out from beneath him, I sit up. Celine steps up in front of me, holds out the platter. I smell iodine, the scent of the sea. I reach out one hand and take a half-shell between my fingers, bring it slowly to my face, careful not to spill the liquid that sloshes about inside it. I inspect it as I do so: I don't know if oysters really are an aphrodisiac, but they can't help but put one in mind of sex, they look so much like pussies, with their plump, glistening wet folds and ruffles. When I tip it into my mouth, its clean, delicate, almost floral taste is what I remember Celine's snatch to taste of. I must experience it again.

Swallowing the fleshy oyster without chewing, letting it simply slide down my throat, I place the empty shell back on the platter. I take another, loosen the oyster inside with my fingernail, and bring it to James's lips. This time he almost leaps back, not expecting the sharp end of the shell followed by the watery sliminess of the oyster. I put a reassuring hand on his cheek, steady him, then bring the shell back to his mouth. Guessing what it is, he opens wide and swallows it, as I did, in one. I bring a champagne flute to his mouth and he takes a swig. Then I take one too.

When I'm done, I take the platter out of Celine's hands and place it on the table. Turning back to her, I bring one arm around her waist and pull her into me at the same time as I lift her little aproned skirt and bury my face in her muff.

She grabs the hair on each side of my head and pulls lightly as she mashes her mons against my mouth. My tongue seeks out her clit, flicks at it again and again, then slips down through her creases towards her wet hole. It tastes how I remember: like a cool fresh blast of the seaside, of air and water and clouds blasted across a blue sky by a coastal breeze. I sigh a long sigh of longing into her as my tongue enters her.

Her hands are tight and fast on my head. I'm perched on the lip of the sofa, one arm around her waist still, the other on one arse cheek, pulling her into me. I'm afraid I'm losing it, but I'm pulled back to reality by James behind me, kneeling up, his cock hard against the small of my back. I ache to be touched by him between my legs, on my breasts, but I remember that his hands are still cuffed behind him. I have to content myself with the pressure of his cock on me and with his lips pecking my shoulders, my nape, the sides of my neck, deliciously.

We continue this way for a while, me lapping at Celine's pool, James nibbling at the flesh of my upper back and neck. Then, as if by a common accord, we start to move in the direction of the master bedroom, melting away from each other by infinitesimal degrees until we are discrete beings again. As we walk across the room, however, Celine, who has taken the lead, reaches back to grasp my hand, and I in turn reach back for James's upper arm, and so we form a kind of human chain heading towards the bedroom. There's a sort of sacredness to it, it suddenly appears to me: the silence, the trust, the concern for one another's well-being and pleasure. There's a carnal aspect to it all, of course, but there's a holiness to it to. I wonder if I have found my religion at last.

The room is low lit. Anne, who must have preceded us, is standing in the window at the end. A street lamp from outside casts her in silhouette, and there's something foreboding to her aspect – perhaps because I can't see her eyes and don't know if she's looking at us, at me. I tell myself that I don't care, that it doesn't matter. I'm not here for her, I'm here for me. Whatever her stake in it all, this is a journey of self-discovery from which I will walk away richer.

Gaining confidence now, feeling that I am among friends

and confidantes, I let go of James's arm and push Celine down onto the bed. Her apron-skirt flaps up again, and I look up at James.

'The box,' I say. Then I remember and reach round him and unclasp his cuffs.

'Where?' he says, pushing up his mask. Our eyes meet. His are warm and brown. They convey nothing but the desire to please me and the desire to be pleased. I am determined to give him the fuck of his life.

He dashes out into the sitting room, in the direction I have pointed, and reappears a moment later with Anne's wooden box of goodies. He places it on the end of the bed. Flipping up the clasps, I peer inside. It's hard to see anything with the lights this low, so after a moment I put one hand in and rustle around. Bringing it up, I find myself clasping what looks like a mini string of pearls, except they're looped only at one end. I look at James, eyebrows raised, and he smiles.

'Anal beads,' he says in a low voice, and then he looks down at Celine where she lies on the bed. 'Here,' he says, holding out one hand. 'Let me help you. But we'll need some lube.' He gestures with his chin towards the box. 'Have another look in there.'

I do so, and find the small square bottle I remember from James's apartment. I hold it up to him.

'Aaah,' he says, and he chuckles.

I unscrew the lid, pour a small pool of the lubricant into the palm of my hand and sniff it. As well as smelling like honey, it has a thick, syrupy texture.

James reaches forwards, dips his fingers into the pool and then begins to coat his cock with the lube.

'Taste me,' he says, climbing into a kneeling position on the bed. I turn away from Celine and bring my mouth down to James's honey-scented groin. With one hand I can reach her pussy, and as I take him in my mouth I caress her lips and clit with my fingertips, trying to keep my touch light and tantalising.

In my free hand I still clutch the anal beads. I know that I should use them on Celine, to enhance her orgasm, but I'm feeling really rather selfish by now, since I'm pleasing two people at the same time. And so, having ensured they've adequately rolled around in the lube in my palm, I bring them behind me. Noticing what I'm doing, James brings one finger to his mouth to wet it then reaches round me. He presses it against the rosebud of my anus until I feel my muscles begin to cede under the increasingly insistent pressure. Then he takes the beads from my hand and begins to insert the chain of them into my sphincter, pearl by pearl.

'These are small pearls,' he says in a low voice, as sweet and sticky as the honey lube, and just hearing him I feel as if I'm falling through space. 'Freshwater pearls. Do you know the legend?'

I shake my head, fascinated to hear there's a story behind them but barely able to stay conscious with what's going on in my back passage.

'*Ama*,' he goes on, 'were Japanese divers, first for abalone and seaweed and later for pearl oysters. They were women who traditionally dived hairless and naked save for a tiny apron in which to stash their find. The pearls themselves were said to be the crystallised tears of Aphrodite, symbolising wisdom and love gleaned through experience.'

Experience, I think through teeth gritted with intense pleasure as bead after bead goes inside, James pausing after every few words to insert one more. Experience is the holy grail, the reason why we are here. And yes, it has involved tears. But I'm so glad, now I'm here, that I've stayed the distance.

When they're in, he lets go of them and then reaches out to locate something in the box while I'm still sucking his cock. Pulling out his hand, he passes me something small. I look down and see glimmering in my palm what appears at first to be a pair of silver rings with two tiny balls on each. When I look at them more closely, I realise they are clips.

'For her,' says James, indicating Celine with a jerk of his head. 'Her nipples.'

Celine is looking up at me questioningly, unable to see what lies in my furled palm. With my free hand I reach down and prise open her black corset where it fastens at the front. Her breasts tumble out, as warm and soft as new-baked buns. I place one of the clips on the bed and concentrate on prising the balls of the other apart. I bring the open jaw of it to one of Celine's erect nipples. For a moment I can't find it in myself to release the balls and let them clamp down on her sweet dusky-pink flesh, but she nods encouragingly, and I know she can take it, that she's probably been here before.

Teeth gritted, eyes squinting, I let go. Celine lets out a high shriek, head thrown back. For a moment I think I'm going to have to take it off her, but no – even as she looks like she's losing herself to the rapture or pain, or both, she summons up the wherewithal to pinch her other nipple with her fingers, pulling it out towards me as if to remind me not to forget it.

I place the other clip on her and then sit back to look at her. James has come behind me now, wrapped his arms around my waist.

'Be careful,' he says. 'Don't leave them for much longer than ten minutes. They can damage tissue.'

'OK,' I whisper. He and Anne seem to be connoisseurs of exotic sex toys, and I wonder that they don't use them together. Or perhaps they did but in time grew tired of each other and needed fresh blood. Is that what Celine and I are: external elements brought in to spice up a jaded relationship?

Celine, too, seems no stranger to sex tools, seems to know what she likes. As if to confirm what I am thinking, she reaches down and peels herself open for me, thrusting her pubis up at me. I bring my lips down to her pussy again, start lapping at her like a cat with a bowl of prime cream. It must be the nipple clips, for she goes crazy, thrashing from side to side, twisting and writhing so that it's all I can do to keep my mouth on her, clasping her hips with my hands, trying to pin her down like an exotic butterfly.

James's hand slides down to my own pussy, his fingers working at my clit. Now she's calmer, Celine is watching his actions, and it's clear that seeing him do that is firing her up even more. She opens her mouth, wider and wider, and her eyes start rolling backwards; she's clearly on the verge of coming. The knowledge brings me close to my personal precipice and my breath quickens. Sensing my body stiffen in readiness for climax, James, with his free hand, starts to tug at the string of pearls he fed into my arse. Unable to hold back, I go rigid in an almost unbearable orgasm heightened by the tugging motion of the little white beads, then I collapse down over Celine who is coming beneath me. As I do so, James slides his hand between us and gently and carefully removes the nipple clips.

Celine and I lie in each other's arms, panting, and it's pure joy to feel her breasts and belly naked against mine. For a moment I'm convinced that I'm in heaven, that I've achieved pure bliss and that there's nowhere to go from here. But I'm summoned from the delusion by James tapping me on the shoulder, and I look back at him and he's smiling at me and I know that I'm just gathering strength, that I want to go on.

He shows me something translucent with a fluid tapered end and a bulbed handle at the other. He's about to hand it to me, when he seems to think again and brings it between my legs, then runs it along my lips where they're still wet with my come juices. When it's thoroughly lubed, he passes it to me and lies back on the bed, looking up at me. There's the old trust in his eyes, the invitation to enjoy and discover. James is taking, asking for his pleasure now, but in a generous way, a way that lets me know I am about to learn something.

His legs are open, his cock like a rod, or an arrow pointing heavenwards. I grip it in my fist and keep a firm hold as I insert the glass toy into his arse, incredibly slowly, millimetre by millimetre, searching his face for signs that it might be hurting more than it should, causing damage. But James is relaxed, smiling, his eyes rolled back in his head beatifically. I carry on.

Beside me Celine stirs from her post-coital languor. Rolling onto one side, she sees what I'm doing to James and lets out a little 'Mmmmm' of approval, her hand creeping back down between her legs to play with her swollen lips. In turn, seeing her do that, James reaches one arm out to the side, around her hip, and pulls her in towards him. Following his cue, she raises one knee and straddles him, then brings her pussy down to his face.

I go down on James now, slurping at his cock still tasting of rich, unctuous honey. With my hand I ease the plug back and forth in his arse. I know the male G-spot is in here somewhere, the prostate, and that when he comes what I'm doing will add another layer of sensation to his orgasm. The trick is to establish a rhythm that I can maintain both with my mouth and my hand. After a few minutes, I have it. I look up, satisfied, to find I have a delicious view of Celine's gorgeous pink rosebud where she's pushing herself forwards onto James's mouth. I lift my free hand and push in one finger, so slowly, so gently. She moans loudly, and within seconds she's coming again.

Unable to contain himself, James starts thrusting into my mouth, and I increase the speed of the plug's movements, and the depth it reaches, trying to match his tempo. He cries out too now, and as Celine falls forwards over him, spent, he starts coming and coming, and I pull out the plug, cleanly. Torrents of him shoot forth into my mouth, so that I'm almost gagging in the effort to take it all in.

We all fall apart, collapsing back onto the bed and back into our separate realities. For a moment, the blink of an eye, that was something almost holy, a communion of both bodies and minds, taking us onto a spiritual plane. It's something I always expected of sex, I suppose, but never really approached until now. Certainly I never got anywhere near it with Nate.

But it's gone, evaporated, and I'm left with a warm, tingly feeling between my legs where the numbness of my orgasm has died away. For a while, we doze on the bed, exhausted in some primal way, sharing warmth as cave-dwellers must have.

I'm the first to wake. My pussy is still warm and tingling. I bring my hand down to it, somewhat half-heartedly, knowing that a quick wank won't keep me satisfied for long and is only an expedient, a temporary measure. As if my very action has stirred him, however, James has pushed himself up from the bed and is leaning over me. Removing my hand, he replaces it with his own, running two fingers up and down my slit,

until I'm creaming for him. Celine, too, has now been roused
from her stupor and is sitting up rummaging in Anne's box,
her magician's inventory. A minute later she's crawling back
over the bed to me, a strap-on looped around her slim hips.

Seeing her, James pulls me up onto all fours and slinks
beneath me. Looking up he smiles at me, winks reassuringly.
I smile back. I'm loving every minute of this adventure that
we've embarked on together, the places he and Celine are
taking me to: uncharted lands from which I'll return forever
changed. Unless I decide to stay there, that is – take up
permanent residence.

James holds up his cock, grazes my pussy lips with its
swollen, questing end. I feel Celine's hand in the small of
my back, gently but insistently easing me down. I lower my
hips, slotting the moist aperture of my pussy down over him.
He pushes to meet me, and for a moment we're still. Celine's
hand is on my buttock now, steadying her. Then the tip of
the dildo, dripping with lube, kisses my sphincter. I hold my
breath and Celine enters me from behind.

There are a few seconds when nobody moves, and we
seem to be hanging in the air, a still life worthy of Anne's
wall of erotic paintings. Then James begins to move up and
down, oh-so gently, and when she's had time to assess his
movements, Celine sets herself in motion, reaching round
me now to let her fingers flutter at my clit.

I struggle to remain in the moment. Paradoxically, it seems
that it's when the physical sensations are at their height that
I begin to feel most estranged from my corporality, as if I'm
having an out-of-body experience. It's as if I'm being lifted,
rising, taken out of my skin, becoming light and untethered
from the Earth. It feels like freedom.

The combined movements in my back passage and my

pussy, the rubbing at my inner walls, begins to have its effect. James, who must be able to feel the dildo through my inner walls, sounds as if he is losing control. I open my eyes and look down at him, and his face bears an expression of utter bliss. He's miles away too. His anchor has worked its way loose and he's bound for distant shores.

Suddenly he freezes, and I know he's trying not to come again, so that I may have my moment. I want to carry on too, but I know I'm not far away, that I can't hold off much longer. Feeling him halt, Celine too pauses, but a minute later they both start up again, and this time it's like a great wave rolling in, crashing over me before I've had chance to get away. As I come, they both carry on thrusting, and then it's like a rip-tide effect – just as I feel I'm reaching the crest of my orgasm, I'm dragged back again, and again, pulled under by the waves, until I'm breathless, afraid I won't make it out again.

At last, when I feel I'm failing, one last wave rolls in and bowls me down. I lie panting on top of James, Celine in turn on top of me, and we are all still.

The room is dark when I awake. I'm alone, or at least for a moment I think I'm alone. Then I see that, although James and Celine are no longer in the room, there is a figure on the other side of the bed, and that figure is Anne. She's not sleeping, but her eyes are unblinking. She's staring out of the window, into the amber glow cast by the street lights, and she looks old, and tired, and lonely. She's not thinking about me, that's clear. I might as well not be here.

I feel a stab of guilt. Perhaps seeing us all enjoying ourselves so much made her feel worse, rather than better? But then, why would she put herself through it, if that were the case? Not for the first time, a twinge goes through me, the instinct to hug her, to hold her, but in a daughterly rather than a sexual way. She looks like someone in need of comfort.

It's like she's read my thoughts, for she turns to me now, says, 'It's not how you think.'

'Then what?'

But she shakes her head, pushes herself up and reaches for her box, grabbing the items that have been used tonight, where they are strewn across the bed, and throwing them inside, any old how. She's impatient to be away.

'You may stay,' she says. 'It's all been paid for. Enjoy it.'

'Are you s–'

'Of course.' She eyes me dispassionately. 'And if you need anything, call room service. I trust you not to take advantage.'

With that, she's away, her box swinging at her side. Away into the London night, in the back of a speeding cab, with all those things that she's seen going round in her head. And to what purpose, to what end? To fuel her own private fantasies, which she will enact, alone, in her room until dawn bleaches the sky outside her window?

I lie there, unable to sleep, running it all through my mind, until finally, realising I am unable to beat the insomnia, I get up, order myself a lavish hot chocolate from room service, and get my notebook out of my bag. Belly down on the bed, I write up the evening's adventures in explicit detail. Doing so excites me but also makes me feel as if I own them in some way. Otherwise, these experiences risk being Anne's alone. By writing them down from my point of view, I am not merely an actor, I'm a collaborator, a co-author.

The room-service waiter rings the bell and I call for him to come in. I don't even bother getting up off the bed.

I hear him in the living room, clearing the coffee table to make space for the tray, and it turns me on to lie here stark naked while he waits on me. I'm tempted to call him to the door of my bedroom and, if he's fit, to lure him in and fuck him senseless. But I won't. I'm too tired, even if I'm wired and sleepless. I've had well in excess of my quota tonight and more would be greedy. So I titillate myself with the thought, for a moment, and then I let it go and carry on writing. Who knows, maybe the fantasy, the germ of an idea, will provide a subject for one of my little vignettes or for a short story?

Check out isn't until noon, so I luxuriate in a deep bath while waiting for my Continental breakfast to arrive. I write a bit more in my diary, and then I go down and hand my room-swipe in at reception, smug in the knowledge that I don't have to pay a penny. When I've done that, I stroll across Mayfair and across Hyde Park back to Bayswater. The breeze takes the edge off the heat, and it's a perfect day for a walk in the park.

I slow down by the Italianate fountains near Lancaster Gate, take the fork that leads to the Round Pond instead of the more direct one alongside the Bayswater Road, which would take me home. I realise then that I'm tarrying, reluctant to return to Anne's. Last night feels like the culmination of everything, as I had thought it would. So what awaits me there? Will I be expected to pack my bags and leave? If not, do I even want to stay? The money is good, the workload minimal. But suddenly it doesn't feel right any more. I won't take money for nothing.

I force myself in the direction of St Petersburgh Place. If there's one thing I've learnt above anything else in the last week or so, it's that we must face up to our fears, otherwise they become bigger, unmanageable – obstacles to our happiness and development. I was afraid of my appetites, but now I know that I was incomplete when I didn't act on them, when I shut them away so firmly that I barely even knew they were there. They have led me to some dark places, but those dark places were inside myself, and I needed to explore them if I was to find out who I really am.

Of course, I'll change some more, plenty. I've not discovered a static 'me' who will last all my life. But I've opened the door to a more honest Genevieve, one who accepts herself in all her contradictions, in all her unruliness, with her strengths and her weaknesses. People pay a fortune in therapy, spend years talking to shrinks, without getting an iota of the self-knowledge I have.

I feel grateful to Anne as I insert the key in the lock and let myself into her hallway, and I feel sorry for her too. All this growth in me has been, in some respects, at her expense, and not only financial – she is still the sad, lonely fantasist she was at the start. But then that's her choice. She's a grown-up and if she can't see her voyeuristic addiction as the dead-end that it is, that's her problem. I can't help her there.

I head upstairs. I'll pack my bag, and then I'll go downstairs and ask Anne if she wants to share a farewell drink with me. I don't want this to end in acrimony, and there's no reason why it should. I'm sure Anne meant last night to be the end too. There was such a sense of finality to it. And the fact that it happened outside of her house was surely symbolic. But I want to make sure, so I'll suggest a drink and we'll have a little chat and then I'll go calmly, without a drama. Where I'll go I don't know, but I'll deal with that when I come to it. Something will turn up.

It doesn't take me long to pack, with the few possessions I

have. Setting my bags on the bed to collect later, I walk down the stairs towards Anne's room. The door is ajar, which is unusual. I rap gently and when no answer comes I poke my head around the door. The room is empty, but I can see that there's a document open on the screen. When I step forwards and look closer, I see that, wherever Anne has gone, she left mid-sentence. That seems to me an unusual thing to do. I doubt she's just popped to the loo or to make a coffee – surely she'd finish her sentence if she was doing that? Then I hear voices from the back garden, and I twitch back the curtain and see her talking to the window-cleaner. She's gesturing up at another first-floor window, and I guess she's berating him for not doing his job properly.

I turn back to the screen. Anne is intensely secretive about her work, always locking her study door. I know because I've tried it a couple of times, when I've known she's not there. I've also – I might as well admit to it now – searched the laptop for anything of interest, looking at 'Recent Items', inside files within files, and even in the 'Trash' folder. I suppose that makes me a bit of an arsehole, but it was only really out of interest. Anne has been such a heroine to me for such a long time, I just wanted to find out more about her and her work. I wasn't planning to use it against her.

It's the same impulse that takes me back to her screen now. She's fed me only titbits about her new book, her work in progress, and suddenly I have the opportunity to find out more. I lean forwards, scan the lines with my eyes, all the while listening for the voices outside, ready to bolt when I can no longer hear them.

As I begin to read, I start, and then a chill runs through me. It's last night, what's written there – everything that happened to me, and James, and Celine. All the permutations of our play, our lovemaking. The characters have different names, but they look like us, and talk like us, and fuck like us. *Exactly* like us.

I read the paragraphs that are visible on the page on the screen, and then I scroll back and forth, to the preceding page and then the following page. There's no doubting it. Glancing over my shoulder, reassuring myself Anne is still out there, I go to the start of the document and read the title: *The Apprentice – An Erotic Memoir*, by Anne Tournier. Then I look at the first few lines. A girl, my age, arrives at a novelist's house for a job interview. I sit down, feeling faint. It's true what they say in the reviews: Anne's inspiration has dried up. She's used me, taken me as the subject of her new novel. Her novel on how people can be changed, bent to others' wills. I've been more than a puppet – I've been a guinea pig, a lab rat. And so have James and Celine, or were they in on it all along?

Anger surges through my veins like pure alcohol. I stand up, fizzing, exploding, with a ringing in my ears. I want to kill Anne. How dare she do this? Thinking back to the interview and her bizarre line of questioning, I realise now that it was all planned in advance, a set-up. She can't even claim that it just happened – that she started writing up events once they'd been set in train. No, it was all calculated, coldly and robotically. She wanted a subject and she went out and found herself one. What a fucking fool I've been.

I want to run down the stairs and into the garden and slap her thin, harsh, passionless face, tell her how disgusted I am. I thought she was a voyeur, essentially harmless, engineering things but playing no part. Whereas there she was, running to her desk, typing it all up, her work of so-called fiction. At what point was she going to mention it to me? When it was on the bookshelves, reviewed in the Sundays? Or was she counting on me being too humiliated to make a fuss about it?

Fists clenched, I stand seething, making a huge effort not to run down to the garden and scream at her. But then, suddenly, something cold comes down over me, like a refreshing blast of icy air. My blood stops fizzing, the clamour in my head ceases. My revenge has spelt itself out to me, and it tastes so sweet, so fucking sweet.

I walk upstairs, calm now, chuckling nastily to myself. Taking my bags, I go back down, shooting a glance into Anne's room. I was careful to leave the document open where I had found it: she won't know I've seen it.

Then I head down and into the living room. Through the French window I can see that Anne is still outside, arguing with the window-cleaner, gesturing impatiently. She's so controlling in everything she does. No wonder she doesn't have a lover: no one would put up with her for a month. There's no warmth to her. It's all cerebral. Everything goes on in her head. I pity her. But still I want revenge.

I leave her a note, something low key, bearing no trace of my real feelings:

Anne – thanks for everything. It's been fun. But it's time to move on. I think you realise that too. Fond wishes, Gen.

Outside on the doorstep, I stand for a moment, my bags at my feet, and take in the soft summer breeze, like a heady blast of freedom. Seeing a black cab drop someone off further down the road, I turn and post my keys through the door. I walk down the steps, stride across the pavement and hold up one hand. The cab pulls into the kerb. I step up to the window. I still don't know where I'm going.

12

Aftermath

I end up, weirdly enough, at Nate's in Brighton, sleeping on the sofabed in the living room of the shared house where we once lived together, trying not to listen to him and his Danish bird humping in the bedroom next door. Not that there's anything between us any more, but it doesn't seem quite right hearing him yelling out for another woman in the way that he once did for me. He comes the same, it seems, for her as he did for me. It makes me feel interchangeable. Which I am, I suppose, in a way. But one doesn't need to be reminded of the fact.

Anyway, I mustn't complain. It's so kind of him to have offered, after I rang him in tears. Vron – surprise, surprise – wouldn't have me. In fact, she was so adamant I couldn't go back to her that I started thinking about the gorgeous Somali guy and of how she had seemed triumphant when I hadn't scored with him, and I began to wonder if she wasn't jealous of me, her baby sis. But that's all by the by. Nate offered me a place to kip while I sorted myself out, and I gratefully accepted. It even turned out that I get on well with Anne-Mette. We have stuff in common, after all.

I even find myself, one drunken night over a bottle or three of cheap wine and one of Nate's spaghetti bologneses, telling them all about what happened with Anne and co. Not in lurid detail, but the bare bones of it – how it started and how it evolved, with me performing ever more outlandish, uncharacteristic acts while Anne looked on, always so impassive, until I realised why: that she was observing me as one does a specimen in a jar, ready to use me as the subject of her new novel.

Nate, throughout the conversation, looks stunned. He can't believe this is the staid girl he went out with, and I feel almost guilty, as if I have betrayed him. I find myself addressing Anne-Mette more than him, and avoiding his eyes, not wanting to see hurt there, or judgement, or a mixture of the two.

She is riveted, I can tell – curious and excited too. Afterwards, alone on the sofabed, I stop feeling guilty when I hear Anne-Mette squealing next door. I've turned them on with my talk, and they're in for a fun night. Just as long as they don't ask me to join in – that would just be too weird.

I put my plan into action right away. Felicitously, one of Nate's friends, Pete, went into web design after uni, and I get him to design my own basic website. While he's doing that, I type up the diary entries I kept while I was at Anne's, editing them as I go along, tightening up the writing, adding a few details. Within a week, we've got something up – my own blog, relating the whole saga from my own point of view. I've trumped Anne, got there before her. It's up on the internet, dated, for all the world to see – she can't publish her book, in the form that I've seen it, without being found guilty of plagiarism.

Of course, I keep it anonymous. I've got my future to think

of, after all. My future as a writer, but also as a girlfriend, a wife, a mother. This is not necessarily something I want everybody to know about. On the other hand, I'm proud of my writing, of my insights, of the whole project. Proud of the fact that I don't overdramatise things, sensationalise or cheapen my experience, but represent things in their true light. And that includes not portraying myself as some kind of victim. Sure, I was tricked into it, lured into Anne's web under false pretences. But I came out of it all with so much. And I was no saint. I took her money and hospitality in exchange for very little work. I spied on her, or tried to. I tried to go behind her back. I admit, publicly, to all those things, as well as to my other shortfallings and to how naive I was before I got involved with her.

I enjoy writing it, but when it's done it's done, and I don't think about it too much, nor do I expect anything to come of it. It's out there, that's the important thing. People can read it or not read it – I'm not forcing anything upon them. But I feel that my experience might be of interest to certain people, and that writing about it has helped me to make sense of it. It's not all about getting in there before Anne.

But what I don't expect is for the blog to take on a life of its own. I don't even understand how it happened – I guess it must have been one of those word-of-mouth phenomena. All I know is that just three weeks after putting it up, I hear from Anne-Mette, who's heard it from a friend of hers, that it's the talk of London. But that's just the start of it: a week later my blog is mentioned in the *Guardian* books page – it seems that literary London is going crazy trying to guess the identity of my voyeuristic literary mentor.

Of course, I covered my tracks. Anne became 'Charlotte', Bayswater became Notting Hill. James became a jazz critic and not an art historian, while Celine – well, I never even knew who Celine was anyway, how Anne knew her or why she was prepared to do the things she did. But she became Lauren, for what it's worth. And I became Olivia, which is my middle name. A little bit risky, but it added a frisson of excitement.

I was very careful not to give anything away, despite the fact that nothing was slanderous. But I respect these people and their right to privacy, even Anne, even after what she did. I'm overjoyed and flattered that so many people are reading me, but I'm apprehensive too. What if someone does work it out, if it's not watertight? I have a few sleepless nights worrying about the repercussions, which culminate in my deciding to take the blog down and forget about the whole thing altogether.

I'm just about to walk to Pete's house to tell him this, since he only lives a few streets away, when my mobile goes and it's a woman called Janine Longfellow of R&K Literary Associates in London, asking for Olivia. My heart races. I wonder how she's traced me. Taken unawares, I'm unable to concoct a cover-up, and I say, when she asks, that yes, I'm the author of www.apprenticeblog.com.

'Great,' she purrs. 'Listen, I'd love to take you out for lunch sometime. You're not free today, are you?'

I tell her I'm not in London but in Brighton, and she replies, 'Not a problem. If you're free, I can be there for lunchtime. Do you know the Sevendials?'

I do know the Sevendials, but only from hearsay, not from experience. I could never afford to go anywhere like that. Suddenly Janine Longfellow is looking like she's got a serious proposition to make. When I've put the phone down, the first thing I do is call Anne-Mette, who's already left for work, and ask if I can have a ferret through her wardrobe to find out if she's got anything halfway decent I can borrow.

Lunch is surreal. Over plates of delicious-looking Modern European food that I can barely touch because I'm so overawed, Janine – blonde and chic, with a coolly angular haircut and Prada clothes – tells me that she's already, on my behalf, sounded out several big publishers about doing a book version of my blog, and she's confident that she will have a bidding war on her hands if I agree to it. She says she's talking six-figure sums, that it's an offer I can't refuse. The only snag is she thinks it should come out under my own name.

I argue my corner. I want a serious literary career, I tell her, and this could scupper all chances of that. And then there's other people to consider – my family, for all their faults, and then my co-protagonists in the drama: Anne, James and Celine. They all have their lives to lead. If it's been possible to trace me as the author of the anonymous blog, then it will be a piece of cake to trace the real-life characters involved if I use my own identity.

Janine won't reveal her own sources, but I strongly suspect Pete. His name or at least an email address must have been buried in the website somewhere, as the designer, and I imagine that Janine must have contacted him via that, more than liberally greasing his palm to get the information she required. Part of me is pissed off at him, but then if it weren't for that I wouldn't be sitting here now, talking to a woman who is promising me fame and fortune.

We go round and round in circles, over main course, desserts, brandy and coffee, until finally Janine sees that I'm going to stand my ground. I'm nothing if not loyal, and I won't let the others be unmasked. There was genuine kindness and affection involved, as well as lashings of sex, and I might be inexperienced but I know enough about life to be aware that those things are all too rare. We do, however, agree that as soon as she gets back to London, she can approach publishers with a firm proposal.

'In fact, why wait that long?' she says as we shake hands outside the restaurant, brandishing her mobile, and I imagine her hurtling back on the London train, making calls that might change the course of my life.

I walk home and I scarcely know what to do with myself until Nate and Anne-Mette get home from work, and then in a burst of generosity inspired by the thought of my imminent wealth – and gratefulness for their hospitality – I take them to a bar and tell them all about my meeting with Janine over two-for-one cocktails. They're astonished, and excited for me, but also convinced that I have done the right thing in insisting the book, if there is to be one, will be published under a pseudonym.

We're just finishing up and talking about going for a pizza when my mobile rings and it's Janine again, breathless, words spilling out of her almost incoherently. Through the confusion of her words and the quickening of my blood, I manage to make out that she's had a great offer from the very publisher that we agreed would be the best for the book. I jump up from my seat, bounce up and down where I stand, barely able to believe that it isn't all just a wind-up. And then I sit down and a bucket with a chilled bottle of champagne appears at our table, Nate having cottoned on to what my news must have been and made a quick trip to the bar to order something special.

Nate and Anne-Mette are almost as excited as I am, and

we sit around getting drunk and silly together – to the extent that, on the way home, I think that it might be fun to have a threesome with them after all. But almost as soon as the thought has presented itself to me, my head screams 'No!', and when we get home I insist that I'm tired and pissed and need to go to bed right away.

In the morning, for a few moments, I lie with my aching head and my parched throat convinced that it was all a dream, induced by an evening on the piss. It takes a while, and a few cups of coffee, for it to sink in that it's real. When it does, I find myself beaming like a loon.

I wind up back in London, in a beautiful, spacious flat in one of the terraces overlooking Regent's Park. Suddenly well off if not obscenely rich, I lead a blessed life, having the leisure to devote myself to what I call a 'proper novel' and to bits and bobs of journalism as well as to go out seeing films, browsing in bookshops and lunching with friends whenever the mood takes me. I made plenty of hip media friends while I was doing promo for the blog – which I did in a foxy auburn wig and rather racier clothes than I would wear every day. I did press interviews, radio, readings and even a bit of TV, which did wonders for my self-assurance, and I met some wonderful people: journalists, novelists, scriptwriters, filmmakers. I hardly recognise myself from the repressed, unconfident girl that I was when I lived at Vron's.

For a couple of months I feel contented and productive, and then something starts to niggle beneath the surface of my apparent idyll, like a worm beneath the soil, and that something, I eventually realise, is guilt about Anne Tournier. Not guilt about trumping her novel with my blog and then my book – I had, I still contend, as much right to write about the experience as she did, and that I got there first is just her rough luck. But I do feel guilty at the way that I left after she taught me so much, or rather helped me to learn so much about myself. For, I have realised, Anne was the best kind of teacher – the kind who stands back and lets the pupil learn everything for him- or herself. I have much to be grateful for.

For a while I contemplate emailing her or writing her a letter, but I know Anne, to some degree at least, and I know she won't respond. If I call her, she'll put the phone down on me – not that she ever really answers her phone anyway, screening calls through her answerphone. So for a couple of weeks I try to repress the idea to make amends, reminding myself of the ends to which she was using me, probably right from the start.

But the guilt won't go away, and so I find myself, one crisp spring morning, in a cab on the way to her house – or rather, to nearby Queensway, where I stop and buy myself some new shades and a hat. Then I walk to St Petersburgh Place and set up camp 100 metres from her house, on a bench with a book in my hand. Doubting that she'll even answer the front door to me – she's the kind of woman to check through her spyhole before opening – I need to intercept her either on the way in or the way out of her house. Which means waiting – for how long, I don't know.

A couple of hours later I'm getting twitchy, needing a pee and a coffee to revive my energy levels, when I see Anne's front door open. It's not Anne who appears, though: it's James, and he looks morose as he hurries down the street on the opposite side of the road from me. Part of me so wants to call out to him, but at the same time I'm afraid. Afraid that he will be angry with me for what I have done to Anne, for betraying all of them, even though their identities are safe.

But afraid, most of all, of this sadness I have always suspected was present in him but only really seen for certain today.

I stand up, needing to get the blood flowing through my veins again, and walk a little further towards Anne's house. She must be in, if James was there. Should I risk it, and knock, or must I wait it out? I'm flagging now. Is this really so important to me?

Suddenly the door opens again, and this time it is Anne. I only recognise her because of where she's coming from – otherwise, she's as disguised as I am, with a headscarf and large black sunglasses, all very Jackie O. and elegant. She turns and starts walking in the direction of Notting Hill.

I follow, remembering the time I stalked her to the art gallery, desperate for an insight into her life and who she was. I never did find out – I just made a fool of myself. Perhaps, even now, she's aware that I'm pursuing her again. Perhaps she's leading me another merry dance, this time as her own form of revenge. The possibility only makes me more determined not to lose her.

She walks all the way through the quiet backstreets of Notting Hill to Holland Park, where she stops at an antiquarian bookseller. For a few minutes she stands contemplatively in front of the window, and I have to take refuge in a bakery across the road, where I pretend to survey the croissants. Then she goes inside, and I steal over and take my turn at the window. There's a mixed bag of works on display, but among them I notice a few erotic classics, many of them special editions in a locked glass display case – a first edition of *The Story of O*, a third edition of *Lolita*, a first-edition Henry Miller.

It's hard to see what's going on inside through the crowded window display and the cabinets, but after a while a hand comes through and removes one of the books – a German book of erotic photographs. I wonder how much Anne is paying to feed this addiction of hers. This is not the kind of shop to broadcast its prices in its window.

It's time to face Anne, I decide. After all, this is why I came to her house. I can't follow her around all day, spying on her. She's a fascinating creature that I would like to decode and understand, but I have a full life now, better things to do. I need to exonerate myself and move on.

She comes out of the shop, a brown paper package under her arm, and I step out in front of her and remove my shades. It's like a violent physical reaction, the way she starts and then steps back away from me, one hand held up in front of her. I can't see her eyes behind her sunglasses, but I imagine them to be full of spite as she rasps, 'What the hell are you doing here?'

I breathe in deeply. I don't want this to turn into a confrontation, a fishwifely to-do in the quiet streets of Holland Park. 'Look, I can appreciate that you don't like me much any more. Probably never did. But can't we go and talk about this over a drink, on me? There's a great place –'

'I know Julie's,' she says, seeing me gesture. 'I've lived in West London most of my life.'

'Of course. I didn't mean . . .'

I stop. Already she's making me feel like a little girl. But isn't that because I, in turn, threaten her? I am the new generation, the potential usurper, hence her keenness to remind me that she was here long before me – both in West London and in the literary firmament.

We walk down the street in silence, and I'm beginning to wonder if this was such a good idea after all. We sit at a table on the terrace of Julie's, despite the chill, and as I bask in the weak sunshine like a cat, wondering what to drink, I wish I was alone, free to watch the *beau monde* go by and let ideas for my novel weave themselves through my head.

Although it's only just approaching lunchtime, Anne orders a gin and tonic, and I think, To hell with it, and follow suit. For a moment, as we wait for our drinks, the silence between us continues, and suddenly I feel constricted, as if a balloon is slowly being inflated, taking up all the space between us, robbing us of air. Our g and ts arrive, and I take a huge gulp of mine. Anne continues to look aloof, lighting a cigarette and gazing off into the distance as if I wasn't here at all.

'Look,' I say finally, a little emboldened by the alcohol. 'I know what you're thinking and –'

'Don't presume to know anything about me,' interjects Anne.

'OK, I'm sorry.' I look at her, so outwardly calm. What turmoil lies beneath, like molten lava threatening to break through?

'OK,' I go on. 'I really am sorry. But you have to realise how I felt, when I found out what you were writing.'

'You spied on me.'

'I did spy on you, but by accident. Your door was open and your computer –'

'Spare me,' she says, taking a drag on her cigarette. 'It really doesn't matter any more. It's not as if you can undo what you did, give me back all the time I put into the novel.'

'I can't do that, no.' I sit back, flummoxed. I've apologised and there's nothing more I can do. Nothing but thank Anne. And so that's what I do. 'I suppose I just wanted you to know that I'll be forever in your debt – not just because of my blog, my book, and everything that goes with that. You gave me

so much more, things that can't be defined in worldly terms
– self-confidence, both sexually and more generally. The
conviction to try things out, even when I'm not sure about
them. That means so much to me. I'm a different person
because of you.'

I still can't see Anne's eyes behind her glasses, but there's
a tremor in the bottom half of her face that alarms me – the
first sign of any real emotion in all the time I've known her.
Part of me wants to finish up my drink and get out, afraid that
I've set something terrible in motion, opened a floodgate.
But the other part – the writerly part – is hugely curious.
What have I said that has touched a nerve?

Anne raises a hand, gestures to the waitress to bring us
more drinks. I'd rather she hadn't: these drinks are strong,
and I've eaten little this morning. I want to be, now more than
ever, clear-headed. I keep my eyes trained on my mentor, not
wishing to miss anything that goes on, to miss any sign that
she is finally cracking. If she is, I want to move quickly, get
my fingers into the cracks and prise her apart so I can at last
see the creature that lives within that hard carapace.

For a while we say nothing, and I'm unable to gauge what's
going on in Anne's head, behind the shield of her glasses.
But then, halfway through her second g and t, she begins to
speak, slowly and more softly than I've heard her talk before,
her waspishness dissolved.

'It's me who should apologise,' she says. 'I tried to use you
in the most terrible way. I was like a vampire, feeding off you,
your growing confidence. But I was . . . desperate. It's the
only word for it.'

'Why desperate?'

'Have you not seen my reviews over the last ten
years or so?'

'I have, but it hasn't stopped me buying – and liking – your books.'

'Then you're the exception, it would seem.'

I still can't see her eyes behind the fug of cigarette smoke, behind her dark glasses, but her voice, brittle as splintered glass, bespeaks her pain and bitterness. As if tapping into my thoughts, she takes the glasses off, places them on the table between us, and then she looks at me.

'Ah, Genevieve,' she says. 'I'm so weary. Nothing I do seems to please them any more. I've thought of giving up, so many times. But I can't. Writing is in me, a curse sometimes as much as a blessing. Maybe you'll realise that one day, when all the furore has died down. We all have our moments of glory, and then the next big thing comes along and we're left to rot in the corner.'

'Is that what I am?' I say anxiously. 'The next big thing? A flash in the pan?'

'You have to realise that the media will hype anybody for a story, but then just as quickly you'll be yesterday's news.'

'But since I'm doing it all under a pseudonym . . .'

'And you're what – writing a serious novel?'

I nod.

'Then good for you. But it's not dissimilar. You might make a splash, but it can't last for ever. The papers need a constant supply of fresh blood. That's how it works.'

I sigh. 'Well, there's nothing I can do about all that. I'll cross that bridge when – if – I come to it.'

'Of course. You're right. I don't know why I'm bothering even talking to you about all this. Except, I suppose, in the hope that you'll understand my desperation and forgive me.'

'Forgive *you*? But I came here wanting you to forgive me.'

She laughs, a low, crackly, worldly laugh that reminds me

of who she is – my literary heroine, sitting here asking for my forgiveness.

There's so much I want to ask her – about James, about Celine, about herself and her erotic past – but I can't bring myself to. She looks tired, and I think we've reached the end of the road. It's not always possible to untangle and explain our own motives, never mind understand those of others – and that's doubly so where the world of sex is concerned. So I content myself with giving Anne a hug, and I leave her then, sitting alone in the pale spring sunlight, finishing her g and t.

It's two months later, and I'm in bed with James, in the bachelor pad that has become our secret love nest. I say 'secret' because Anne doesn't – mustn't – know about us. Not that we're at all serious: James doesn't want to be seen around London with a girl young enough to be his daughter, and I don't want to be tied down again, to deny myself the possibilities that I once did – which are a hundredfold since my erotic *succès de scandale*. We're fuck buddies, I suppose you'd say. We understand and accept each other, know each other's body, like to help each other push our limits.

Not that Anne has been muscled out altogether – she and I have actually become good friends since our little chat and we meet regularly to discuss her new novel. I'm thrilled to be able to help out. Mine – which deals largely with my relationship with my mother and my boarding-school days, with a sort of Colette-ish lesbian subtext – has sold for a modest sum, and I'm eagerly awaiting the proof copies from the publisher.

We've also talked, Anne and I, about setting up a publishing company of our own, producing literary erotic fiction and photography books. It's still early days, but we're both very excited about it.

I never have got up the guts to ask Anne about her sex life, or lack of it, but James filled me in a little on that, when I badgered him about how he knew her and got involved in her weird games. It seems that he loved her once, when they met as students in Paris in the 1970s. He pursued her for years, with a relentless passion that grew only stronger the more she turned him down. This has been his only way of being near her, and also a way of satisfying her at one remove.

I ask him why she is so frigid, and he tells me it wasn't always so. In Paris she was a sex goddess, well known in St Germain for her love of both men and women, and sometimes both at the same time. There was nothing, it was rumoured, that she wouldn't try. Then she fell in love with a famous artist, a married man and a womaniser who devalued her, made her feel she wasn't good enough. But she couldn't break away. For years she jumped through hoops, trying to find ever new and more exciting things to do, ways of binding him to her. She wasted a decade, perhaps even a bit more, attempting to please him. When he rejected her for good, she developed an aversion to sex, at least to doing it herself. James doesn't know for sure, but he feels that watching is her only way of getting pleasure. Or perhaps a way of punishing herself, in perpetuity.

There's a knock on the door. James sits up, slips into his kimono. I lie on the bed. I'm conserving my strength. We've fucked twice already this evening. James bought me a new copy of the *Kama Sutra* and we flipped through it together over a glass of wine, then tried out the Dancing Position – him standing, me with my legs wrapped around his waist and my arms around his neck. We were backed up against the wall to start with, and I thrust against him as he drove himself into me. Then he moved slowly away from the wall and we graduated into the Crab, with me arched over and back, supporting myself on the floor with my hands as well as my legs while he, with slightly bent legs, continued to pump in and out, one hand supporting my buttocks, the other on my breast. When he moved his hand to my well-exposed clit, I came like a train, massively turned on by the way my body was on display to him.

I hear his voice as he comes back across the living room towards the spiral staircase, at the top of which I lie, on the bed, like a regent awaiting her subjects. I know these people so well, and yet I know, by now, that whenever we get together there are surprises and discoveries in store. Last time we made a daisy chain, which is as sweet as it sounds – each of us going down on each other simultaneously in a circle. Then the guys watched for a while as Celine and I made out, first dry fucking, rubbing our vulvas together, then, lubed up, fisting each other. Afterwards we all had some champagne before starting again.

It came as a shock to me to find out that Celine has a boyfriend, is basically hetero. She'd become a sort of gay idol to me, an idealised version of myself had I chosen to take that route. I was surprised when James told me the truth about her: that she, like me, was an aspiring writer who had lived with Anne as her assistant, and for a time, like me, been Anne's alter ego – the self who would do things that Anne no longer could.

I was shocked, but after that wore off, I actually found it funny, and through James I got in touch with Celine and we went out for a drink and had a good laugh about it all. Although she's given up on her literary ambitions in favour of photography, she followed my fortunes with interest and was glad to meet up and hear all about both my experiences following the publication of the blog-based book and my novel itself. She told me that she'd never felt used by Anne, that she'd accepted everything she did as payment for the world of experience that Anne opened up for her. There'd been no animosity when she'd left, of her own accord, to pursue her photographic studies, and she'd been happy to step in again when Anne contacted her.

Then Celine's boyfriend turned up to pick her up from the Notting Hill pub where we had met. They were going to see a film – or that was the plan. But when I set eyes on him, a thrill went through me as I recognised the toy boy with whom Anne had set me up after that first time with James. The boy Venus I'd thought I'd never see again.

The boy's name is Ed and, though he can't be mine, Celine has shown her worth as a friend and occasional lover by sharing him with me, from time to time, when the mood takes her. And the mood took her that night, when instead of going to the cinema the three of us took a cab back to their flat in Ladbroke Grove, had a few beers, and then, by the glow of candlelight, reintroduced our ardent, adventurous bodies to one another, in a multitude of glorious ways.

Also available from Black Lace:

DARK SECRET LOVE

by Alison Tyler

'I knew what I wanted – Someone who wouldn't laugh or scowl or turn away in disgust when I confessed my darkest fantasies. Someone who had a brush, and a belt, and a set of cuffs and was not afraid to use them.'

Based on the author's real life experiences, this is a fictional account of a submissive and her quest for the perfect dominant. *Dark Secret Love* is a modern-day *Story of O* with a kinky fairy-tale twist.

'A sulphurous personal memoir of past sexual activities which puts Belle de Jour's timid exploits in the shade'
The Guardian

BLACK
LACE

Also available from Black Lace:

THE ACCIDENTAL MISTRESS

by Portia Da Costa

Seduced by a billionaire...

After being mistaken for a high-class call girl when they
first met, Lizzie now enjoys a fiery relationship with John,
her gorgeous and incredibly rich older man. Devoted,
romantic and devilishly kinky, John knows exactly how to
satisfy her every need.

But John has a dark side – and a past he won't talk about.
He might welcome Lizzie in his bed – and out of it – but
will she ever be anything more than a rich man's mistress?

'A powerfully seductive, modern-day *Pretty Woman*
fantasy – with loads more sex!'
Reveal

**BLACK
LACE**

Also available from Black Lace:

A PRIVATE VIEW

by Crystalle Valentino

Welcome to the world of the elite...

As a model, Jemma is used to being the centre of attention. And when Dominic Vane, the world-famous photographer, asks her to pose for him, she knows it's not just her pictures he's interested in.

But in a world where pleasure is pursued above all else, will falling for Dominic's masterful touch come at too high a cost?

From the glamorous South of France to the luxuries of Monte Carlo, *A Private View* will take you on a wild journey of sexual discovery. A classic *Black Lace* romance.

BLACK
LACE

Also available from Black Lace:

AFTER HOURS

by Crystalle Valentino

It's getting steamy in the kitchen. . .

Venetia Halliday, a go-getting entrepreneur, is trying to make it in London's fiercely competitive restaurant scene. And her new chef – East End bad-boy Micky Quinn – has tricked his way into her business, and her bed.

Cheeky, well-built and confident, Quinn embodies everything she loves in a man, but with wild sexual abandon on the menu, can Venetia keep her mind on the job?

Black Lace Classics – our best erotic fiction ever from our leading authors.

BLACK LACE